Praise for Nixon Under the Bodhi Tree and Other Works of Buddhist Fiction

"A MILESTONE. Kate Wheeler has assembled a marvelous collection of stories, inspired, in one way or another, by Buddhism. They range in length from a few lines to several thousand words, and cover topics as diverse as driving, acting, politics, food, birth, rebirth, love, death, murder, suicide, animal adoption, and lawn mowing. Certain themes emerge—we meet monks and nuns and earnest and not-so-earnest meditators—but there are plenty of surprises. A book that fiction lovers, Buddhist, or otherwise will very much enjoy."
—*Tricycle: The Buddhist Review*

"An extraordinary collection. These beautifully crafted stories are poignant, ironic, compassionate, and inspiring. They are a testimony to the ability of the literary imagination to provide glimpses of the mystical dimension of everyday life and illuminate the beauty, frailty and yearning of the human soul."
—Jeremy D. Safran, editor of *Psychoanalysis and Buddhism*

"Some of the best Buddhist-themed fiction to come around since the likes of Kerouac and Salinger."
—Paul W. Morris, editor of KillingTheBuddha.com

"This fine collection of stories introduces a strikingly diverse range of voices who tell their tales with warmth and wit. I enjoyed it very much."
—Stephen Batchelor, author of *Buddhism without Beliefs*

Nixon Under the Bodhi Tree and Other Works of Buddhist Fiction

Nixon Under the Bodhi Tree and Other Works of Buddhist Fiction

Edited by
KATE WHEELER

Foreword by
CHARLES JOHNSON

Wisdom Publications • Boston

Wisdom Publications
199 Elm Street
Somerville, MA 02144 USA
www.wisdompubs.org

Library of Congress Cataloging-in-Publication Data

Nixon under the bodhi tree and other works of Buddhist fiction / edited by Kate Wheeler ; foreword by Charles Johnson.
    p. cm.
  ISBN 0-86171-354-0 (pbk. : alk. paper)
  1. Buddhist stories, American. I. Wheeler, Kate, 1955-
PS648.B84N595 2004
813'.6080382943--dc22
                        2003027339

Cover design by Nita Ybarra
Interior design by Potter Publishing Studio. Set in Monotype Apollo 9.5/16

Printed in the United States of America.

Table of Contents

Foreword

The [monk] would grin when he saw the cake. He would take
each bite and savor it, but when the cake was gone, he
would let it go.
   —"In the Sky There Is No Footstep" by Margo McLoughlin
in *Nixon Under the Bodhi Tree and Other Works of Buddhist Fiction*

ACCORDING TO A CAUTIONARY *sutra* (as the
teachings of the Buddha are called) entitled "The Drum Peg,"
one of twelve talks by the Buddha in the *Opammasamyutta*,
connected discourses with similes, he predicts that his teachings will be in danger of decline if monks become seduced by the sensuous
beauty of art and prefer that to the Dharma teachings of liberation from suffering. "So…[monks]," he says, "…(this) will happen with the bhikkhus in
the future. When those discourses spoken by the Tathagata [the Buddha]
that are deep, deep in meaning, supramundane, dealing with emptiness,
are being recited, they will not be eager to listen to them; and they will not
think those teachings should be studied and mastered. But when those discourses that are mere poetry composed by poets, beautiful in words and
phrases, created by outsiders, spoken by their disciples, are being recited,
they will be eager to listen to them, will lend an ear to them, will apply

their minds to understand them; and they will think those teachings should be studied and mastered."

But this replacement of the teachings by lovely speech is only one side of the problematic relationship between the Buddhadharma and art. What of the danger to the artist? One of the Buddha's most poetically gifted disciples, Vangisa, felt taking pride in his Orphic creations was such a deleterious temptation, he found it necessary to take a step back from joyful outbursts that praised his teacher and examine his own mind; then he composed these lines, which appear in the eponymous sutra, *Vangisasamyutta:*

> Drunk on poetry, I used to wander
> From village to village, town to town.
> Then I saw the Enlightened One
> And faith arose within me.

For both Vangisa and the Buddha, as well as any creator who is also a spiritual seeker, there can sometimes be a daunting challenge involved in reconciling the Path of nonattachment, desirelessness, and liberation with the enchanting yet evanescent beauty of created things. (I'm reminded of a story about Martin Luther, who once created a simple artifact—a piece of household furniture it was, or pottery, but he fashioned it so beautifully that he couldn't stop admiring his handiwork, its pleasing form, and finally had to smash it in order to free himself from attachment and his creation's spell.) Here's the question, one I've pondered and been returned to repeatedly during the more than thirty years I've devoted to trying to deliver something of Buddhist principles and insights in novels and stories like *Oxherding Tale, Middle Passage,* "China," and "Moving Pictures": How in heaven's name can a student or practitioner of the Buddhadharma *write* about nonconceptual insights that are ineffable and must be directly experienced to be authentic? Haven't centuries of Zen masters explained that language and concepts—the very stuff of stories—are themselves impediments to true awakening? How does one depict the holy? Can a fiction *about*

the Buddhist experience ever be anything more than merely a finger pointing at the moon, and never the moon (or goal) itself?

Remarkably, those thorny questions are answered, and then transcended
in *Nixon Under the Bodhi Tree,* the world's first volume of "Buddhist fiction." I read these twenty-nine stories, each and every one, with a rare aesthetic pleasure *and* an ever so subtle deepening of my appreciation for such
leitmotifs in Buddhist practice as suffering, impermanence, dependent orig-
ination, the status of the self as an illusion, lovingkindness toward all sentient beings, and emptiness. So many of these contemporary stories succeed
as literary art, and overcome the problem the Buddha pointed out (as well
as bringing a momentary quieting of our "monkey minds") precisely because *as* stories they are limpid, finely wrought fictions that never preach,
never become didactic, and never proselytize. Rather, they dramatize the
Dharma by taking us intimately into the lives of numerous characters, world-
wide, and by faithfully exploring the very universal dilemmas each faces.
Because of such attention to craft, to character and event, the writers collected in this one-of-a-kind book show us, time and again, how the Buddhist
experience is simply the *human* experience, and that the transcendent can
be found in the pedestrian, ordinary texture of our daily lives and doings.

Start with Gerald Reilly's O. Henry Award–winning story "Nixon Under
the Bodhi Tree," a powerful and moving tale of Dallas Boyd, a gay actor
whose stage portrayal of America's thirty-seventh president becomes a spiritual Way. Then treat yourself to Francesca Hampton's deeply satisfying
"Greyhound Bodhisattva," where a young, fallen Tibetan—"the twelfth incarnation of the Pawoling Lama"—is down and out in southern California,
ruined by his desire for all things American until redemption appears in
the form of a drug-ravaged, tattooed young woman he meets in a bus station. Somehow, by some miracle of inspiration, Keith Heller takes us in a
time machine called "Memorizing the Buddha" back to that pivotal moment two thousand years ago when the Buddha's followers decided to finally move from the oral transmission of his teachings to "convene in the cave

temples at Aluvihara with our best scribes to copy out what we've memorized onto the dried *ola* leaves of the talipot palm tree," and one young man
named Deva, "who had too perfect a memory," unexpectedly finds himself
enlisted for this monumental project.

From the distant past you can move to the blue-collar present in Easton
Waller's delightful "The War Against the Lawns," and meet there both Jerry
Mistretta, a boorish, ambitious man with his own lawn-mowing business,
and his Cambodian helper Suchai, whose tendency to enter into single-
pointed concentration, *samadhi,* when working leads to thalian results—and
liberation. You will meet Shakyamuni Buddha's mother, Mahamaya, before
his birth in Jeff Wilson's "Buddherotica"; just maybe the Awakened One
himself in a Wisconsin animal clinic, courtesy of Ira Sukrungruang's tale,
"The Golden Mix"; and the spirit of a famous Japanese author (I won't tell
you who or in what story).

On and on they come, an embarrassment of literary riches—inventive,
imaginative, and intellectually stimulating. Ironically, these accomplished,
spiritually-attuned writers may well find themselves with Vangisa's
dilemma—the need to wrestle their prideful egos to the ground after giving us prose gifts of such perfection. That, I will let them worry about in their
practice. For myself, I can only say that I've waited all my life for a book
like this. I feel grateful for it. And I believe you will feel the same way, too.

Dr. Charles Johnson
Seattle, Spring 2004

Preface

ALTHOUGH A FEW of the stories in this book have been published before, to the best of our knowledge, this world has not yet seen an anthology of Buddhist fiction. The inspiration for it arose in the mind of Rod Meade Sperry. Meade Sperry meditates and writes, and he has several Maori-looking tattoos. He likes to read, which is good because he reads a great deal, working at Wisdom Publications. One day, as he tells it, it occurred to him that he would like to read a book of Buddhist short stories. "If you're a Buddhist in the world right now," he explained to me much later, "you'll see something that has never been seen before. And if you write about it, then you're going to say something that has never been said before."

The courage to make it happen came from Wisdom's editor Josh Bartok, and Wisdom's publisher, Tim McNeill. Josh was always available to support good ideas and gently discard the bad.

But the main credit goes to everyone who sent us their work (I lost count after the 108th submission but they filled two large cardboard boxes in my house) and also to the innumerable beings who surround and help those writers. Thanks. May all of us everywhere be happy, healthy, prosperous, creative, fearless, safe, and free.

Kate Wheeler
Somerville, Massachusetts, Spring 2004

Publisher's Acknowledgment

The Publisher gratefully acknowledges the generous help of the Hershey Family Foundation in sponsoring the publication of this book.

Kate Wheeler

Introduction
"That's How It Is"

GOOD FICTION makes me say, "That's it. That's right. That's how it is." In Buddhist meditation, I also feel like that—I know I'm seeing clearly, coming close to the way things are. Fiction and meditation are forms of attention, giving life to life. We turn our awareness onto the most ordinary details and they begin to sparkle, bop, and shift to flash out unexpected depths.

Still, you can't just lump Buddhism and fiction together, and start talking about "Buddhist fiction." I want to take my royal seat as the editor of the world's first anthology of "Buddhist fiction" and say there is no such thing, or at least that "Buddhist fiction" is a rather strange and impossible category. It exists like the horn of the rabbit—only because we have thought of it, not inherently. Please don't think I'm just being ornery. I think it's riskier, more delightful this way, to luxuriate in a story that knows it belongs nowhere, like savoring the idea of ice cream when it first arose in the mind of its inventor.

"Buddhist fiction" is just too problematic a notion to solidify, anyway. Why? Because from the point of view of fiction, there can be no "Buddhist" fiction. A story is a story and that's that. A story can be good or bad, satisfying or unsatisfying, innovative or banal—whether it's "Buddhist" or not is irrelevant. Then further, from the Buddhist point of view, to invent more stories, full of more characters who love and fight and die without ever having truly been, is a redoubled version of the existential mistake that lies at the heart of all suffering. Everything that seems to be happening to "you" and "me" is already like a fiction, from a Buddhist's standpoint, and the thing to do is to unravel your involvement in the story, not become entranced and follow it to the end.

Yet nonetheless the Buddhist tradition is rich in stories, remembered and retold. The sutras, sermons of the Buddha, often begin by telling us the story of where he was preaching and the situation of the audience who was listening. The sutra on loving-kindness, for example, was delivered to a group of monks so tormented by tree spirits that they came asking to be assigned to a different meditation grove. (When the monks emanated unconditional love, as the Buddha suggested, the tree spirits calmed down and became helpful). Some stories in the sutras are tragic, like Kisa Gotami's, a woman who went insane at the loss of her child and was cured only after the Buddha sent her to retrieve a single mustard seed from a family in which no one had died. The impossibility of her task caused her to realize the universality of grief.

In the Chinese and Japanese Buddhist traditions, there are many koans—teaching riddles—reminiscent of short-short stories ending with surprising, even shocking punchlines. And throughout the various other branches of the Buddhist tradition, there are spiritual adventures, like the story of Milarepa murdering his evil relatives through sorcery, then retiring to a cave where he ate nettles and wore nothing but a small piece of cloth—and this was in freezing-cold Tibet!—purifying himself so ardently that his effort is said to echo still today.

Great stories, surely, but even if we sneakily delight in their texture, characters, depth, or dramatic qualities, their convincing aspects are meant to seduce us toward a moral. Nearly every Buddhist story has a happy ending, where its characters discard their self-centered point of view and thereby end their suffering.

And the stories of Buddhism are also regarded as "lower" than its instructions, either textual or oral, which point beyond the existence of anything like a solid character.

However wonderful that may be, it's a little different when we read stories for their own sake. In the Western fiction tradition, there can't be too much goody-goodiness or authoritarianism, or else the reader starts to feel coerced and his or her interest falls away. Writers are required to be unflinchingly true to the story first of all and to conceal their ideological motives, if any, under a thick cloak of delightful verisimilitude. If you want to prove something but you can't be convincing—off with your head!—no one will read you.

Mere, bald words won't work. A good story won't say, "She was sad." Instead its heroine will go out and scream at the driver of a truck delivering a Port-a-Potty to the vacant lot next door, where a mansion is about to be built in place of the small house where her beloved neighbor burned to death a year ago last April. Her screaming unleashes a flood of consequences (comic, tragic, romantic) that a Buddhist might call karma. Step by step we are eased toward seeing that no life is complete without complex motivations; unforeseen consequences; all the words we wish we had not said; and the proven irrelevance, over time, of many of our pet opinions. Finally, as readers, we begin to see we aren't alone. When the story ends, we'll sigh with relief and amazement. "Life is like that," we'll say. "Yes, that's how it is."

Which brings us back toward Buddhism again. Our boisterous, fleeting, coincidental world appears before us full of instantaneous vividness, conflicting emotions, and tangled plot. The full story is so full that the only complete description of it is silence.

And then, words.

As the great Indian writer Nagarjuna, one of the writers I admire, said: If you believe that things exist, you're dumb as an ox; but if you say nothing exists, you're dumber—practically hopeless!

BEFORE ENTIRELY GIVING UP the stance that there is no "Buddhist fiction," I should probably admit that in one review and innumerable casual conversations, I've been called a "Buddhist writer." I'm always glad of any recognition yet remain squeamish about the label. To be honest, I've ended up deciding that fiction writing and Buddhist practice feel different to me, and that this has to be okay. Buddhism simplifies, untangles the mind; while writing seems to require the mind to fold and turn back on itself, as the critic Jeffery Paine has pointed out. My work contains Buddhist characters, situations (and perhaps at times, insights), in the same way that any writer who happened to be a farmer might likely write about living on a farm.

Both can be ecstatic, total experiences. Or miserable, fragmented, excruciatingly boring and humiliating. But I'd take a bad moment in meditation over a bad moment in writing any day.

Reading, on the other hand, seems almost too easeful, like a sin.

WHEN WISDOM APPROACHED ME to edit this anthology, I'd already been pondering this problem of "Buddhist fiction" for quite a while. I wrote an essay about the topic for *Inquiring Mind*, a Buddhist journal, without agreeing it was fair to use the term "Buddhist fiction." However, in the course of researching that essay I had to recognize the existence of dozens of wonderful books and stories by major writers—Rudyard Kipling, Charles Johnson, Peter Matthiessen, Roger Zelazny, Herman Hesse, Ursula K. Le Guin, Jim Harrison, J. M. Coetzee, and Alice Walker—who were influenced by Buddhism. And as I meandered onward, eagerly reading more and more, I found new Buddhist-influenced writers sprouting across the cultural landscape like mushrooms after a rain.

When I agreed to take this project on, I did it with the stipulation that we would not define what the nature of the Buddhist connection had to be. Rather, we'd leave that to the writers, and they didn't have to identify themselves as Buddhists.

Submissions came from all over the world, including two in French and one in Spanish. Some writers identified themselves as Buddhist practitioners or sympathizers. Sometimes the content of the story was Buddhist. In a few cases the "message" was vaguely or explicitly Buddhist. Somehow even notional Buddhism seemed to open up some unconventional creative possibilities: other realms, other ways of seeing the mind, the person, circumstances. No formal strictures seemed to apply; we got stories of every shape and hue.

In the end the main criterion I rigorously applied to the selection process was that every story be *satisfying*.

And in the end I felt lucky. The submissions were like gifts, the contributors like family, or fellow alumni of some vast alma mater whose literary magazine this anthology became.

"NIXON UNDER THE BODHI TREE," the title story by Gerald Reilly is an O. Henry Award–winning, finely honed traditional short story with visionary content. There are a handful of short-short stories, hip and informal, each one rearranging the brainwaves momentarily. A couple of barely fictionalized memoirs include Pico Iyer's tender, elegant account of a romantic stroll near Kyoto, and Diana Winston's hilariously rotten experience in a Burmese monastery. "Rebirth," a short-short story by Lama Surya Das, embodies a single blip of creative inspiration, while Victor Pelevin's "The Guest at the Feast of Bon" (published here in English for the first time) leads us on a sustained associative journey far beyond our bearings. And Sharon Cameron's intense depiction of personal experience is written with such finely wrought pragmatism that it comes off as almost equally bizarre.

Some stories have a Zen flavor, like Dinty W. Moore's "No Kingdom of the Eyes." A flourishing secondary reality takes over in Anne Klein's "The Mantra and the Typist" and then, from the opposite point of view, reading Marilyn Stablein's flatly realistic accounts of dream events, we may wonder what to think is real. Several works—like Jeff Wilson's lightly outrageous "Buddherotica" and Keith Heller's "Memorizing the Buddha"—re-imagine Buddhist history into fiction. And then Keith Kachtick takes us into the mind and heart of a trendy Buddhist who also happens to be a bit of a sexual predator.

Several of the writers are internationally famous, like Victor Pelevin and Doris Dörrie, who's better known for her films. But others are unpublished before this, and one said he'd never written any other fiction. Even the biographical sketches seem more fascinating than regular bios. Kira Salak, as one example, emailed me from somewhere along her 1,000-mile bicycle trip across Alaska to fill in details of her copyrights. Leah Sammel claims her life is "unremarkable." How provocative!

There were certain common themes. We ended up including, for example, three stories about how your karma can veer off between one life and the next. There are also several very different stories about unassuming characters who possess amazing hidden qualities. And the contributors who practice in the Tibetan tradition seem easily to enter visionary experiences, not too surprisingly, given the deities they tend to hobnob with.

Yet despite these common threads, the stories remain wildly varied. And as this collection began to take final shape, I kept feeling glints and hints of something extraordinary gleaming out from it, as if, together, the pieces had become facets of a jewel.

But what is at its core, exactly? I still can't pinpoint a common essence—and I think that's good. Let this be less of a summation than a start.

"*Gyuma, milam,*" as the gentle old Tibetan saying goes, "Like a dream, like an illusion." Such is our life. Fleeting, poignant, we take it for more solid than it is. Let's enjoy it, and these stories, while we can.

Nixon Under the Bodhi Tree and Other Works of Buddhist Fiction

Mark Terrill

Acceleration

PEOPLE TALK ABOUT *theater* or *drama* in reference to everyday experience but when did the curtains ever part to reveal you sitting there next to me in our old BMW while crossing the bridge over the Stör on a clear winter afternoon with a sky like blue glass *scratched* as you said from all the various jet trails you turning your head to the right looking off towards the western horizon across all those flat green acres of northern Germany me glancing over at you without you being aware of it seeing you sitting there content in the warm sunlight coming through the windshield absorbed in your own personal thoughts of god knows what & then the attendant cascade of psyche-encompassing emotions that suddenly engulfed me as I caught a glimpse of the tiny set of wrinkles at the corner of your eye immediately remembering how seriously you took your fortieth & most recent birthday then me being catapulted into that crushing orbit of conceptual thinking dealing with time & age & destiny & what it means to be alive & how we all deal with getting old & the passing of time & the laying aside of certain dreams & desires in favor of various creature comforts & a predictable easiness into which we all are slipping deeper & deeper from day to day ultimately precluding even the remotest possibility of any manifestation of true happiness or satisfaction & then us coming down off the bridge & onto the autobahn me putting the gas pedal calmly and purposefully to the floor leaving what I had been thinking about behind us like the clouds of blue exhaust as we accelerated in a mechanical rush of pure power & motion the tachometer & the speedometer both rising steadily the car hurtling forward on the smooth asphalt temporarily eclipsing all thoughts of time & the passing thereof & cleanly bringing to an end the inner spectacle of today's particular drama in a manner so thorough & final that it's bordering on the surgical.

Gerald Reilly

Nixon Under the Bodhi Tree

EVERY NIGHT IT TAKES Dallas Boyd at least two hours to become Richard Nixon, and after the performance it takes just as long to get cleaned up and find a taxi to drive him home. He has started spending nearly the whole afternoon before a show getting ready, and the people at the theatre are used to it, they've already let him bring in some furniture, a reclining chair, an old oriental carpet, even a hot plate so he can brew his herb teas, whatever he needs within reason to make things a little more comfortable. He loves his dressing room. *I could live in a dressing room* he has confided to the makeup artist named Gwen. He tells himself this is more than just a juicy part: it's become Dallas Boyd's defining moment, his crowning achievement. His entire life has shrunken around the role, he doesn't have energy left over for anything else.

The play is called *Nixon at Colonus,* and he's never liked the title, this play is more Mamet than Sophocles, it hardly offers Tricky Dick anything like the apotheosis that he deserves, but he loves the play all the same. The script is pretty hard on the president by way of being sympathetic. Tough love. Whatever softness Dallas has been able to insert is purely around the edges.

No ducking the truth here, no claims that the only problem was being too soft-hearted, as though Nixon was ever soft-hearted.

Dallas Boyd loves the author too, a sweetheart of a playwright named Lester Feltzer who still shows up occasionally at performances. Feltzer is straight, but the most soft-hearted, gushiest heterosexual friend that Dallas has ever known. At the end of the summer Les moved out to Los Angeles to write for the movies, but things haven't gone well for him on the coast, the studio declined to exercise its option, and so Les is already planning a return to New York. Whenever he visits the theatre he brings tasty health food offerings with him that he dispenses to Dallas like a Jewish grandmother, and then they sit down and talk.

On the very last visit, he told Les that he felt he was finally starting to get deeper into the part. He's been doing the play for more than fourteen months already, but at last it feels like all the unyielding discipline and concentration is paying off. With Feltzer he never talks about his fears. Or that he has no idea how long he's going to be able to continue. Even as he's drawn himself in and focused all his energies, inner and outer, on the role, he can feel the life forces fading. The ironies of this are rich: almost Nixonian. Forty-three years old, after twenty years of freak shows and supporting roles, he lands the perfect part, complete with terrific notices and interest from film casting people; all this, and he doesn't have the slightest idea how much longer he can stick it out. He knows for certain he will not be able to move on to some other role, so he has no choice but to keep settling deeper and deeper into the personality. In his recent performances he feels like he has finally mastered the physical Dick Nixon. He never had to struggle to achieve the unmistakable clipped speech cadences that always seemed to be uttering just the wrong sentiment, and early on Gwen managed the pasty-face makeup that forever appeared in desperate need of a shave; but now he effortlessly takes on the awkward play of the shoulders as the president thrusts yet another, absurdly inappropriate victory sign with both hands. Gwen needs well over an hour to do the hair and face, but he knows the resemblance wouldn't add up to much if he doesn't inhabit that makeup with the bristling awkwardness of the man himself.

When he is in character, all the lighting technicians and stage hands call him Mr. President. This started out as a joke but right away the star understood this helped him get deeper into the part. At one point when he was struggling to improve his Nixon shuffle, he actually requested Vinnie, the chief stagehand, to do the same. At first Vinnie looked vaguely insulted, as though he was outraged by the notion, as though going along with such absurdity was not only *not* required by the union handbook but absolutely against all good sense.

"It helps get me in character," the actor explained. "If you feel I *am* the president, I'll feel that way too."

Over time Vinnie has turned out to be his best friend at the theatre. Every week or two he brings in Italian food that his wife has cooked up, and whether his appetite is strong or not, Dallas tries to eat it as best he can, even on those nights when the smell of meatballs and veal nearly turns his stomach, and he always follows the dining with extravagant compliments to the chef and insistent requests for more.

But even Vinnie has been acting strangely tonight. Earlier he noticed something was wrong with Gwen, when she put on his face, but for once he didn't press her for details. Instead it falls to Vinnie to bring him the news. It is almost six-thirty, and Gwen has long since finished her work and left him alone, sitting in character when Vinnie knocks on the door.

"Want some tea?" Dallas offers as he always offers. He knows right away something is wrong. Vinnie shakes his head about the tea and stands there with an awkwardness that Dallas picks up immediately.

"How are you today, Vin?"

"Okay. How you feeling, Mr. President?"

"Terrific. Is something wrong, Vinnie?"

"You haven't heard the news?"

"No. What news?"

"That's what Gwen said. She didn't think you knew yet."

The stagehand removes the *New York Post* carefully from behind his back. For once Vinnie looks utterly abashed, like he's doing something that has to be done but gives him no pleasure. The huge front page announces that Richard Nixon is dead. A *New York Times* follows. The news overwhelms Dallas, surely more than it should have. Nixon's health has been shaky, he was in the hospital early in the week, but before this exact moment Dallas has never been willing to allow the possibility of Richard Nixon's death, much less to explore its potential symbolic significance to his own inner life. And this is especially odd because he has so often contemplated his own death.

His eyes search for details to hang on to. One columnist is named Apple. The time of death is listed as nine o'clock in the evening. Which means he was onstage even as the president died. It occurs to him fleetingly that it might be good for box office receipts, at least from a short-term perspective, and then Dallas blushes deeply at the utter shallowness of that reaction. He thinks that everyone must have been shielding him, avoiding any mention of it with him, as though he were too fragile for the shock. Who knows, maybe they were right. He lives in such a focused world that he hadn't even gotten the news on his own. He blushes again, realizing that he has been ignoring Vinnie, who has been standing in the dressing room, watching him the whole time.

"I just thought you should know."

"Of course you were right. Thank you Vinnie." Their eyes meet. "I guess I'm living in a cocoon. Even news like this comes to me a day late."

Alone, Dallas looks in the bright makeup mirror and asks himself what he is going to do. He considers medication but settles on a mere pair of aspirin that he extracts from the forest of medicine bottles. Prescription bottles are laid out on surfaces everywhere, and Dallas carries a satchel packed with medications wherever he goes. He has become an expert at painkillers, and Dr. Reynolds has given him considerable latitude. There's Vicodin and

Hydrocodone. When things get more painful there's Ativan and an open prescription for morphine, which he doesn't imagine needing till much later on but which is a reassuring presence even in prescription form. He feels like he's been enormously lucky. He's gone for monthly blood tests and he keeps track of his Tcells but he's resigned to the course of the disease. They tried AZT for almost six months, and he's happy to be free of that drug's ugly side effects. He keeps reducing the circle of his days, reducing distractions of any sort. His performances are all that he can manage to get through. And the round of performances never ends. On Mondays, when he finally has a day off, he doesn't budge from his apartment. He lies in bed all day, dressed in a bathrobe with slippers no matter what the temperature outside. Lately he always feels a chill. Silk long underwear, the thick wool Irish leg warmers, double layer of socks—nothing helps much.

He begins doing the now-familiar *tonglen* meditation, and it feels different with the news that the president has left the human realm. His mind roams back over the career, and for once he doesn't fight his wandering mind, he only tries to keep the bare touch of the rhythm of his breathing and the exchange, the dark light in, the white light out, and slowly he feels himself steadying. It is simply indescribable doing this meditation with Dick Nixon. Some days he finds himself thinking about Cambodia and all the bombs that were dropped and the black karma coming so thick that it clouds out the sun until Dallas feels he can barely keep breathing and then just before he panics, he is letting go, all bliss and blue skies exhaling out to Nixon. It works counter to everything in the life of a struggling, up-and-coming actor, what's supposed to make up your most basic nature, your survival instinct. *You've changed* friends told him. He knew he had grown altogether more somber, he felt like he was wearing a jacket and tie all the time now. He was dying and yet he was worrying about poor Dick Nixon.

He often wondered what the president would think about his performance, even while knowing beyond the slightest doubt that Nixon would never have subjected himself to such a play. For years he's hated Nixon in that strange, superficial way that you can feel emotions about somebody existing so far from your daily life. He knows the written record only too well. At home he has two shelves overflowing with Nixon books, and he keeps a few beloved duplicates on hand in the dressing room but rarely needs them. The sight of himself made up as Nixon is inspiration enough. There's so much juicy stuff. All the swear words that embarrassed Nixon so terribly afterward, all the anti-Semitic jabs, the compulsive hate talk. How he ranted about all the Jews and liberals out to get him just because he wasn't as charming or Ivy-League connected as Jack Kennedy. It's only gotten worse since he left the White House. Nixon has remained totally unrepentant. He claims only that he was too soft-hearted even as one after another of his underlings and friends went to jail for him. In the media every few years there arises that periodic drone: Nixon is back, Nixon is back, every chorus of it more carefully orchestrated than the last.

But maybe the real Richard Nixon, the spirit Nixon, will finally get the chance to perceive his performance in this latest, disincarnate form. Watching a play must be entirely different for a consciousness that has left its body. Maybe Richard Nixon will be able to see past the prejudices and stubborn self-images that would have marred his appreciation in the first place. Maybe Nixon will feel Boyd's performance for what it is: a life-and-death role, a veritable inhabitation of the dead man's just departed career and life story.

He has already journeyed through a lifetime of his own karma in the last few years. Jorgen went back to Stockholm as soon as he tested positive, and back then Dallas knew it was only a matter of time before he tested positive. A few months later he got the call to play Nell in *Uncle Tom's Cabin* and two years after that he was chosen to become Richard Nixon but only after a pair of unsuccessful tryouts separated by almost a month. From transvestite glitter to the White House, but by then Dallas was utterly alone with his diagnosis. Such isolation was just perfect for Nixon. It was the way Dallas first slipped into the part. Nixon was a genius at loneliness, and now Dallas Boyd was utterly alone and undistracted with him too.

Dallas doesn't know how long he's been sitting by himself when there's a knock on the door and he answers, "Come in," and the dressing room door opens to reveal Les Feltzer.

"As soon as I heard the news I thought of you."

For the first time Dallas feels like he might start crying. For the first time he feels like part of himself has died tonight. He motions to the empty chair.

"Sit with me for a few minutes."

Dallas knows Lester understands, maybe Lester alone in the entire world. They'd had long talks about the role. "I understand why you're acting even though you're sick," he said after the first week of previews. "We do what we do right up until the end," Lester said. "I'm exactly the same. I'll write until I can't hold a pen up. Then I'll probably talk into a microphone and have it transcribed. We're all terminal cases, and the lucky ones, like you and me, we know what we want—no what we *have* to do right up till the bitter end." That was months ago, and the stakes have only gotten more intense in the interim.

"Want some tea, Lester?"

"Do you have something stronger?"

Suddenly Dallas is laughing at the obvious *just rightness* of the idea of sharing a stiff drink. Of course it has to be booze. He looks quickly around the dressing room. It is not often that he drinks anything much stronger than green tea, but he sees that he's better stocked than even he realized. He goes out and returns with a tiny cardboard pail of ice courtesy of Vinnie's refrigerator.

"I can just about manage martinis."

"Just the thing."

"I think I'll join you too. One for the president, that bastard. A stiff one for the road."

He pours quantities of gin and vermouth into cups used for his tea rituals and mixes them carefully, even using the bamboo tea whisk; he'll worry about cleaning that off later. Yes, just the thing. Both of them clink their cups as gingerly as if they are drinking highballs at Sardi's or 21.

"I'm glad you're here tonight, Les. I hope you stay for the show."

"Wouldn't miss it for the world."

"You know I've been thinking a lot about Cambodia. I keep thinking about what he did, what we all did, how it's all been forgotten."

Les nods. He is listening with great care. He has spent the afternoon apartment hunting, planning his move back to New York in the next few months, and certainly he hadn't expected to have this impromptu wake in honor of Richard Nixon. He watches Dallas sniff the martini and then they both take deep draughts of their respective potions. Les has been startled by the signs of physical deterioration that he sees up close, behind his friend's makeup. The actor looks haggard, appears to have aged even since the last time he visited, barely a month ago. All of it only contributes to the character, no question. Because it's not just the physical appearance.

"I've taken your play and turned it into a religion," Dallas whispers only exaggerating slightly. "I live and breathe and shit Richard Nixon. I dream his dreams."

Lester leans forward but doesn't answer. He senses that the actor, this particular terminal case, is a vehicle for something special tonight.

"Most people, if I told them I was playing Nixon right up until the day I died, you know what they'd say. Say I was crazy. Absolutely certifiable crazy. Sometimes I think that too."

Lester says nothing, staying focused, centered.

"But you know why I'm doing this?"

Lester admits he doesn't have a clue exactly what he's getting at.

"I'm teaching Nixon to forgive himself." He empties his cup. "I've already forgiven myself. It's all for Tricky Dick from here on out. Every night the soul of Richard Nixon is going to be hearing me, hearing all these prayers you wrote for him. And feeling the play too."

Lester cannot speak now. He feels like he's seen a ghost, it's not just this figure that looks like Richard Nixon, it's everything he knows about Dallas, about the fact that the actor is going to die.

"The real Nixon's with me tonight," says Dallas. "I've been reaching out to him night after night . . . ," he reaches up toward the ceiling of the dressing room, " . . . and now he's reaching back from wherever he's journeying."

"You *feel* him?"

He nods. "I felt him last night. I didn't know it then, on stage, but now I know what it was. All that suffering. No wonder I didn't want to see a newspaper. But now I'm going to be able to reach him so much easier. There's nothing separating us anymore. We're all suffering, but poor fucks like Dick Nixon and me, we're just *swimming* in all the suffering." Then before Les can finish his martini or say no, Dallas has slipped a religious book in front of his friend and placed a Xerox copy of the same text on his own lap. The actor has a huge stack of meditations and prayers for the dying, but his favorite one is right on top.

"What's this?" the playwright asks, not dreaming for a moment of offering the slightest resistance.

"The Heart Sutra. One of the most sacred Buddhist texts. Now I'm going to read this slowly, and don't worry if the words don't exactly seem clear or even make much sense. The important thing is the feeling you have. And imagine that Nixon's in the room with us. Just meditate on the words as I say them."

Lester is visibly moved, if nothing else by the intensity with which Dallas is directing this improvised moment. And as always Dallas—while he knows that his Tibetan teacher wouldn't agree with whatever extras he's adding, how he's turning a simple prayer recitation into something closer to a séance—Dallas feels completely right about what he is doing for the dead president and for himself. Already, even as he begins to read, Dallas is certain that Nixon is with them, his soul is present in the room. Lester is completely spooked by now, goose-bump-flesh spooked, he cannot see any of this of course but his body is registering that they're not alone in the dressing room. The five skandhas are enumerated, each of the components of the psyche, and they are liberated in the text, found to be no different than the selflessness of pure experience, all things marked by emptiness—not born, not destroyed. In the few seconds it takes for Dallas to finish the text, scarcely a page long, Lester sees again that the actor is going to die very soon: first Nixon, then Dallas Boyd. They sit in silence for a little while after the prayer's finished. They can hear backstage sounds, but they are listening to something else.

Then Vinnie is knocking on the door. "Ten minutes to curtain."

Lester reaches out and squeezes his hands, "I love you, man."

"I love you too," Dallas answers back.

The actor spends the last few minutes by himself. Already he feels exhausted. He looks at himself in the mirror and doesn't know how he will have the energy to perform for two hours. Outside, the theatre seats will be filling up. The electronic bell tone will be signaling that the curtain is about to go up though he can only hear this in his imagination.

He stands up. He is sure that it is not merely his own power carrying him forward any longer. He pauses before opening the door and pauses again in the darkness outside the dressing room. Ahead the bright rim of stage lights awaits him. A few more steps and he can feel the audience in the darkness, all of them focused on his movements as he enters their view and sits down at the replica presidential desk. The dark space around him has evaporated: he feels as though they're sitting in a space as large as an airplane hangar, but a hangar so very vast that you can't even see the walls supporting it. Thousands of Cambodians are sitting in long aisles, the four dead youngsters from Kent State are there; the actor's parents and his grandparents and poor Jorgen Lindgren too. Even Pat Nixon has joined the rest of them: saints, arhats, martyrs, bodhisattvas. But by far mostly simple people, as flawed as Dallas, as flawed as Richard Nixon, all of them merely seeking a glimpse of the truth. What do the souls say to each other in the endless space after their bodies are shed? Soon enough he will know. He looks up through the branches and sees the Milky Way twinkling clearly above. Then he looks down at the dark space that is his audience and begins speaking with a resonance that surprises even himself, loud enough so even the backmost rows can hear clearly.

"I *am* the president."

M.J. Huang

Martyr

DARK LIMBO. It might have been a cave except there were no walls. Silence consumed the space. A white blur floated like light. It was a man's face. Bloody cuts and scrapes tattooed his skin. He possessed the expression of a child waiting to unwrap Christmas presents.

"Am I . . . ?" Tendrils of hope crept into his voice.

"Yes," a female voice confirmed.

He felt relief.

"Tell me," said the Interrogator, her face no longer cloaked by the shadows. She was an enigma, simultaneously containing no emotion and all emotion.

"About what?"

"Your mission."

"What is this? Some kind of trial? I don't need to tell you anything."

"Tell me."

He fidgeted in the steel folding chair and looked across the plain sappanwood table that separated him from the Interrogator. He could barely discern her colorless tunic, much less the shape of her body.

"It's fairly self-explanatory," he scoffed. "Boom. Beginning, middle, and end of story."

"Don't make a mockery of these proceedings," she said.

"Nobody said there would be a trial!" He felt betrayed.

"Does this look like a courtroom, Hani?" The Interrogator gazed at a dossier and rummaged through the unseen contents of a rusty toolbox on the table. There was a faint clatter of wood, like dominoes bumping together.

"I was promised a better life. I've done everything that was expected of me." Hani didn't like being cheated.

He noticed a strange orange henna marking on the back of the Interrogator's right hand: a triangular circle made of three convoluted arrows. (Where had he seen that emblem before?) Perhaps she belonged to a radical faction working against the holy crusade.

"Tell me about your mission."

"I was recruited because I was fearless."

"You mean *determined*."

"I mean *brave*."

"Bravery involves a risk to yourself. You were determined."

Hani was indignant. His face flushed, matching the color of his cuts and scrapes. "I was brave!" he screamed. "*You* go get girdled with C-4 and slip past security into a baseball stadium to detonate yourself! I sacrificed myself for the greater good!"

"But you had nothing to lose. You did it because you wanted the reward. You were determined to get the reward," she said.

Hani stared at the Interrogator as if she were insane. "Of course I did it for my reward! Why else would *anybody* do it?"

"I thought you did it for the greater good."

"I—I did! The Book says infidels must be killed, even if you have to sacrifice yourself to get it done."

"Which book?"

"What do you mean *which* book? The Book. The only Book."

The Interrogator laughed heartily. So unexpected, the sound terrified Hani.

"Everybody thinks their book is The Book," she said.

Hani recovered himself but his growing dread milked the meager reserves of his brazenness. "Where am I? What is this place?"

She ignored his question. "Finish your tale."

Hani shifted his weight in the cold chair and muttered, "I'm a hero of the crusade."

The Interrogator began hunting through the toolbox on the table.

"If it's all the same to you, I'd like you to end these *proceedings*," he said, feeling the extreme lateness of the hour.

"That's what I'm doing," she assured him.

Sweat glistened on Hani's forehead.

"It's such a struggle against the atheist swine," he wailed. "I suffer."

"We all do," she replied.

Hani fell silent for a moment, then appealed to her sense of justice. "I just want what's due to me."

The Interrogator selected old-fashioned wooden rubber stamps from the toolbox. She overturned them on the table. Hani could see only two. One looked like a snake or worm. Another, a bird in flight.

Patience was a virtue . . . one that Hani never had. "I've earned it! It's all rightfully mine! I want my mountain of pearls, my throne of silver, and my one hundred vaults of gold brighter than the sun!"

"Your book may as well have promised you one hundred dancing bears," she said.

"What kind of nonsense is *that*?" he shrieked.

The Interrogator merely studied him in silence. She inked a beat-up rubber stamp. Twisted silver wire ensnared the wooden handle.

"Here you are," she said, stamping the top page of his dossier. Stapled to the left corner of the sheet was a passport photo of his head.

Again, Hani noticed the orange henna arrows on the back of the Interrogator's hand. Only now did the significance of the symbol break through the membrane of vague familiarity and trigger recognition of his surroundings, or rather, the lack of surroundings.

He was trapped in a Recycling Center.

"You're all set to go, Hani," she said, not unlike a flight attendant.

The Interrogator handed the form to him. In a region *For Office Use Only,* under the stenciled word *METEMPSYCHOSIS,* the silhouette of a pig stood out in fresh black ink.

He stared at her in horror.

Lama Surya Das

Rebirth

T WAS MIDNIGHT when he was once again surfing Indra's cosmic net of consciousness, seeking a doorway, a hint in the karmic wind, a numinous womb like a crack between worlds to alight in—when a young married couple in Marin County climaxed together with a rush like freight trains colliding.

And he sailed toward that chink in the iron mail of time and infinity, overlooking the fact that the clear light of eternity also beckoned. When suddenly, sensing the tantalizing fragrance of bacon, he found himself inside the belly of a sow.

There would be other lives and other lights, other worlds, he dimly knew or at least intuitively remembered. But this one would prove to be a short, dull existence: not without pleasure certainly, but full of pain too, and confusion, and dense dream-like images flickering through his obscured consciousness—not at all what he had come back to this world to do...

Doris Dörrie

Where Do We Go from Here

N THE MIDDLE OF THE NIGHT Norbert gives me a shake. It's a quarter-past five, he whispers. Get up! Meditation!

I turn over with a grunt, but once awake I can't get off to sleep again. I sit up, swearing. Theo, seated on his mattress, is pouring hot water into a cup from a vacuum flask. He produces some Nescafé from his bag. Coffee! I inhale the scent longingly. He sees the look on my face. Like some? he asks, and holds the cup for me to take a sip, a sublime, glorious sip.

He signs to me to follow with a jerk of the head, so I climb into my trousers and stumble down the stairs in his wake, not forgetting to give my head another crack on the beam.

I put on my shoes, which are proving to be very impractical because I have to keep tying and untying the laces. Blearily, I shuffle outside into a dawn light as soft as a teenager's first kiss.

Gliding along in slow motion, figures are converging on the white tent from all directions. I hear a bell ring and a nun singing in Vietnamese. The combination of her singing and the baby-pink sky is sweeter than sugar, simply entrancing, so all at once I, too, glide slowly down the hill to the tent.

Shoes off again. I get in everyone's way because it takes so long to undo my laces. Maybe I should have acquired a pair of stupid sandals for this trip.

They all make for their cushions. I park myself on one near the entrance, so I can escape. It's terribly flat and compressed by long use, and the mat beneath it smells of sweaty feet. A gong sounds, and from then on nobody moves. Except me.

The cross-legged position I've adopted proves extremely uncomfortable after a few minutes. I surreptitiously try to adjust it, but the resulting noises are embarrassingly loud. My joints creak, the planks beneath me groan, the cushion rustles. The others are quiet as mice. No idea how they manage it. I could cry out, my knees hurt so much after another five minutes. I re-adjust my position, but now my back hurts instead. By the time I've more or less relieved that discomfort, my right foot has gone to sleep. It's all I can think of until a mosquito comes whining around my ears. I try to blow it away, but even that sounds loud in this reverential hush. The pain travels to my upper thighs, my left foot imitates my right foot and goes to sleep too. I swivel my wrist for a glance at my watch. Less than ten minutes have elapsed. I can't stand this, I know from Claudia what one has to do: simply let one's mind wander.

But how can I, if all I can think of are my various aches and pains? At best, the mosquito will distract me from my numb feet, the pain in my knees from the mosquito, and my numb feet from the pain in my knees.

Interesting, really, that one pain should take my mind off another and one torment be replaced by the next. Is there ever an interval between them?

That thought itself was the interval, it seems, because I forgot about my knees, my feet, and the mosquito while thinking it. Now that it's gone, the whole process starts again: cramp in the shoulder muscles, another mosquito, a sudden urge to sneeze, an unendurable itch in the balls. If I don't scratch this minute, I'll have hysterics.

Just before I reach that stage my left knee becomes so painful, I forget about the itch.

Meditating is sheer torture. How will I be able to stand an hour and a half of it?

Furtively, I glance to right and left. Antje is sitting two cushions away. She's looking delightfully drowsy. What's going on in her head? What are they thinking about, all these stoically motionless people? How can they bear it?

Not me. That's it, I'm off. Just as I'm about to get up, however, the gong sounds again. They all stretch and get to their feet. Great, it's over. In slow motion—so slowly I almost tread on the heels of the person ahead of me—we shuffle around the tent in single file. Making for the exit, I think, but no: at the next gong, they all halt in front of their cushions and sit down again.

I stand there fractionally longer than the rest, uncertain what to do. I could perfectly well thread my way through them and leave the tent—nothing to it. Except that I'd be a failure, a weakling. So I sit down again, and the next bout of torture takes its course.

The whole procedure is repeated four times, and I stay with it only because, during the second session, I experience a tiny, wholly unexpected moment of time that opens up before me like a treasure chest on the seabed.

I see a blackbird hopping around on the grass outside, where the light is growing by degrees, and suddenly I hear the dawn chorus.

I hear it as if I'd only just been equipped with ears. I don't know anything about birds, so I can't identify them, but I hear them not in the usual way, as an incidental twittering sound, but as a unique occurrence unrepeatable in this particular form. This dawn chorus will only occur once—now, this very moment—and if I don't hear it now I'll never hear it again. I'll have missed it once and for all.

Euphoric as this realization makes me feel, I'm simultaneously shattered because it means I'm forever missing my own, unique life—because I'm blind and deaf.

After an hour and a half I totter out of the tent like a zombie. It's an effort to stoop and put my shoes on. Once again, being the only one who has to tie his laces, I'm jostled on all sides.

ALTHOUGH THE SHOWER in the communal bathroom yields only a trickle of lukewarm water, I feel as if I've performed some mighty feat. I'm a hero. I've sat cross-legged and motionless—or almost—for an hour and a half without screaming and running away. My whole body hurts, my head is a void. I let the water trickle over my scalp and stare at hand-written, trilingual notices hanging on the door: *Brothers and sisters, kindly remove any hairs from the plughole when you're through.*

While cleaning my teeth I read: *Brothers and sisters, use water sparingly.*

On the loo: *Brothers and sisters, kindly refrain from putting paper in the toilet. It can cause blockages!*

If there's one thing I hate about loos in Southern Europe, it's those little waste bins brimming with shit-smeared toilet paper. I refuse to observe that revolting custom. My used loo paper goes down the pan, and that's that.

When I emerge I see Norbert, with a hand towel around his waist, disappearing into a shower cubicle. Norbert of the three balls, charged with manslaughter and deserted by his wife. He catches sight of me and raises a cheerful hand in greeting. I'm about to open my mouth—I feel it incumbent on me to make some belated comment about his terrible predicament, to react in some way, but how?—when, just in the nick of time, I'm reminded of noble silence. So I raise my arm likewise, and we exchange a majestic wave.

I'M TOO LATE FOR BREAKFAST. Meditation hasn't done much for my fellow inmates' looks. Grey-faced and exhausted, they sit shivering over their muesli in fleeces and trousers, staring at me like a herd of cud-chewing cows. The children are unwashed, fretful, and food-bespattered. The breakfast table has been thoroughly grazed, the muesli bowl scraped almost clean. There's nothing left but a slice of wholemeal bread—wholemeal bread in France!—and a smidgen of jam, plus soya milk or herb tea. Although I know there's no coffee, I seek it like the Holy Grail. An equally hopeless quest.

I sit down and munch my slice of bread, overcome with melancholy. Where the devil is Franka? Without her I feel as forlorn as if I were soaring through space on my own. It's not even eight o'clock yet.

An interminable day lies ahead of me.

I feel a draught on the back of my neck. There she is at last! Laughingly, without turning around, I reach behind me two-handed and grab a pair of firm, slender thighs. Unfamiliar thighs. Franka's they certainly aren't. To her mother's chagrin, Franka has legs like Doric columns. Hastily releasing them, I turn to look.

Antje is standing behind me.

So sorry, I say, I thought you were—

She puts a finger to her lips and signs to me to come with her. I give the cud-chewers an apologetic smile, get to my feet, and follow her, afire with curiosity.

We've barely rounded the kitchen building and are out of sight of everyone when Antje breaks into a run. Along the gravel path, past the lotus pool, to the parking lot. I catch her up, panting hard.

Which is your car? she asks.

I point it out and open up. She flops down onto the passenger seat, produces a lipstick from her bag, lowers the sun visor, and paints her lips bright poppy-red in the courtesy mirror.

Then she smiles at me and says, *Un grand café au lait, s'il vous plaît.* I turn the key in the ignition.

Martha Gies

Zoo Animal Keeper I, REC-SVC-ZK

2 April

WAS QUITE AMAZED to see an ad for Animal Keeper in the Maui News. The zoo is run by Maui County Recreation Services, a division of our local third-world county government, which is made up of haggling factions—Japanese, Chinese and Portuguese. I thought you couldn't get a job with the County unless your brother or uncle worked there. But since the savings I brought from the mainland are nearly gone, I have decided to apply.

Disadvantaged by being a male—worse, a haole male—and having no relatives working for the County—or anywhere else—I also wrote my old boss at the Seattle Zoo for a letter of introduction.

I have now moved to Ka'ili'ili Road, where I serve as caretaker for the house of my tea master while he is in Kyoto. The old Sensei wished to visit Daitoku-ji Monastery once again, and to be a pilgrim at the many Buddhist shrines. I love this secluded tropical farm, where Sensei has electricity, hot and cold running water, a telephone, and many rooms.

But I miss the Sensei, and especially our tea lessons. In his absence, I study the seven secrets of the way of tea: *prepare an umbrella even if no rain falls, attune your heart to the guests,* and so forth. They appear obvious, but there is much to be mastered.

3 April

At 8:00 this morning, I was in the County office building, filling out a job application. I submitted my application along with a humble cover letter. About one hundred people applied. We shall see.

Afterward, I went to have a look at the little zoo, which has twenty goats, eight ducks, some chickens, a pair of ostriches, and a water buffalo. A real zoo I could not handle, what with gardening for the Sensei and studying tea, but this is perfect.

I met Luke Santos, the supervisor. He is an upcountry Portuguese, an energetic little man with a shock of white hair and much zoo experience. Together we "talked story" while walking through the zoo, which is set in a little jungle valley. Though I did not mention it to Luke, I did note that the viewing platform over the koi pond might be replaced and expanded. We visited the water buffalo, a lumbering creature, and I saw something of the Sensei himself in those tremendous sorrowing eyes. I scratched the animal's forelock fearlessly.

For two years, Luke was saying, he has been trying to get the pair of ostriches to breed. They lay, but won't tend the eggs. I told him of Seattle and my many attempts to get the ostriches separated from the springbok, whose sudden leaps made them jumpy. Sadly, Luke told me he had nothing to do with the hiring, though he said he respected my credentials. He offered me a small cigarillo, which I wrapped in a handkerchief and placed in my pocket.

It was during this visit with Luke that I began low-level political lobbying in earnest: I volunteered to help him set up for ZOOFEST!, a local event sponsored by the zoo's primary patron, the Maui County Philharmonic

Society. An amphitheater is needed in a grassy hollow adjacent to the zoo, and many citizens are planning to help construct it.

Back at home, I made a bowl of tea. With the Sensei absent, the sound of soft evening rain fills the house.

Tonight I am reading about the remarkable sixteenth-century tea master Sen Rikyu, who was also a zen monk:

Alone in his tea house, meditating, Sen Rikyu senses someone creeping up behind him. Without turning around, he raises the bamboo water ladle up over his right shoulder and strikes the assassin's sword. The bamboo shatters steel.

10 April

It is still another two months before the Sensei returns from Japan. From the Hundred Rules of Sen Rikyu: *If anyone wishes to enter the way of tea he must be his own teacher.*

Today I received a reply from Winston Donnelly, my old boss at the Seattle Zoo. He sent a "To Whom It May Concern" letter to the Maui Department of Personnel Services in my behalf. He also gave me a bit of news:

It seems the female European Brown Bear killed one of her cubs in a dispute over an orange thrown into the enclosure by a visitor. In the ensuing scuffle, the cub bit its mother, and she turned and cuffed it. After eating the orange, the mother turned to lick the heavily bleeding wound of the cub, then proceeded to kill and eat it. All of this occurred at 6:00 P.M. on a warm spring evening, in front of many parents and children.

Reading this letter, I was saddened at the zoo's harsh and reactionary decision to suspend public feeding. I was also reminded of the many arguments and controversies stemming from the contradictory purposes of the zoo, and how relieved I was to finally leave it. Fame and profit are both dispensed with, was my thought in resigning. This is the exact phrase from which Sen Rikyu took his tea name.

The good news in Donnelly's letter is that they've put the patient, oxlike eland on display with the ostriches and they are getting along so well that the entire group beds down together at night. A welcome change from the flighty springbok. Could the little Maui zoo invest in an eland, I wonder?

One of Sen Rikyu's sayings: *If you wish to follow the way of Buddha it is only this: lead a life of leisure and don't take things seriously.* Clearly, Sen Rikyu did not have to contend with Maui County bureaucracy.

ZOOFEST! brought to the attention of the Maui County Council the use of volunteer labor and donations to construct the amphitheater without approval of the Council. The Council has attacked Bud Hokoana, the director of Recreation Services, for being sloppy and unprofessional. Hokoana is a rare native Hawaiian in a position of power. The Council's attack on this man was intense, though many citizens supported him through letters to the editor in the Maui News.

Today I begin clearing an old taro terrace, the site of my newest project, a low altitude garden, in accordance with the poet Soji: *A glimpse of the sea through the trees and the flash of the stream at my feet.*

It's 4:30 A.M., dark and damp. The dew creeps into the Sensei's screened-in back porch where I have set up my old typewriter. Trying to write letters is not an easy task in the jungle, which is dripping around me. The writing paper is soggy, the stamps stick together, and the envelope glues itself shut. I've filtered a cup of dark roast Kona coffee and have three kerosene lamps gathered around my table. Outside the screen are many gardenia bushes, heavy with buds soon to go off.

I have decided to offer my support to Bud Hokoana, the director of Recreation Services, with the following letter:

Dear Mr. Hokoana:

The "amphitheater controversy," with its thorny birth in Council budget scrutiny, reveals a very positive picture of the

hard work of County Recreation employees and the inspiring ini-
tiative of volunteers. Especially to be admired is your department's flexibility in using whatever is at hand, and in not being
bound to useless rules. As the famous tea master Sen Rikyu noted:
Only a stupid person will glue the bridges of a harp in place.

I myself helped Luke Santos with ZOOFEST!, and I was amazed
by the sheer volume of volunteers, from many diverse factions,
all working together. Your notion of the community "accepting
responsibility for their own leisure pursuits" seems especially
fundamental in these low-budget times.

The extraordinary and inappropriate assault of Council members Cordova and Tsutakawa strikes me as an attempt to cover
up for their own deficit in attention regarding the workings of
your department. Though I respect the vast scope of information
and data that must be assimilated by these elected officials, your
position aroused much empathy from this County resident.

This letter also serves to introduce myself as a potential County
of Maui, Recreation Services employee. I worked as an animal
keeper at the Woodland Park Zoo in Seattle, Washington, from
July 1987 to June 1992. There my primary responsibility was
the bird collection. Animal care and feeding, exhibit cleaning
and maintenance, medication and breeding programs, record-
keeping and dealing with the public are among my capabilities.

I hope I may put these skills at your service as a Maui County
employee.

My sincere aloha,
William Rivers

P. S. I append a well-known haiku which I thought might be of
use to you in this (I hope brief) time of political strife:

Wind comes to bamboo
Wind passed by
Bamboo retains not wind.

28 April

Today I received a reply from Bud Hokoana, thanking me for my letter of support. He reminded me that the County Personnel Department handles the hiring process, but says "your empathy for our cause is welcome."

I also learned that I survived the first screening of applications, and have been given a date for the exam—6:00 P.M., the day after tomorrow.

29 April

This morning I perused data previously checked out from the library. I began by taking a sample federal civil service exam for janitors and custodians, but found I could not focus on the many multiple-choice questions involving the virtues of single rotor and double rotor floor buffers. I moved on to almanac reading, all sections having to do with animal gestation periods, what the young of animals are called, what groupings of different animals are called, etc. From there, I went right into GED sample math tests. Though I can answer quickly, I am wrong 90% of the time. Fortunately, the answer section states the specific data necessary to solve the problems, so I am still at it.

Among the Hundred Rules of Sen Rikyu, we read: *One who is ashamed to show ignorance will never be any good.*

30 April

Tonight, approximately 100 people appeared in the Kahului School cafeteria to be tested. Most were taking carpenter tests. Only five were taking the zoo animal-keeper exam, which indicates some severe pruning. Although we had two hours, I finished in 18 minutes. I sat waiting for a local to finish so I wouldn't have to turn in my exam first. A young Japanese man finished, and I turned in my paper and left. We shall see.

2 May

Though it's still a month away, I am already thinking about a party to welcome the Sensei's return from Kyoto. I am guided by the spirit of a famous story about Sen Rikyu:

Once he invited the famous General Hideyoshi to tea. The night before the general was expected, snow began to fall. Sen Rikyu went into the garden and set cushions on each of the stepping stones which led to the tea house. At dawn he took them up again. When the great general arrived, the entire garden was covered with snow and only the stepping stones were smooth and bare.

Of course, we have no snow here in the jungle, but it is hoped that I can prepare in a way that will show my eagerness to honor the old Sensei without being merely clever.

9 May

They sent me the test results: I got the highest score, and a #1 civil-service rating in my category.

12 May

I was called in for an interview today. I expected it to be with the Personnel Department, but it was with Bud Hokoana and the zoo supervisor, Luke. Hokoana is a large man, perhaps 50, with a sweet round face. When I admired his native shirt, a black-and-white palm-leaf print, he told me with a smile that he bought it at The Gap in San Francisco. I was relaxed and the interview was brief. When asked to expound my zoo philosophy, I quickly made one up: *Each animal is a guest; we must attune our hearts to the guest.*

I waited at the zoo for Luke to get back from the other interviews. He told me I had his vote for sure, and he thought I had Hokoana's vote also. However, Luke did warn me that the other applicant has strong family connections in County government. He gave me another cigarillo, which I graciously accepted and put in my shirt pocket.

13 May

Today I am hacking back the tangle of guava trees that encroach on the hibiscus hedge I planted last year along the south property line. I alternated varieties, planting a lavender-pink species mixed in with a hybrid double-blossom orange. Among them are a few of the Oahu white hibiscus with its six-inch petal. They will bloom soon if the guava jungle doesn't take over. The sun is completely up, and it's extraordinarily beautiful.

14 May

A letter arrived from the County Personnel Department saying June Tsutakawa has been hired to fill Zoo Animal Keeper I, REC-SVC-ZK. It was a cordial letter, reminding me that many qualified persons applied.

I phoned Luke Santos at the zoo. He seemed uneasy, and grumbled a bit about so much training required for the new employee, yet I raised the point with him that this woman (who turns out to be Councilman Tsutakawa's niece) will have *"the humble but eager heart of the beginner."* It is this quality that the great tea masters remind us to preserve in ourselves.

As we talked a bit, I thought Luke relaxed. I thanked him for his support. Then I described the eland, with its backward flying horns, and mentioned the possibility of his acquiring one as a way of increasing the comfort of the ostrich family. Luke chuckled and said next they'd be asking him to breed eland. That is probably true.

I invited Luke to come to Ka'ili'ili Road after work to have a bowl of tea, and he said he just might do that, which sounded to me like he would not. We shall see. I have placed two of the cigarillos that he likes in the Sensei's humidor, just in case he drops by someday.

I only wish the Sensei could be here to drink a bowl of tea with me now. He has written a long letter describing his visit to the monastery of Daitoku-ji. There is a postscript, which I recognize as Sen Rikyu:

If even one guest is missing, then the haunting and lasting flavor of the tea must take his place.

Keith Kachtick

Hungry Ghost

THE BEACH dogs are barking again, though this time not at the *federales*. The little herd of sand-covered mutts—two have their ears painted purple, one wears a red bandana—has sniffed out your hiding spot in the late-afternoon shade and is splashing toward you from the surf. For the better part of a minute they snap and yelp at where you lie high up on the dunes, clearly not as well concealed by the shadows as you'd thought.

Once the dogs finally get bored and trot off along the shoreline, you sit back up, run a hand through your hair, adjust your sunglasses, and continue spying on Greta, a blond, blue-eyed, thirty-one-year-old sous chef from Berlin, who you've known for three days and who is now naked and preparing for a swim in the ocean. You gape at the slope of Greta's breasts and run the back of your wrist across your mouth. Though alone on the beach, she seems unconcerned about the dogs. Without so much as a glance over her shoulder, she drops her black bikini top and diaphanous, burgundy-colored sarong, strides across the damp sand, and dives into the breakers.

Over the last three days you've come to think of this long-legged German woman in specific physical terms, individual pieces of an exotic, big-boned puzzle. Greta is taller than average, heavier than average, ample but in an understated, competitive-sculler sort of way. A pre-Raphaelite mop of sandy blond hair. Broad shoulders. Muscular calves. Collarbones you could rope a horse to. A drowsy, full-souled smile. You can't get enough of her smoky German accent. At times she works so hard at finding the correct word in English, her wide, Old World face scrunched from the effort, that you want to take her hand. But you haven't—not once. And thus far you've managed to stay out of her cabaña, too.

Today is the final day of your three-day shoot. All of your photo gear has been re-packed in the brushed-silver Anvils in preparation for tomorrow morning's departure. Less fruitful than it might have been (you exposed only nineteen rolls of film of the fifty you brought), this unexpected "adventure travel" assignment in southern Mexico will nonetheless pay much of the balance due on your new $2,900 Minolta laser printer and last month's $1,800 rent on your East Village apartment. The details of your arrival here in Zipolite back on Tuesday now seem blurred by heat: New York to Mexico City to Oaxaca on increasingly smaller planes, five hours by rickety bus along the winding mountain roads of the Sierra Madres to the fishing village of Puerto Escondido, hitchhiking to San Augustinillo and then crossing by foot the beachfront dunes that lead, ultimately, to this hedonistic Pacific coast sanctuary. Despite the halfhearted professional effort, you're in no hurry to leave—the warm winter weather has proven intoxicating.

Zipolite is located on the tip of the country's southernmost peninsula, about as far from the United States as one can get and still be in Mexico. You were hired and sent here by Men's Agenda's art director to illustrate with your photographs a 2,700-word article titled "Bohemian Paradise: A South-of-the-Border Shangri-la." For three days you've remained barefoot, worn the same pair of oversized Abercrombie & Fitch canvas cargo shorts, stayed either high or within arm's reach of a frosty Negra Modelo, and been surrounded by comely beachcombers wearing little more than coconut oil and toe-rings. Each morning you meditated hidden behind dunes taller than your outstretched arms. After a breakfast of papaya or watermelon, you wandered from one end of Zipolite's half-mile beach to the other, bliss-fully stoned, photographing with either your new Mamiya M645 or your rugged little Canon Elan, discreetly and usually with permission, the occa-sional semi-naked woman lying on the dunes. You discovered that among the semi-naked women you photographed were a high school English teacher from Ontario, a Brazilian journalist covering the Zapatista rebels in the neigh-boring state of Chiapas, an Italian sculptor with a name you couldn't pro-nounce, and Greta, the dripping-wet sous chef from Berlin whose body is so sun-darkened that the palms of her hands seem to glow, and who—eyes lowered, arms crossed—is presently hauling herself from the roaring, early-evening surf back to her towel.

What to do? As another high-tide wave unfurls close to your restless, lust-prickled toes, you lean over and secure yourself higher on the dry dune, your water bottle and black North Face daypack stuffed an hour ago with your seduction supplies: travel-size chessboard, pack of Marlboro Lights, Spanish-riddled Cormac McCarthy novel, Sony Discman and pair of minia-ture speakers, five self-mixed, computer-burned, thematically-titled CDs *(Caligula, Dharma Groove, Faster Pussycat to the Library, McInerney's Love Dogs,* and *Music for the Bong)*, $100 in pesos, deck of Red Bicycle playing cards, and what's left of the quarter-ounce of marijuana you brought from New York. You turn back to the cove and watch Greta refasten her bikini top. Seated and facing the horizon, heels digging into the wet sand, thighs and shins covered again by the maroon sarong, she shields her eyes from the setting sun. The prickling rises up your brainstem. Struggling neophyte Buddhist that you are, you blow out a breath and dutifully remind yourself about the cause-and-effect reality of karma, and the Buddha's maxim that sensual pleasure is like saltwater: the more you indulge, the more the thirst increases.

You first laid eyes on Greta shortly after your arrival in Zipolite Tuesday afternoon. Trudging from the Sendero registration hut with your backpack and photo equipment, already sunburned from the hour-long hike along the beach from San Augustinillo, you caught sight of her swinging in a hammock and reading a paperback novel. Pausing before unlocking the neighboring cabaña, you jiggled your oversized key to get her attention, and conspicuously tilted your head in order to see the book's title. Without saying anything, she straightened the cover for you. Rainer Rilke's *Die Aufzeichnungen des Malte Laurids Brigge*. "Ah," you responded knowingly, though the only book by Rilke you've read is *Letters to a Young Poet*. "Do you speak English?"

Greta's blue eyes returned to the weathered pages. With the hint of a smirk she replied, "That depends to whom I speak."

That night, showered and dressed in your multipocketed cargo shorts, mala beads, and an ocher-colored linen shirt purchased expressly for the trip, the loaded Elan slung low around your neck, you joined her for a beachfront dinner at Lo Cosmico, an open-air restaurant set up directly on the sand, the waves breaking fewer than fifty feet away, the wooden tables so close to the surf you could feel its salty spray on your cheeks. A boisterous, eclectic-looking group of European backpackers and local artisans sat around a long picnic table, eating seafood and drinking cuba libres from plastic cups. A boombox hanging by rope from the thatched roof blasted American rock music. Everyone at the table was barefoot and tan. Most smoked cigarettes. Several were already drunk. Though you were the oldest and palest of the assemblage, after two drinks you felt comfortable. To your right sat a woman named Kaja, an amber-eyed vendor of Mexican silver in Austria who wore a green halter top and a black headband high on her forehead, her tousled brown hair erupting skyward like the plume of a volcano. To your left sat a young Oaxacan painter named Morro, almost feline-looking with his black goatee and ponytail, who warned you of the dangers of Zipolite's notorious surf.

Between mouthfuls of red snapper and steaming corn tortillas, you slurped *sopa de mariscos* from an enormous bowl that appeared before you out of nowhere. While at Lo Cosmico, in part because of the noise and commotion and free-flowing rum-and-Cokes, you failed to keep your "meal mindfulness" vow (suggested by your Tibetan Dharma teacher, whom you plan to join on retreat later this month) to always lower your spoon or fork between bites. You were further distracted by the spectacle of Greta, laughing and drinking with an Australian surfer, at least ten years your junior, at the far end of the table. Wolfing down another tortilla, you sized up Greta's tight white T-shirt and faded jeans, the beaded necklaces, the loose blond braid. You stared and stared until you finally made eye contact. The blue-eyed Berliner responded with a coy smile and subtle nod and shortly came around the table and demanded that you join her with the handful of others who had begun to dance in the sand.

IN FEBRUARY you'll turn thirty-nine. Five years ago a female editorial manager at *Elle* told you over dinner that she thought thirty-six was the red-flag age for never-married heterosexual bachelors, a red flag that signaled in most females' eyes a man's fundamental difficulty with commitment and perhaps even an unhealthy regard for women. In a word: broken. You've questioned for half a decade whether this assessment is true of you. Though you've not had a steady girlfriend in three years, you feel okay about your love life, which you would semi-seriously describe as semi-serial monogamy. All in all your life is . . . okay. You sleep well. You rarely get sick. You volunteer at the Chelsea AIDS Hospice. You hope one day to be a father, and understand that to be a good father you must first be a good husband. And for the last six months you've been attentive to your daily Dharma practice, which consists of a self-concocted pastiche of cardiovascular exercise, seated meditation, mantra chanting, precept vows, and (with an increasingly strained rationale) moderate marijuana consumption.

In fact, the shot of yours that will eventually be chosen to accompany the *Men's Agenda* article was taken less than an hour after Wednesday morning's palm-shaded meditation. You would like to think the two events were connected. While trolling through Zipolite for more pictures, a little bow and Buddha-like half-smile bestowed upon everyone who crossed your path, you came upon the Italian sculptor with the unpronounceable name as she practiced yoga on the beach. The moment you looked through the Elan's viewfinder at the small Sanskrit tattoo between her shoulder blades you knew that this would be the image. "It's the symbol for the mantra Om," the sculptor explained of her year-old tattoo over the crabmeat *quesadillas* and Negra Modelos with which you repaid her, twisting her shoulders sideways to give you a closer look. Greta watched the two of you from behind her sunglasses and Rilke novel at a corner table.

Late Wednesday afternoon you caught your first sight of Greta skinny-dipping in the ocean. Early Wednesday evening you invited her to dinner. By midnight, before a small driftwood campfire on a quiet dune near the Sendero compound, you and Greta found yourselves squared off again across your chessboard, a peso and a surprisingly savvy hermit crab serving as White's two missing bishops. Greta was in her purple sarong and the same white T-shirt from the previous night, with a light bone-colored shawl pulled over her shoulders. Between moves you discussed German fashion designers and your favorite non-American films—*The Bicycle Thief, Nosferatu, Lawrence of Arabia.* By the beginning of your second game—you lost the first one, Greta explained, because of your overly aggressive rooks—all of the open-air cafés on the beach had turned their lights off for the night.

THURSDAY AFTERNOON, shortly after lunch, you exposed four final rolls of color film in Zipolite's village and then packed your gear for Friday's departure. You'd not seen Greta all day. Intent on finding a dinner companion for your last evening in Mexico, you showered, stuffed the daypack, and, leaving your mala beads, set off down the beach in your cargo shorts and the last of your new linen shirts. For an hour you prowled the beachfront cafés in search of the dark-eyebrowed Italian sculptor (whose name, as best you could figure out yesterday, is either Emelise or Amelisa), before spotting Greta and her book on the empty shore. Rather than wave, you decided to perch yourself on a dune behind her—the better to keep your dining options open.

You spied on Greta for almost an hour before she disrobed and plunged into the water to cool off. And after she marched past you en route to her cabaña, dripping wet and surprising you with her coy smile and comment about the weather, you remained on the dune for another fifteen minutes, flat on your stomach, alternately staring at Greta's white towel and damp black bathing suit draped over the railing, and her shadowy movements behind the shutters.

In recent weeks you've wondered if it isn't better for people always to think of themselves in second person, fully to disassociate their awareness from the obstructing, lower-self "I" that thinks in terms of "me" and "mine" and "may I unbutton your blouse now, please?" You tell yourself again that to spiritualize your desires, you must desire to be without desire. That the spiritual path takes willpower. In your heart you know the truth of this, that you're the captain of your fate, that who you are right now is based on what you did in the past, and that who you'll be in the future is determined by what you do next. Nevertheless, you sigh and flip onto your side, scratch your belly, and stare hungrily at the partially opened door to Greta's cabaña, the warmth draining promptly from your heart into your loins, the lust suctioned southward so forcefully that you sit up, remove your sunglasses, and let out a long, miserable groan.

Ten minutes later you bang on Greta's door with the side of your bare left foot. Daypack slung over your shoulder, chessboard in one hand, an ice-chilled six-pack of Negra Modelos in the other, you beam broadly as your blond-haired prey swings open the portal and invites you to enter.

TWENTY MINUTES AFTER YOUR ARRIVAL, two beers already under your belt, your rolling papers and lighter tossed on the mattress, you lean back in the cabin's one chair and watch Greta examine the labels of the self-mixed CDs you brought for the Discman, now unpacked and positioned strategically with its two miniature speakers on her bed's head-board. Most of Greta's dark, dewy skin is now hidden beneath the sarong and a man's long-sleeved cotton shirt. Apple-scented lip balm adds to her smile a sexy shine. While you crumble the biggest, red-fringed bud from your baggie into a snorkeling mask secured between your knees, Greta flips over and reads the CD's band list. Spotting the red Bicycle deck among the items tactically extruded from your bag onto her bed, she asks, "Do you play the cards?"

"I do. Wanta see a trick?"

"Yah—of course. Please."

You scoot your chair closer to where Greta sits on the bed's edge. Joint lit but as yet unoffered, you shuffle and then nonchalantly cut the deck with a single hand, fanning the cards face-down with a graceful, "ooh"-inspir-ing sweep. "Pick a card," you tell her. "Any card." Made nervous by your card-handling skills, Greta examines and cautiously inserts her selection back into the deck. You shuffle the cards three more times, flip the deck over, and present her with the bottom card: the Jack of Clubs. "Is this your card?"

Greta shakes her head. "No."

As you show her each of the next three possibilities, you ask, "Is *this* your card?"

"No," she replies repeatedly, unsure if the trick is unfolding as you in-tended, though confident that her card is not among the four you place face-down before her on the mattress.

You hand Greta the remainder of the deck. To verify that her selection is not among those you've shown her, you reveal the four cards again, con-firming with each as you turn it over, "This is not your card—correct?"

"No," she replies, crossing her arms and shaking her head. "None of those are my card."

You arch an eyebrow, make a show of rolling up your nonexistent sleeves, and dramatically extend for inspection your empty palms. "Choose a num-ber between one and four."

"And tell you?"

"Mm-hmm."

" . . . Three."

Pointing to the row with an index finger, you count from right to left to the third card. You take a long, theatrical breath, administer with your fingertips an ambiguously magical *smack,* and with a flourish flip the card over to reveal that—*voilà*—it has become her selection: the Queen of Hearts.

Greta clutches her chest and instinctively leans away from you. "Oh, my God—Carter. How is this so?" Mouth gaping, eyes wide, she inspects the remaining three cards with disbelief. "How did you do this?"

You answer darkly, "Magic," promptly gathering and returning the repacked deck of cards to the depths of your bag, as Greta grabs your arm and implores you to show her another of your tricks.

"Please," she begs, but you lower your eyes and wag your head: a good performer always leaves his audience wanting more.

An hour later the two of you are naked and in her bed. Six empty bottles of Negra Modelo are clustered in the corner behind your discarded shirt and cargo shorts. The tangled mosquito net lies on the floor. Greta moves onto her stomach on the mattress beside you wearing nothing but her beaded necklace, lightheaded from the beer and her first puffs of marijuana in two years. Eyes closed, she rolls her head and hums along with Erykah Badu.

"Are you hungry?" you ask, as the two of you eventually pull yourself from her bed and dress on opposite sides of the one-room cabin.

Greta shakes her head.

"I'm gonna go get something to eat," you tell her. "Do you want anything?"

Her back turned to you, Greta sighs but remains quiet.

The moon is out by the time you return to Greta's cabaña with two more bottles of beer and a plate of four fish tacos, the rolled-up soft flour tortillas steaming, the shredded shark meat inside smelling of cilantro.

Back in her long-sleeved shirt and purple sarong, silent, even more pensive than when you left her, Greta stands smoking one of your cigarettes by the screenless window as you enter without knocking, set the plate of food on the wobbly wooden table, and resume your seat in the room's lone chair. The ceiling fan and Discman have been turned off. The bed is made. The mosquito netting is nowhere in sight. She feels queasy, her mouth dry and her eyes red from the cannabis.

Because you're chewing the first fish taco and already thinking of the next, you don't observe that Greta is near tears. Because you've not bothered to ask, you're unaware that she has come to Mexico seeking respite from the pain of losing a miscarried child, buried in October, fathered by a boyfriend to whom she said nothing about the pregnancy for fear of jinxing it, an architect who routinely beat her in chess and who drove away with their four-year-old Audi when he moved out, without explanation, the Sunday before she lost their child—a boy she planned to name Rainer. You're unaware that on the plane ride to Oaxaca, Greta promised herself not to drink alcohol before dark or while alone, and to do her best not to fall in love with anyone—especially not an American photographer who dances like a teenage boy. You're unaware that the false promise implicit in your short but intimate time together will help her decide to leave Berlin for good, to start elsewhere what she hopes might be a better life, that she will eventually marry a wealthy estate lawyer in Paris, fifteen years her senior, with a thirst for saltwater worse than yours, that because of her marriage to this man she will never again work professionally as a chef, a loss that will lead her to give up on her drinking vows altogether, and that she will die while scuba-diving alone in the Mediterranean Sea on her fortieth birthday.

You're halfway through eating a second fish taco before you speak. Wiping your lips with a finger, you notice the line of ants crawling across the straw mat beneath your feet. "You okay over there?" Greta nods but stays turned toward the darkened sky. You glance at her opened duffel bag, at the stack of her paperbacks leaning against the wall. You ask, "Would you like to see a picture of my dog Marley?" Before she can respond, you withdraw from the back pocket of your cargo shorts your passport holder, and from that a wrinkled 3" x 5" self-portrait of you and your shaggy, eight-year-old mongrel dressed as Batman and Robin for last Halloween's East Village street festival. Marley, looking up goofily at the automated flash-box, wears four little green boots, a red cape, and a crooked gold mask. Greta smiles politely, the image bringing more tears to her eyes, which force her to blink and tilt back her head lest they spill.

"He is a cute dog, Carter," she says, stepping away. "He looks like he is a good friend to you."

You lean back in the chair even farther, returning the picture and pass-port to your pocket, willfully oblivious to what Greta is feeling, and give the North Face bag—half-hidden beneath the bed—a nudge with your toe. You fear Greta expects you to spend the night with her.

"I like your hair, Carter," she says wistfully, turning back after wiping her eyes, gamely trying to change the subject as she reaches down to touch your bangs. "How do you make it to do this?"

"Turn gray?"

"Puhh—no it's so—mmmm . . . how do you say, it's—"

"Messy? I don't do anything, really. It just comes out this way."

Arms crossed below her belly, she asks, "What will you do with the pictures you took of me?"

You clear your throat and think hard for a moment. "I don't know," you answer, which is more true than not.

Greta gazes out the window at the ocean and moon. Dogs are barking on the beach again. "Hmmm. I have to smile about myself some—I *hate* being looked at with a camera. It takes your soul, you know? It possesses you. And I saw you with so many other women, Carter."

You look down at the plate, which now holds only one of the original four fish tacos. You smack your lips and wince, tasting in the back of your throat the biliousness, the weakness, that would lead Peter O'Toole's self-hating

Lawrence, bloodied by a battle wound, to nod and mumble, "Good, good." With an embarrassed shrug, forearm drying your chin, you smile feebly and extend the plate toward Greta—but it's too late: Arms still crossed, she's turned fully to the sea and sky. She's no longer listening to you. She's no longer thinking of you. She's no longer even in the room. She's in the future. And the future, she realizes, has not come out quite as she had hoped.

Ira Sukrungruang

The Golden Mix

T'S BEEN COLD HERE in Chester, snowing at night, leaving fresh powder in the morning. Anders bursts in and tracks some of it into my apartment, real inconsiderate. He rolls up here like it's his place, throwing his wet leather on the couch, shaking his green hair like a dog after a swim. Lucky, I'm not in the mood to criticize.

Chester's south of Madison, and so small nothing's a secret. You can tell you're in Chester because suddenly everything's pastel. On the main downtown strip, about a mile long, the buildings are the color of spring. Lou Ann's, where I work, a real man's man bar, is pink; the hardware store next door, sky blue. About fifteen miles north, on 218, is the university the town doesn't like; it's the reason people like Anders and I mill around.

Once, a regular at Lou Ann's asked about Anders, only he referred to him as the "weird one." "What's the story with that friend of yours, the weird one?" And I'd tell him the story. We met at the University of Wisconsin three years ago during a protest to stop experiments on cows. UW was planning to remove a chunk of skin from the side of a heifer and replace it with a window so students could see the working anatomy. Painless, they'd said. I was still with Michelle then, an activist who wore leather, who made me move to this town because she thought it was cute and pretty. Exact words. She got hyped up about this rally and begged me to come out and support the cause. "What the hell," I said. "I'd just stand here and wave a grotesque sign of a bloody heart. Cool." At the protest, this guy with green hair jumped over the barricade and ran around the administrators like he was hyped up on NoDoz. Then he stopped in front of them, pulled down his pants and bent over, talking between his legs, asking if they'd like take a look at his working anatomy. A guy like that I had to meet. The story made the regular groan. "The shit that damn university brings in," he muttered.

Anders takes a seat and rubs his hands together then blows in them.

I toast a coffee mug and ask, "You want some tea?"

He shakes his head and hunches over, as if the Egyptian cross around his neck weighed him down, as if he has a secret he wants to share. "Buddha came to the Shack today," he says.

"Who?" I ask, thinking Anders said a girl's name, maybe a one-niter, someone he thought he'd never see again. He's like that, the Swede in him. He leaves more shit than he could clean. Funny thing is, that's what he does. Cleans shit. Every day at the Shack: Chester's Humane Society. He likes it.

"You're not listening," he says.

"I am," I say, but I'm really not.

"Buddha," he says again. "Open your ears. Oriental God. Dude we see in Chinese restaurants all the time."

The teakettle whistles. I look at him hard before turning the burner off.

"Did you smoke up?"

"No," he says.

"Drop a yellow?"

"I'm not kidding," he says. "Buddha came in today wanting to adopt a dog."

I just stare at him, thinking he's lost it, sniffed one too many lines. Finally, I say, putting him on, "Was he fat and bald? Were his ears real long? Buddha always looks like he's drunk."

"Real skinny," he says, all serious, not cracking a smile. "In some parts of Asia Buddha's a skinny dude. I saw it on *National Geographic*."

I sip my tea, but the water is so hot I spit it out and say fuck.

"Slow down," Anders says. "Let it cool."

The tea stains my shirt, the last clean one. I take it off and throw it into a pile of dirty laundry by the fake ficus. The tree is layered with so much dust that if anything shook the plastic leaves it'd sprinkle snow. The entire apartment is layered with dust. You can't wear black without walking out of my place with streaks of gray on you. I have dishes from a month ago, soaking in cloudy water. The other day Anders said my apartment smelled like canned dog food. The place needs serious cleaning, but I've been unmotivated, thinking about my life here in Chester, about the Psych degree that went for nothing because I lost my faith in people, and how Michelle upped and left, saying I'm going nowhere. Fuck her for being right.

I take another shirt from the pile, smell the pits, and put it on. "So what dog did Buddha get?" I say.

"I was cleaning Patches' cage," Anders says. "The little pup got sick. Shit and puke everywhere. Martha took him to the vet. I was cleaning the cage and in walked this bald-headed Oriental dude. At first I didn't see him. I kind of felt him, like when someone leaves the door open and cold air comes in. I thought Martha left the door open. I turned around and here's this bald little Oriental guy outside the cage, looking at me. I didn't hear him come in. Suddenly, he's just there."

The tea steams. I leave it alone. "How the hell do you know it was Buddha?" I say.

"I'll get to that," he says.

"Was he wearing robes?" I say. "Like the monks in Kung Fu Theater?"

"Jeans," he says. "Levis and a leather jacket that went to the thighs."

I laugh a little too loud. "Bullshit," I say.

Anders ignores me and continues with his crazy story. "He wasn't tall or anything, but he felt tall. He felt like a giant. You've met people like that, right? People who feel much bigger than you?" He pauses and waits for my nod. "When I saw him, I jumped back a little because it's not all the time you see an Oriental dude in Chester. I said to him, I didn't hear you come in. And shit, he said, Sometimes silence awakens the inner heart."

"What the fuck?" I say.

"Like a fortune cookie."

Anders cracks his neck by snapping it to the right, then left. I hate that.

"I stood there a while with Patches' puke in a bucket. He didn't say anything, just stared and smiled. Finally I said, Can I help you? He said, Yes. Nothing else. This guy, he was a strange one, but I wasn't scared. I was feeling okay, better than okay. I was feeling like I smoked a tenth. I asked, Are you interested in adopting? I am, he said. Cat or dog? I asked. He opened the cage door for me. Cats have their own roads, he said. Dogs need a push to find theirs. Do you believe that? What do you say after that?"

"What did you?"

"Nothing. I just showed him the dogs."

Anders stops and hits his forehead. "Dammit! I forgot to tell you about the weirdest detail. When he came in, the whole place got quiet. No noise."

At the Shack, you talk like at a Prodigy concert. You have to kick it up a notch over the barks, whines, meows, everything. I brought Anders a hoagie for lunch once and thought about the qualities of a person who worked in a place that was loud and smelled like piss and shit. Anders gave me the tour. The Shack was small, had cages outside the front door in case someone found a stray after hours. On the left side of a narrow hallway was a room with small cages: the cat room. On the right side was where they kept "other creatures," like domesticated snakes and ferrets. The back of the Shack was dedicated to the dogs.

I got sad watching Anders work. I wasn't into animals, but I wanted to rescue them all and give them a good life. I thought, Who would dedicate their days dealing with so much sadness? And then I looked at Anders. He gave them scraps of his turkey. He was talking up a storm, so happy I was there. Then Martha came in from her break, smelling like a couple shots of JD, like she hadn't bathed in a while. She called Anders a dummy for feeding the dogs people food. She asked why the hell I was there, looked at me like how some of the regulars at Lou Ann's looked at me, a mix of disgust and curiosity. I said to her, "Keep your panties on," and walked out of the place. I told Anders I was never going back because of Martha, but the truth was, I didn't want to feel all that sadness again.

Anders stares at my mug. "Sip your tea. It's probably not too hot now."

I sip. "What next?" I say.

"Fuckin' silent," he says. "Even Bobo shut up, that yappy bitch. She didn't say a word. I went along the cages, and the dogs just stared at us. I asked the dude what kind of dog he wanted—small, large, young, old— the usual things, the standard things to ask. What kind of attitude was he looking for? What about energy level? He didn't say anything. He moved his fingers along the cages, and all of sudden, these dogs were jumping and licking at his fingertips. These dogs wanted him. They never acted like that. Not all of them. Some go to the corner, whimpering, scared. But for this guy, they were jumping. Except one. Bobo. She sat still."

I lean against the stove and cross my arms. I'm hooked in by Anders' strange story. I don't take my eyes off him.

"Bobo," Anders says, "well, she's at the end of the line. Her date was coming. She wasn't baring teeth or anything. Just sat there, pretty-like, like a girl showing off her tits. The dude was heading for Bobo, and I said, You don't want that one. She's a mean sucker. She bit a boy. How about this one, I said. I showed him the golden mix, my favorite dog in the place. It was wagging and singing a tune for him. The man put his finger through the gate, and the golden kissed like crazy. I don't know how it got lost. It's so good. How can anyone lose this good dog?"

"People," I say.

"Yeah," he says. "People."

We don't talk for a while, thinking about people. Anders cracks his knuckles, and I know it is a good day for him because the iguana on his ring is looking at me, the tail pointing at him.

"This dog is on the right path, the guy said, one that does not cross with mine. He looked at the golden again, such a good dog. And on cue, the dog stopped licking and looked at me. Man, I love that dog. The dude, he started walking toward Bobo again, and the crazy bitch didn't move. You'd think she was the National Obedience Champion. I told him, No. You don't want that dog. She's close. Probably next week some time. And he said—get this—he said, Close to what? And I'm not good with shit like that. You know what I'm talking about, right? I'm not good at telling people that—you know. Martha says it like nothing, like it doesn't matter."

When Anders told me about Bobo two months ago, I couldn't stop shaking. The story reaffirmed my thoughts about people. Bobo bit a boy. Anders thought the boy provoked the dog, since there were little puncture wounds all over her body like someone was poking her with a sharp stick. The boy's father beat the shit out of her, beat her until she couldn't move anymore. This was a small dog with short little legs. The fuckin' guy brought the dog in, laid the bloody and broken body on the Shack's counter, said one thing, "It bit my boy," and left, screeched away in a pickup. People like him you can't help. Seems to be more people like that in the world.

The guy should've killed Bobo, just ended it. She was suffering big time. I bet you she wanted to die, but Anders patched her up. "There's always room for a second chance, right?" he said. I suppose there is room, except Bobo, four months later, is a real bitch, mean and scared, the worst combination.

The snow drifts down again. The springtime-green diner across the street is barely visible. "What'd you say to him then?" I say. "How'd you tell him—you know?" I can't say it either.

"I didn't say anything," Anders says. "He didn't let me. He put his hand on my arm and I got this feeling, real strange, like when my mom put her hand on my head when I was sick and it made all the difference, like tomorrow I knew I was going to be out with my friends picking on the girls again. I knew 'cause her hand told me so. His hand told me so. You know what I mean?"

I nod, understanding perfectly.

"Then the dude said, Dogs, you like them, yes? I loved dogs, loved all animals. I told him how I wanted to be a vet, but was too stoned to go class, so I dropped out. Hell, I began telling this Oriental dude everything, the time my first dog, Mick, died, how I wished I could breathe life into him. I told him about the jay I tried to save, how I made a brace for its wing—remember, man?—but it died anyway. I told him everything, spilling my guts."

I remember all the times Anders made me stop the car so he could help a stray, and how then, it annoyed me because he was wasting my time. I feel guilty now. I envy Anders' heart; how he'd do anything for an animal, even risk his own life by throwing himself onto a car once to save a little garden snake. Stuff like that defines a person, and it doesn't matter how much weed he smokes, or whether his hair is greener than the grass you keep up with those chemicals. It doesn't matter because shit like that is artificial.

"After I was done, I looked at my watch and forty minutes had passed. Forty minutes! and he never interrupted me. I'm sorry for taking up your time, I said. He said, Time is a mountain. You really don't want that dog, I said again. You look like a good guy. Maybe you'd like this one or this one. You don't want that one. She bit a boy. But he wanted to see Bobo, sitting so pretty. He went to her cage. She bit a boy, I said again. He squatted to this mean dog—some sort of terrier mix with a purple tongue and thick fur like a Chow. And Bobo pushed her nose through the cage. Believe that? Usually, I have to sedate her so I can clean her cage and the shit off her poofy fur. But this time, Bobo wasn't mad. She wasn't baring teeth. She just put her nose through the cage."

I take another sip of my tea.

Anders stands up and helps himself to a glass of water. He takes a little sip and sets the glass on the table. I don't know what's going on in his head, but he's thinking real hard about something.

"Well," I say.

He says, "Well."

"Finish," I say.

Smiling, he says, "The dude adopted Bobo. He did it! He said, I want this one. He said, There is no other dog here I want more. Look at her. She is ready. I wasn't going to talk him out of it. Bobo had this second chance, and she *was* ready. I could tell. I opened the gate. She jumped right into the guy's arms, her purple tongue going to town. Her leg was twitching every time he scratched her ear, like this was the first time anybody patted her. We did all the formality shit, filled out the forms. He paid the adoption fee, the whole time with Bobo in his arms."

"Wait," I say. "What was his name on the forms? I can't make myself believe it said Buddha."

Anders laughs. "John T'sai," he says. "I checked as soon as he finished filling it out."

"How the fuck do you know, then?" I say. For the past hour, the snow steadily falling, I've listened to Anders' story, gotten into it, and now it sounds like a joke, like he had me on a leash all along.

"I'm not done," he says. "Everything was set. Take care, I said. I reached over and patted Bobo behind the ear and she didn't even snap at me. She let me. She even kissed my hand. Fuckin' A."

Anders's eyes are wet and red. He digs his palms into them before going on. I give him some time.

"The dude put Bobo on the ground and she stayed there, so obedient, looking up at him. She knew she had another chance. She was a new dog. I asked, Do you have a leash? No, he said. I reached under the counter and pulled one out for him. He stopped me with his hand. She is on the right path, he said. We will walk it together. I could tell Bobo wasn't going to go anywhere. She was stuck to him, he to her."

Anders takes another sip of water. He leans back in the chair and looks smug. "This is the part where you call me a liar. But it's true. I swear it." He sucks in some air. "This guy, John T'sai, started walking out of the Shack with his new dog, and I couldn't believe what I was seeing. Bobo was weaving in between his steps, in figure-eights, back and forth. She circled one step then the other. I saw it once on the Discovery channel, doggy disco or something, and the owners said it took months to train. Months! John T'sai walked like normal, like there wasn't a dog weaving in between his steps. But there was—Bobo with her little legs working fast to catch up with his strides, around and around. Divine shit! They walked together like that right out the door."

Anders looks me in the eye. "It's hard to believe," he says.

"Yeah," I say. But I do, and Anders knows it.

"As soon as John T'sai and Bobo left, in walked Martha. She had Patches on a leash and he was pulling her, looking so much better, jumping on me, wanting to lick my face. Real cute. Martha saw Bobo's cage empty. Where is she? she asked. Didn't you see her? I said. She got adopted. The small Oriental dude adopted her. Did you see them? You must've passed each other. He went out then you came in. You must've seen them. Martha said she didn't see a damn thing but a pickup pull in and out of the lot. Then she started yelling at me, her fat cheeks red and jiggling. She was calling me dumb. How could I let Bobo go? Did I want her to bite another boy? Am I that stupid?"

"Fat bitch," I say.

Anders is all worked up, face so red it looks like Christmas with his green hair. "I hate her so much," he says. "She's always on my case and I know it's because of the way I look. I'd been so patient with her. Tried to be real nice. Never talked back and took her shit because people are allowed to be assholes sometimes. But she didn't stop. Got up in my space and started jabbing me with her finger. I couldn't take it, man. Patches' puke bucket was right beside me. And I was so mad, madder than I have ever been. I picked up the bucket and threw it at her. She was covered in vomit, dripping with it. It got her quiet. Quiet enough for me to say I quit."

Throughout Anders' whole strange story, this is the part I don't believe. Anders loves animals, how could he quit? I say, "How could you quit? You love animals. What are you gonna do?"

He gets up and digs deep into his pockets. "Try to be a vet," he says. He walks to the door.

"Where you going?" I say.

He pulls something out of his pocket, "I still got the key to the Shack. I'm thinking about stealing that golden, that good dog. I think I'm gonna bring him home."

Anders leaves.

My tea is cold, not worth drinking anymore. I take it to the sink and pour it out. Outside, it is getting darker. The imprints of shoes in the snow are disappearing under fresh powder. I fill the sink with hot water. I take a plate and start washing, scrubbing hard. I wonder whether John T'sai is Buddha. I think about second chances. I think about how in the morning the snow will cover everything up and make it new.

Jeff Wilson

Buddherotica

EVEN THE FRUIT BATS and serpents of the forest have gone to their dens, but the festival continues gaily in the court-yards and pleasure rooms of the palace below as you wearily mount the steps to your bedchamber. A silent maidservant walks before you with a lamp, and behind you another holds your royal train lightly. Your husband is somewhere in the throng you have left, perhaps enjoying the dancing girls in the harem, or the Bhutanese acrobats in the throneroom. He will not come to you this night.

The wine and dancing have finally sapped your strength, and with quiet delight you spread your tired limbs upon the goose-down bed. A servant is pouring you cool water drawn from Kapilavastu's sacred well, but already you are drifting away, your eyes half-focused on the leering monkeys and strutting jungle-cocks carved into the bed. Another servant, her eyes properly downcast, sweeps the huge palm leaf fan back and forth through the humid air. Somewhere far away the sound of drums and laughter drifts; the room is blurring and soon you are asleep, your tangled black tresses fanned out over the silk pillows.

But all too soon the room is growing brighter and brighter. Your eyes slit open, you turn slowly toward the window. The sun is not rising. All around you radiance illuminates the room, a shifting glow of indefinable color. Four figures stand at the corners of the bed. They are not your maid-servants. It is hard to make out anything in this unearthly light, but you see arms, too many arms, muscled and limber and blue as emerald, grasp-ing at your bed. Are those gems set into their foreheads, or eyes? A voice from between the stars speaks at the foot of the bed: "It is time."

And suddenly you are soaring through the dark night sky far above the land. Your four escorts hold the bed firmly, and you do not even think to fear. The air is full of music the likes of which has never been heard in all of great India, teased lovingly from harps strung with moonlight. Kapilavastu is far behind, and soon the fields and villages give way to untamed jungle. And then beyond the jungle the mighty Himalayas stand impossibly tall, loom-ing over you even at this intoxicating height. They stand protectively and proud as your bed comes to rest at their doorstep, and your heavenly guides disappear.

A small pool set with fiery gemstones sparkles nearby in the starlight, and silent young women beckon from its edge. Despite the heat your skin prickles as they slip your royal robes away and lead you down the jeweled steps into the water's waiting embrace. It is cool and perfumed with jas-mine, and seems to move of its own accord, gently washing away the sweat and exhaustion with slowly swirling ripples. You rise, and the maidens comb out your hair and wipe away the water from your body. They rub you with oil scented like cinnamon, and return you to your bed.

You are naked and open beneath the sky and mountains, and anticipa-tion charges your limbs. Somewhere above, the gods are looking down boldly at you, and you search the constellations for signs of their approval. There is a star shining brightly directly above the bed, brighter than any star you've seen before. It is coming toward you, dropping from the dark tapestry overhead to join you on earth. Ever larger it approaches, until its white bril-liance floods the countryside. The light resolves into a mighty form, too large to be a man. Your breath catches in your throat. It is a majestic white elephant, his back broad, his curled trunk strong, his six gleaming tusks sharp and hard. His long-lashed eyes gaze upon you with intelligence. Huge like the mountains, he stands over the bed, and held in his trunk you behold a thousand-petaled lotus flower.

Now the flower is moving over your flesh, as the great trunk tenderly tickles you with its petals. He runs it across your breasts, your torso, over your navel, and down, down your legs and back again. The anticipation is swelling in you, building and building as the flower strokes you like a thousand soft fingers. The elephant fills your whole field of vision. You can feel the strength of his massive snakelike trunk moving upon you, and the air is full of the joyful cries of watching deities. The scent of the lotus is thick in your nostrils and suddenly you are carried away on a wave of bliss as the elephant melts into you and you see for a flickering moment the face of a man more wise and loving than any god. The ground gives a tremendous shake and in the city blind men cry out as vision crashes in on them, cripples dance as they are made whole. And in the bedchamber the maidservants exchange a sly look of knowing over your sleeping form, a fierce blush hot upon their cheeks. For from this sleep will come an awakening like no other, to change the world forever.

Leah E. Sammel

Morning

THE SUN tastes good, like gold. I sit and reach for my breath, elusive as a shadow. I sit, a shadow, in the sun, slowing settling. . .

The texture of sun in my mouth, I feel my son crawl over. He scales the heights of my sitting body, tumbles over my back, shrieks with glee.

I sit with the sun, as he kicks me and grabs at me like crags of a mountain. He tumbles over me and I tumble into quiet. I hold myself and my world in one breath, my face pressed to the sun's face. I breathe in the sun and breathe out thought. I breathe out the smoke that smothers me, and in the warmth that tickles me. I breathe in the sun and exhale shadows and mishaps and the memory of how I should feel.

My eyes closed, without definition, I am the sun, in a moment, I am light.

"Mommmmeeeeee!" The TV has changed and my daughter calls to me.

I have turned, like a compass, flickering and falling north, drawn into and contained by breath. I sense the air in my body, nourishing, the air leaving, an empty still space.

"Wake up, Mommy. *Wake up!*" She is perturbed by my quiet. My eyes are closed, my back straight, my spine travels upward, to the sun.

I breathe in. And out. I open my eyes.

"I am awake," I say.

She giggles, a burst of light in my body. I smile and she is my smile.

I am awake.

Judith R. Peterson

Meditation

HER MEDITATION was continually interrupted by small pieces of her so-called self drifting haphazardly into space. Snow lion, sleeping, startles awake. Snow lion leaps up. He dances among the meteorites, delightedly fetches, gently replaces all with an affectionate swipe of his tongue. Snow lion flops at her feet. Stretches, yawns, back asleep.

Meditation done, she swirls upward. Flaming lapis lazuli, ruby, crystal, gold spin out into the universe as she ascends. Her halo softly pulses red/green light. Glistening black hair coils and writhes about her face, neck. The universe looks down, the halo signals are studied. Quiet appropriate adjustments are made by most. Some could not read the signals, and some did not understand the signs. A whisper vibrates along the threads of night sky, *"OM TARE TUTTARE TURE SOHA."*

Tara suspends, sighs. She smoothes back wild tresses and steps down from the cool blue lotus to another busy day.

Margo McLoughlin

In the Sky There Is No Footstep

THE CHIEF MONK'S BIRTHDAY fell on the day of the full moon. One of the novice nuns, Anagarika Liz, had decided to make a cake. Nobody knew her plan. It was to be a surprise. Though how she was going to produce a cake large enough to feed twenty monks, seven nuns and six *anagarikas,* plus at least ten laypeople, without anyone noticing, well, she hadn't figured that out. She was counting on a measure of inspiration and a cup and a half of luck.

Liz was Australian. Her family were sheep farmers. They had no idea why she had taken it into her head to put on the white robes of a novice, shave off all her lovely red hair, and take the eight precepts. Her father was so confused, in fact, that he said to her, in a mournful tone, "But Lizzie, it's very quiet here on the farm. I promise we'll turn off the telly in the evenings." As if she could be lured home by the promise of a silent living room, with her mother sighing heavily on the sofa, and her father doing his best to look hopeful and interested.

The Ajahn had a weakness for chocolate. It was common knowledge. Sometimes on cold mornings there would be hot cocoa at breakfast instead of tea. Then the Ajahn would grin and take each sip with great care, inspiring everyone to pay attention. Anagarika Liz wanted to make him a chocolate cake. A double-decker chocolate cake with vanilla icing.

On the day before the full moon Liz was in the kitchen early. She was on cook duty that day, and for the next three days as well. She had it all figured out: if she and her helpers made large enough quantities there would be leftovers for the next day and she would have a good excuse to send the laypeople away. Then she would be alone in the kitchen to create her masterpiece. The trouble was, whatever she made for lunch (which was the only substantial meal of the day) had to be good enough that the monks might want it again the next day, but not so good that the laypeople would come back for seconds and eat it all up at once.

She decided to make a curry, with lots of potatoes and mushrooms. Rice, boiled eggs, and slices of bread would fill them up. And maybe a fruit salad, since apples were plentiful at the moment and there had been a donation of grapes and melons. (No one ever donated mangoes. If there had to be just one fruit, Liz had often thought, it should be a strawberry mango, like the ones she remembered from her childhood—large, soft, tender and sweet, with a slim little pit.)

When she had given her instructions to the lay visitors (one Czech, two Hungarian, and one Polish), Anagarika Liz lit a candle in front of a little altar beside the kitchen sink. A small Buddha *rupa,* a china teacup with three short-stemmed roses, and a photo of Achan Chah, plus a small earthenware pot filled with sand, in which a stick of incense stood, made up the altar. Anagarika Liz rang a small brass bell and waited while the others gathered in a semicircle. Then she read a verse from the *Dhammapada,* the wisdom sayings of the Buddha:

Irrigators guide the water.

Fletchers bend the arrow shaft.

Wood the carpenters bend.

Themselves the wise ones tame.

They stood in silence for a few moments. Outside the window, one of the *bhikkhus,* a German who liked to sing, was whistling as he swept the path behind the building. Inside there was only the sound of the faucet dripping. The candle flame flickered, the smoke from the incense went straight up, and a petal dropped off one of the roses. Anagarika Liz felt her break sink into a deeper rhythm. It often happened to her now, between one activity and another, when talking had ceased, her breath and her body resting in the space between thoughts. She felt her breath coming and going, deep in her chest. She counted four breaths, then she rang the bell again but left the candle and incense burning.

The meal preparation began in an atmosphere of calm. Anagarika Liz felt the calmness, but underneath was a hovering, frothy excitement. As though she were planning some elaborate, solitary prank. As she chopped and stirred and added spices, the young Czech woman would occasionally ask a question, more it seemed for the opportunity of practicing her English than because she needed instructions.

"Anagarika Liz," she would say, "How would you like the potatoes chopped?" Or, "Anagarika Liz, do the monks prefer spicy food?"

Anagarika Liz liked her new title. It had a formality to it, and it pleased her to think that when she became a nun, her own name—her childhood name—would disappear. She had been Liz, Lizzie, or Elizabeth since birth. Now she was Anagarika Liz. Her name, she thought, was like the skin of an orange which changes color as the orange ripens. In order to see and taste the fruit inside, however, the skin has to come right off. When she was ordained, Liz would be given an entirely new name. The Ajahn would choose one for her. A Pali word. She hoped it would have at least three syllables.

When the cooking was well underway Anagarika Liz began a thorough inventory of the baking supplies in the room next to the kitchen, which served as both a larder and a meeting place for the *anagarikas* and nuns. In one cupboard she found a large sack of whole wheat flour. That was probably donated for Ajahn Virasana, she thought, because he likes to bake homemade bread. But whole wheat flour was too heavy for a cake. In another cupboard she found smaller sacks of white flour, rice flour, and one marked "KAMUT." Kamut? It sounded like a German breed of dog. Now she remembered. The previous summer a guest had arrived with a knapsack full of peculiar foods. He was an American from Oregon and had recommended the monks and nuns try blue green algae supplements. The Ajahn had happily accepted the donation of green capsules, and each monk, nun, and *anagarika* was issued one at mealtime until they ran out.

Liz put a hand into the sack and felt the flour. It was light and grainy. It would probably do in combination with the others. She found baking powder and baking soda and a sack of white sugar. She knew there were lots of eggs in the big walk-in fridge—they bought them with cash donations from the farm down the road. The Ajahn was very solicitous about the community members getting their protein. Protein and generous amounts of leafy greens—that's what the Ajahn liked best. He often talked about his time in Asia, and what it was like to go to the village with his begging bowl, standing head bowed, while the villagers offered rice and vegetables, usually some starchy, fibrous root vegetable that was almost inedible, even when thoroughly cooked.

There was milk in the fridge as well, because all the British monks and nuns had to have milk in their tea, lots of it. There was cocoa, the unsweetened kind that comes in a round tin, and the instant stuff that tastes sickly sweet. That must have been a donation. The only thing missing was icing sugar. And a slab of chocolate would come in handy, to grate on top of the icing. Could a cake really be complete without icing?

It was a problem, but not an insurmountable one. Anagarika Liz filed it away and let the day unfold. At ten-thirty she sent Slava, the Czech woman, to ring the bell in the center of the courtyard. The nuns and monks came in with their bowls and arranged themselves in sitting positions on their cushions. They faced each other in four rows, the monks in their amber-colored robes, and the nuns in brown, the *anagarikas* in white. The lay visitors and the workmen came in, unrolled the bamboo mats and sat cross-legged or on cushions.

After the chanting, one of the lay visitors came up to lift each dish off its mat while one of the senior monks blessed the food. Then the monks served themselves (it was astonishing how much they could eat—some had bowls as big as mixing bowls) and then the nuns. Anagarika Liz loved to watch the monks and nuns at mealtime. Especially when she had done the cooking. There were exclamations, and delighted faces bending over the steaming pots. They were like children at a continual birthday party.

The lay visitors were the last to serve themselves, lining up with growling bellies, trying not to look anxious about the dwindling supplies on the platters and in the pots. Anagarika Liz would sometimes (but not very often) pretend that she had run out of dessert. She would shrug her shoulders, and give a sympathetic smile while she stood there at the door to the kitchen. Next she would frown, as though she were remembering something, and then she would run back through the swinging doors and produce another dish of apple crisp, or another bowl of fruit salad. The gratitude on the faces of the lay visitors was almost comical.

Today there was more than enough. When she had eaten her own meal and returned her plate to the kitchen, where a huddle of monks had begun the cleanup, she received a number of smiles and nods. She was a good cook, and the monks appreciated the variety of meals she served. One of them had even gone so far as to say he hoped she would stay and complete her two years there, even if the opportunity arose for her to go down to Arundell, the training monastery, where there wasn't a continual string of renovation projects under way.

Anagarika Liz smiled to herself as she put on her shoes and went out the back door of the kitchen. She pictured her father in his straw hat, leaning back against the hood of his old blue truck, holding a beer in one hand, and looking out over the green fields of his farm. That's where he belonged. That's where he was happy. But not her. Liz had come home to something else.

A light rain was falling and the far side of the valley had disappeared in the mist. From the neighboring village came the sound of church bells. Steady, rich, ringing gongs. She counted twelve. Sometimes on Friday evenings there were lessons in bell-ringing down at St. Stephen's and the bells would ring for an hour or more. Liz liked to walk down the road towards the village and listen, trying to guess who was the teacher and who was the student.

All the *anagarikas* and nuns had their own rooms in one of the low wood-frame buildings along a walkway from the main temple and the dining hall. Liz was the most recent arrival. Sister Kovaka had shown her all around the monastery and given her the history of the place. A Buddhist monastery in the middle of the English countryside was an anomaly to start with, but the fact that the place had been built before the war, with cedar shipped out from Canada, added another dimension. It had been a summer camp at one time and the buildings were forever under repair. Among the novices and lay visitors the monastery was known as the "Gulag" because there was always work that needed doing.

When she first arrived Liz was given a tour, cloth to make her own robes, and a paintbrush. She had heard about the monastery, she knew it wouldn't be easy, certainly it wouldn't be like practicing in Asia. In Burma the European laywomen weren't allowed to do any work at all, not even cooking. And yet to practice and live in a temperate climate! To hear the English songbirds, eat nice thick English porridge in the morning, and never be so hot and exhausted that mindfulness meant straining all one's faculties to stay awake. And constipation, it never crossed her mind anymore. She walked every day and most of the time the food agreed with her, especially as she often got to cook it.

Liz had first tasted the dharma at a Zen center in Sydney. Her gut response was so strong that she found herself, only a few months later, sitting the rainy season retreat in Burma. Her parents had tried everything to stop her from going. Her father had even offered to pay for Liz to study aromatherapy at an alternative health center in Auckland, an idea she had once mentioned to him. Her mother had suggested, with all sincerity, that she join a support group for young people recovering from cult experiences.

Well, Liz said to herself, what are my choices? Please them and be safe. Please myself and take a risk. She decided to please herself. All summer she worked at a candy factory, lifting down heavy trays of chocolates amid a cloud of corn starch, and earned enough to pay her airfare to Bangkok and from there to Rangoon. When she stepped down off the plane she was met by a wave of hot air, like the breath of giant tiger bearing down on her. There in the distance she saw the Shwe Dagon, the Golden Pagoda. She felt a shock of recognition, and with it, a surge of hope that her life might turn out to have meaning after all.

Among the many rules in the Vinaya—the book of discipline set out by the Buddha for the monastic community—were several about personal habits. Anagarika Liz kept her room neat, which wasn't hard because she had pretty well given up all personal possessions. Besides two sets of robes (which she had sewn herself with fabric donated by the London Thai community), she had only her sturdy walking shoes, four pairs of knee-high wool socks, a small suitcase, a pad of airmail paper, one pen, and a copy of the *Dhammapada*.

Of course, no one came around and checked to see that the windowsills weren't covered with knickknacks and other objects of attachment. No, Buddhism wasn't like that, at least that's how Liz saw it. Buddhism offered a voluntary renunciation. The freedom she felt when she looked in the mirror and saw her familiar round face looking back at her, unadorned by the waves and curls of her unruly red hair, well, it was difficult to describe. Writing to her old friend Penny, Liz called it "the sort of feeling you get when you lose your wallet, and suddenly all those little pieces of hard plastic with your face on them, and a number somebody's assigned you, they're gone, and so then, you can be anybody. You can make yourself up from scratch."

That's how it was for Liz. She was making herself up from scratch. And not just once, no, she was re-inventing herself all the time. If she committed a misdemeanour, like interrupting the Ajahn in the middle of a dharma talk (it had happened more than once), or taking the last boiled egg at lunch, even though she knew that Anagarika Françoise needed more protein than she did, well, she forgave herself and vowed to do better next time. She had given up filling a sack of faults and lugging it around with her. She was practicing being herself at each moment. She was learning to be a beginner in all things.

Of course, she was still the same Liz who had played on the high school volleyball team, serving her beautiful underhand serve that curved its way across the net and always landed just inside the line. She was the same Liz who had worn black oxfords to a high school dance, and trousers that were two inches two short, and though her best friends Penny and June had teased her, they were the ones who spent the evening leaning up against the gym equipment while Liz danced and danced. These stories were true, they were parts of her, but just as true and rich were her memories of the four months at the monastery in Rangoon, the sound of the nuns and lay-women—more than four hundred of them in the hall—beginning the evening *metta* chant with one voice: *"Sabbe satta?, sabbe pana?, sabbe bhuta?, sabbe puggala? . . ."*

Giving up dancing was hard. Giving up music was hard too, but it was just a choice like any other. She explained it to herself this way: any choices you make require that you give up something else. You may want two desserts, but, the fact of the matter is, you can only eat one and enjoy it. And there was something very sweet about this practice. Sometimes, after the morning *puja* in the women's meditation hall, Anagarika Liz would wait until all the others had left. Then she would step outside, look up at the sky and watch the clouds. The words from the *Dhammapada* would come to her: "In the sky there is no footstep . . ." The movement of the clouds was great and peaceful, unhurried and full of a rich, momentary beauty. At those moments Liz felt a softening of her "Lizness," and that softening tasted so very sweet. What other choice could she have made and been so happy in it?

Being an *anagarika* meant two years of wearing white robes, and then Liz could taker her ordination vows and put on the brown robes of a nun. Then maybe she could go down to Arundell, and spend six months there, studying. That would be a relief. Liz didn't mind all the sanding and painting, but at times her eyes were itchy from all the dust and her ears always seemed to be ringing with the sound of saws and hammers.

The monastery was quiet as Liz crossed the courtyard—a brief lull before the afternoon work period began. Since she had been on cook duty in the morning Liz had the afternoon free. Usually she wrote a letter and then went to the women's meditation hall. Only Anagarika Françoise, and the Ukrainian *anagarika,* who made her think of a Russian Pinocchio, went there in the afternoons. Often she was entirely alone in the hall. No one's breath or rustling to listen to but her own. But today, just before she reached the nuns' quarters, an impulse took her past the building along the walkway where the rosebushes were still in bloom.

The walkway made a neat rectangle about the buildings, and on one side was a low grassy hill, where young oak trees were growing. Liz stepped off the path into the wet grass and climbed up the hill. She knew what was on the other side, she'd found it on her first day, but still, when she reached the top and saw the brilliant white stupa in the middle of the green meadow, she felt an inner gasp of awe and gratitude. And she knew how she would finish her cake.

On lunar observance days there were no regular work periods. Sitting and walking meditation began in the afternoon and continued all night.

Whoever was on kitchen duty made a special effort to prepare a good meal since there would be no afternoon tea. At eight o'clock on the morning of the day of the full moon, the chief monk's birthday, Anagarika Liz had her helpers slice apples for an apple crisp (just in case there wasn't enough cake) and make an enormous cabbage salad. Then she put on two kinds of rice, and took out the rest of the potato-mushroom curry, ready to be reheated in the double boiler.

She was alone in the kitchen by nine o'clock. Quickly she set to work. The recipe came from a cookbook she had found in the library. It was called "Magic Chocolate Cake." She had already done the math to multiply the quantities, so now she just had to make sure she measured carefully. She lined up her ingredients, the utensils she would need, the bowls, and the cake pans. She felt quietly amazed at her own efficiency, the way she cracked the eggs so expertly, the way she sifted and resifted and then measured the flour, resisting the temptation to skip steps in the recipes that she had always considered unnecessary when she baked cakes at home. She had quadrupled the recipe and now she poured the batter into four nine-by-thirteen-inch pans. The pans went into the oven and Anagarika Liz sat down on a kitchen stool to think.

The flowers by the kitchen altar caught her eye. The roses were a pale coral pink. The petals had begun to drop off in the heat of the kitchen, their perfect shapes making a delicate offering of pinkness in front of the small Buddha *rupa*. Liz smiled. Rose petals would do just as well as icing. She glanced at the clock, took a pair of scissors and a basket, slipped on her walking shoes, went out the door and down the kitchen steps. The sky was clearing and the sun was about to come out. The rickety old buildings shone with friendliness. The oak trees quivered with purpose and joy. Anagarika Liz began to chant to herself as she cut the roses.

When the cakes had cooled a little she brushed the tops with egg white and arranged the rose petals. On one she made a wheel with eight spokes, symbolizing the wheel of dharma, set in motion when the Buddha gave his first teaching. On the other cake she made the figure of a sitting Buddha. It demanded some skill to achieve the impression of a full lotus position with rose petals, but again, Liz surprised herself with her intuition about how best to do it. The result satisfied her. It was simple and uncomplicated and beautiful.

Liz made several trips through the swinging doors, carrying out the pots and bowls. The young Czech woman appeared in the kitchen and began to help. Together they arranged platters and plates for the chief monk's birthday lunch. Then Slava went to ring the bell. Anagarika Liz had thought of bringing out the cake at the last minute, perhaps with birthday candles on it. But now, it didn't seem to matter. Everything was so beautiful. The crisp purple tangle of the cabbage salad, the soft crumble of oats and brown sugar on the apple crisp, the double-decker chocolate cakes with their decorations of rose petal forms—they all had their own beauty, their own truth.

The Ajahn would grin when he saw the cake. He would take each bite and savor it, but when the cake was gone, he would let it go. As the monks and nuns came in with their bowls, Anagarika Liz took a last look at her masterpiece. One of the Buddha's petal elbows had slipped. Liz smiled. She thought to herself, I wonder if there is a Pali word for "cake-maker."

John Rueppel

Enlarging the Zendo

A LMOST-WHITE LIGHT comes in the windows and illuminates the old carpet, the little shrine, the almost-white walls, and gives a sense of space and depth to the little basement zendo. Since no one can enter, and no one can leave, how does the light get in?

In the center of the room there is a hole in the floor and inside it is so black that you can't tell how deep it is. Yelling into the hole, you receive no echo. Looking into the hole, you become empty and dark and of undetermined depth, and while you are looking into it, no one can see you.

Upstairs there may be other rooms with furniture and a kitchen and perhaps a cat. When the cat sits down, it doesn't have to try to catch the mice, and the geese honk "meow" all the day long.

Even if we eventually make the zendo bigger, it will still seem to be the same size, but we won't be able to walk around it, not even in a million early morning *kinhins*. How will you figure out how to buy enough carpet to cover the whole floor? Can you know how much area the hole takes up, and how do you put the new carpet down while you're standing on it?

Either the zendo will never be finished, or perhaps, after a *kalpa* of toil you realize it already was finished. But when the expansion is over, there will be no zendo in which to sit, no carpet to sit upon, no cat at all, but there will still be enough space inside for everyone.

Pico Iyer

A Walk in
Kurama

ONE DELICATE AUTUMN DAY a few days later—
the sky now gray, now blue, always like a woman's uncertain heart, a light drizzle falling, and then subsid-
ing, and falling once more—I met Sachiko outside an
Indonesian store for a trip to Kurama. She was, as ever, girlishly dressed,
her hair falling thickly over one side of her face, held back on the other by
a black comb with a red-stone heart in its middle; the tongues of her black
sneakers hanging out from under lime-green legwarmers.

As we traveled toward the hillside village, she set down her backpack
beside her on the train and began telling me excitedly about her friend
Sandy, and how it was Sandy who had first introduced her to Zen, Sandy who
had first taken her to a temple, Sandy who had first encouraged her to try
zazen meditation. "I Japanese," she said softly. "But I not know my country before. Sandy my teacher." More than that, she said, it was Sandy who
had shown her another way of life and given her the confidence to try new
things. Sandy, supporting two children alone in a foreign country and at

the same time embarked on a full-length course of Zen studies, had shown her that it was possible, even for a woman, to have a strong heart.

Now, she went on, Sandy was planning to send her children back to America for high school. "I dream, maybe Hiroshi go your country, Sandy's son together. You see this movie *Stand by Me?*" I nodded. "Very beautiful movie. I want give my son this life. I dream, he little *Stand by Me* world feeling." And what about her husband's view on all this? An embarrassed giggle. "I don't know. Little difficult. But I much dream children go other country." She paused, deep in thought. "But I also want children have Zen spirit inside, Japanese feeling." I asked her to explain. "Example—you and Sandy, *zazen* very difficult. Japanese people, *zazen* very easy. I want my children have this spirit."

"But if your children go away, they may grow distant. Maybe never talk to you. Maybe forget all Japanese things. Wouldn't that make you sad?"

"*Tabun*. Maybe."

"It's very difficult, I think."

And so we get off the train, and climb from shrine to shrine, scattered across the steep hills of Kurama, and the rain now drizzles down, now stops again, and the two of us huddle under her umbrella, sweaters brushing, her hair almost falling on my arm. "*Ai to ai gasa,*" I say, thinking of the phrase I had read in a Yosano Akiko poem, describing two people sharing a single umbrella. "Maybe," she says, with a lilting laugh, and we climb some more, the hills before us resplendent now, and then still higher, in the gentle rain, till we are sitting on a log.

In front of us, the trees are blazing. "I like color now," she says, pensive. "Later, I not so like. More sad. Leaves die. Many thing change." And then, carried away by the view, perhaps, she recalls the only other time she has come to this hill. Kurama is only a few miles north of Kyoto, a thirty-minute train ride. But Sachiko has not been here for fifteen years, and all that time, she says, she has longed to return. "I so happy," she whispers, as if in the presence of the sacred. "I so excited. Thank you. Thank you very much.

I very happy. Very fun. Before I coming here, little teenage size, together three best friend. We climbing mountain, I very afraid, because I thinking snake. Much laughing, many joke. Very fun. My friends' names, Junko, Sumiko, and Michiko. But Osaka now. Very busy, marry ladies."

We walk down again, through the drizzle and the mist, then up slippery paths, between the trees. "I much love Kurama," she says quietly, as if in thought. "Sometimes I ask husband come here; he say, 'You always want play. I very busy. I cannot.' And come here together children, very difficult. Soon tired. Thank you very much, come here this place with me."

This is all rather sad. She tells me of her adventures, and the smallness of it all makes me sad again: how, when she was a little girl, she went with her cousin and brother and aunt to a cinema, and her aunt allowed her to go and see *The Sound of Music* alone. "I very scared. All dark. Many person there. But then, film begin, I soon forget. I much love. I dream I Julie Andrews." She also describes reading about Genghis Khan. "I dream I trip together Genghis Khan. I many trip in my heart, many adventure. But only in my heart." She tells me how once, last year, for the first time ever, she went alone to Osaka, forty minutes away, to see the Norwegian teeny-bopper group a-ha in concert, and then, exhilarated by this event, went again that same week to another of their concerts, in Kobe, with her son and her cousin, all three of them sharing a room in a luxury hotel. The night she spent in the hotel, the trip to the coffee shop after the concert, the way she had chanced to see the lead singer's parents in the coffee shop and then to meet the star himself in an elevator—all live on in her as what seems almost the brightest moment in her life. "I very lucky. I very excited. I dream, maybe next summer, I go this hotel again. See other a-ha concert."

And when she says, more than once, "I live in Kyoto all life; you come here only one month, but you know more place, very well," I feel again, with a pang, a sense of the tightly drawn limits of a Japanese woman's life, like the autumn paths vanishing in mist around us. For I could see that she was saying something more than the usual "Tourists know more of towns

than their residents ever do," and I could catch a glimpse of the astonishing circumscription of her life. Even while her brother had been to Kansas
City to study for three years and was now in his third year of pursuing
Jung in Switzerland, she had never really been outside Kyoto. She now
worked two mornings a week in a doctor's office, but it was the same place
where she had worked in during junior high school and high school va-
cations, just around the corner from her parents' house. Her cousin, a kind
of surrogate sister, sometimes worked in the same place. Her own house
was in the next neighborhood down, within walking distance of her par-
ents-in-law's house. And her mother still called her every night, to see how
she was doing.

Every year, she said, her husband got three or four days of holiday, and
the trips the family took together on these breaks—to the sea once, and
once to Tokyo Disneyland—still lived within them as peak experiences.
Even a trip such as the one today, for a few hours to a suburb, seemed a rare
and unforgettable adventure.

"Please tell me your adventure," she begins to say. "Please tell me other
country. I want imagine all place," but I don't know where to begin, or how
to convey them to someone who has never been in a plane, and what cloak-
and-dagger episodes in Cuba, or nights in the Thai jungle, will mean to one
who has scarcely left Kyoto.

"I dream you lifestyle," she goes on, as if sensing my unease. "You are
bird, you go everywhere in world, very easy. I all life living only Kyoto. So
I dream I go together you. I have many, many dream in my heart. But I not
have strong heart. You very different."

"Maybe. I was lucky that I got used to going to school by plane when I
was nine."

"You very lucky. I afraid other country. Because I thinking, maybe I go
away, my mother ill, maybe die. If I come back, maybe no mother here."
Her mother, she explains, developed very serious allergies—because, it
seemed, of the new atmospheric conditions in Japan. (All this I found in-

creasingly hard to follow, in part because Sachiko used "allergy" to mean "age"—she regularly referred to the "Heian allergy," and when she was talking about "war allergy," I honestly didn't know if it was a medical or a historical point she was making. I, of course, was no better, confusing *sabishii* with *subarashii,* and so, in trying to say, "Your husband must be lonely," invariably coming out with, "Your husband is wonderful. Just fantastic," which left her frowning in confusion more than ever.)

"When I little children size, my mother many times in hospital. And Grandma too. And when my brother in Kansas City, my grandma die. He never say goodbye. She see my husband, she think he my brother. Very sad time. So I always dream in heart. Because many sad thing happen. But dream stay in heart." This seemed a sorrowful way to approach the universe, though eminently pragmatic. Yet she held to it staunchly. "Maybe tomorrow I have accident. I die. So I always keep dream." That was lovely, elegant, Sachiko: Sachiko, in her teenager's high-tops, keeping a picture of Sting in her wallet and sometimes losing sleep over him—a thirty-year-old girl with daydreams.

All this gets us onto what is fast becoming a recurrent theme in our talks, the competing merits of the Japanese and the American family systems. I, of course, argue heartily for the Japanese.

"It makes me so happy to see mothers and children playing together here, or going to temples together, and movies, and coffee shops. In America, mothers and daughters are often strangers. People do not know their parents, let alone their grandparents. Sometimes, in California, parents just fly around, with very young girlfriends or boyfriends, and leave their children with lots of money but no love." (My sense of America, in Japan, was getting as simplistic and stereotyped as my sense of Japan had been in America.) "So fifteen-year-old girls have babies and drive cars, and have money, many boyfriends, and lots of drugs."

"Maybe. But in your country, I think, children have strong heart. Do anything, very easy. Here in Japan, no strong heart. Even grown-up person, very weak!" I think she means that they lack adventure, recklessness, and freedom, and in all that I suppose she is right, and not only because twelve Japanese CEOs have literally collapsed this year under the pressures of a strong yen. And she, of course, as a foreigner, sees only the pro ledger in America, while I, over here, stress only the con—though when I am in America, I find myself bringing back to American friends an outsider's sense of their country's ever-green hopefulness.

And as we continue walking, a few other people trudge past us up the hill, elders most of them, with sticks, the men in berets and raincoats, the women in print dresses, occasionally looking back through the curtain of fine drizzle at the strange sight of a pretty young Japanese girl with a shifty Indian male. Sachiko, however, seems lost in another world.

"What is your blood type?" she suddenly asks, eyes flashing into mine.

"I don't know."

"True?"

"True."

"Whyyy?" she squeals, in the tone of a high school girl seeking a rock star's autograph.

"I don't know. In my country, people aren't concerned about blood types."

"But maybe you have accident. Go hospital."

"I don't know."

"Really? True??"

"Really. Foreigners think it's strange that Japanese are so interested in blood types."

"Really? *Honto ni?*"

"Yes." I am beginning to feel I am letting her down in some way, so I quickly ask if she is interested in the Chinese calendar, or astrology. All this, though, is frightful to try to translate, and when Sachiko says that she is the sign of the "ship," and I say, "Ah, yes, you mean the waves," she looks very agitated. "No, no waves! Ship!" Now it's my turn to look startled. What is going on here? "The Water Bearer?" "No." "The Fish?" "No. Ship!" She is sounding adamant. Then, suddenly, I recall that Aries is the ram. (Thank God, I think, for all those years in California!) "Oh—sheep! You are the sheep sign." "Yes. Ship."

Then, of a sudden, she plops down on a bench and draws out from her backpack a Japanese edition of Hesse and shows me the stories she likes and repeats how he had struck a chord in her when young. "When I little high school size, I much much like. But Goldmund, not so like. When I twenty, it not so touch my heart, not same feeling. Now thirty, maybe different feeling. Which you like?"

"I don't know. That's why I'm reading it again now. When I was young, I liked Goldmund. Then, later, I understood Narziss a little better. For a long time, I spent one month living like Goldmund, traveling around the world, and one month like Narziss, leading a monk's life at home. Now I'm trying both at the same time, to see which one is better."

Somehow the world has misted over as we talk, and time and space are gone: the world, I think, begins and ends on this small bench. And as we sit there, sometimes with her dainty pink umbrella unfurled, sometimes not, I pointing to the yellow trees, or the blue in the sky, and saying, *"Onna-no kokoro, Kurama-no tenki"* (The weather in Kurama is like a woman's heart), I can see her perfect white teeth when she laughs, the mole above her lips, a wisp of hair across her forehead, another fine strand that slips into her ear. She bends over to look at the magazine in my hands, and her hair falls all about me.

"You tell parent about girlfriend?" she says, looking up.

"Well, for many years, I haven't had—or wanted—a girlfriend."

"So what am I?" A long silence. "I man?" She giggles girlishly, and I don't know where that puts us: our discourse is soft and blurred as autumn rain.

"I think you're a very beautiful lady," I say, looking down at my outstretched legs like a bashful schoolboy. "Your husband is a very lucky man."

"I not so think. I bad wife."

And then, seizing the closeness in the air, she tries to formulate more complex thoughts. "I very happy. Today, time stop. Thank you very much, coming here this place together me. I only know you short time, but you best friend feeling. I think I know you long time. I no afraid, no weak heart. You foreigner man, but I alone together you, very easy. I think maybe you very busy man. But talking very easy. I very fun, thank you." All of this is a little heartbreaking, I think, together on a bench on a misty autumn day, and she so excited to see me after only two weeks of acquaintance.

Standing up, we start walking slowly down the hill, through faint drizzle, talking of her closeness to her mother, and the poems of Yosano Akiko. And as we leave the hill of temples behind us, she turns and bows toward the shrine, pressing her palms together and closing her eyes very tight.

THAT EVENING, I read Yosano Akiko late into the night and try to recall the short *tanka* Sachiko had recited to me on the hill. But I know only that it begins with *kimi,* the intimate form of "you," as so many of Akiko's poems do. Falling asleep over the book, I awaken with a start in the dead of night, imagining that I am holding her by the hand and saying, "Sachiko-san, I'm sorry to disturb you. I know you have a husband, and I'm very sorry, but . . ."

And later in the night, I think of the two of us under her pink umbrella, and flip hurriedly through the book in search of the phrase *"ai to ai gasa."* When I find it, my heart seems almost to stop: it is, it seems, a classic image of intimacy, and one of the most famous figures in Japan for lovers.

Marilyn Stablein

The Prediction

ENTER A LAMA'S ROOM. He is going to predict my future. With an X-Acto knife he slits a neat rectangular gash on my right arm. The wound doesn't bleed.

"Peel off the outer layer," he tells me after stamping my skin with a navy blue stamp of some kind. "Then give me the skin."

I don't like the idea of peeling my skin. I wince but finally take a breath and peel a rectangular patch the size of an address label. The skin peels off easily. I hand the skin to the lama.

He holds the small patch to the light. His face is expressionless as he peers at, around, under, and through my translucent skin. He is neither pleased nor alarmed. The reading seems fine.

Marilyn Stablein

Teeth

GROW A SECOND SET of teeth, an extra row on my lower jaw. In the mirror: corncob mouth crammed with pointy canine teeth. The teeth start to fall out one by one when I chew on nails and a sour green mat. I'm relieved. I don't need so many teeth.

Teeth fall out of my body like *ring sel,* the miraculous jeweled bits that appear in the cremation ashes of very high lamas. People covet tiny particles the size of mustard seeds or rock salt granules. In my palm bits of teeth shine like pearls.

"Wait! There's more!" My mouth feels crowded. A tiny Hindu statue emerges from under my tongue. In my mouth Ganesh, who removes obstacles, is himself an obstacle until I spit out the porcelain elephant-headed deity.

Kira Salak

Beheadings

I.

W HAT I SEE before anything else, is space. The unadulterated space of central Cambodia which gives me the feeling of reaching the end of something. I look away from the window and wait for the other passengers to get off the plane. Everyone else has come with someone, and they stare at me, the lone woman in no hurry. What they don't know is that I consider this just another place, another destination, and there are so many in this world. But I think I can guess why my brother, David, came here, and why he refuses to go home. He must like the privacy of so few people, and a sun that always keeps the country warm. No winter, only a dry season and monsoons. The greenery barely has time to fade before it sprouts uncontrollably in the rains, giving the air its sultry, overripe scent as foliage invades the rice paddies and colors the fields.

The last time I heard from David, nearly four years ago when I was back in Chicago, he'd written to me in this excited scrawl that Cambodia is "clean." He explained what I already knew: at least 1.7 million people dead from Pol Pot's scourge, a fourth of the total population. All the bad karma has washed over this place, he wrote. It's annihilated past sins. This is the cleanest place on earth.

Cambodia, a "clean" place. That alone told me that this was just another one of his escapes. It sounded like he'd become a Buddhist. Or something close. I wasn't surprised by his new incarnation, and Cambodia? Well, why not. It sounded as good a place as any. He didn't have to worry about the American authorities pursuing him in a country where the Khmer Rouge was still actively collecting foreigners' heads. Hell—I doubted even his own ghosts would have the courage to follow him there, particularly when there were so many others to compete with. Nearly two million, give or take. A country aching in sin. Cambodia had always depressed the hell out of me. Even the Associated Press didn't like to send me there, and they knew I didn't care where I went as long as it wasn't home. To me, Phnom Phen had always looked like it'd been bombed. Crumbling buildings, shit in the streets, child beggars who'd had their legs blown off. The first time I went there, it took me a week to discover that all of this tragedy was normal—actually represented a country at peace—though I'd been in these kinds of places before and had seen much worse. But there comes a time when your life catches you off-guard and you suddenly pay attention. What did it for me was seeing a scrawny dog with its head caught in a clear plastic jug, running around the streets of Phnom Penh, banging into laughing people, getting kicked away, taunted, and eventually forgotten. Reminded me of David, somehow. Just the fact that no one tried to get the jug off—not even me; I could do nothing but watch. I knew right then it was time to go home. I'd had enough. I took a couple weeks off and flew back to Chicago, not leaving my apartment for days. I ate stale Frosted Flakes, leafed through year-old copies of the *Washington Post* which had been catching run-off from the radiator, and tried to figure out how in hell I could forget the world.

The problem is, memory claims everything—good or bad. David realized this long before I ever did, which has kept him running ever since. Me, it took a while. I kept thinking I could disappear from the past. My apartment off Lake Shore Drive had just enough windows to convince me that I was a part of something greater than myself, a huge maternal city, aloof and resplendent at night, skyscraper lights usurping the stars. All I saw was everyone else, all the lives, all the destinations as the cars edged by before my windows.

But Siem Reap notices me. It's back to that unfamiliarity that makes me feel so much at home. Out the window, I can see the crowd of young men with their American hand-me-down T-shirts from aid organizations, looking like a bunch of poster boys for Nike and the University of Virginia. They sit on mopeds in the airport parking lot, waiting for someone like me, the rare and foolhardy "rich tourist" willing to brave Pol Pot and beheadings for a single glimpse of that fabled kingdom of Angkor Wat lying outside of town. Supposedly it's more incredible than the Pyramids, if only I went to places for the sightseeing. If only this time I didn't have to find David wherever he's hiding in this land of lotus pools and killing fields, where a fourth of the people greet you from mass graves.

I leave the plane and walk across the tarmac. Already I'm sweating, and put on my baseball cap and sunglasses. A water buffalo chews its cud in a nearby paddy, watching me, its jaw unhitching from side to side like the arm of a record player. I stop to watch it, and try to imagine the afternoon when my brother had arrived at this very airport. I picture this same animal chewing away, gazing at him with its Buddha eyes, casting no judgment.

II.

I CLAIM MY BAG and pause at the airport doors to stare outside. A few disinterested palm trees sag along one side of the parking area, yellow fronds clattering in the wind. I've never had reason to come to this part of Cambodia, yet I like it. It is clean. Pure. I walk outside, leaving my sunglasses off for a moment, the sun always brighter when I notice it. The moto drivers soon surround me, assailing me with offers to drive me into town.

I know they all want my U.S. dollars, the hard currency that is more widely used here than the Cambodian riel.

A young man practically runs me over, pulling up and beckoning me on behind him. He starts his script. It is always the same tedious script the world over.

"C'est bon marché, Madame."

"I'm not French," I say.

"Cheap for you. Ten dollars."

"Two dollars."

"No profit for me. Okay, six dollars."

"Two dollars or forget it."

We stare at each other in silence. I cross my arms and wait.

"Okay, okay." He pats the seat behind him. "You come. Two dollars. But no profit for me."

He balances my bag on his handlebars, and I sit behind him. The motorbike putters out of the parking lot and down the narrow asphalt road toward town. No trees anywhere now, just the flat green rice paddies. Paddies and blue sky and a horizon at 360 degrees.

I shut my eyes and sigh, the wind whipping hair from my baseball cap and sending it flying about my face. I think of my mother, ninety pounds in a hospital bed, dying. Whenever she's upset, she mumbles in Czech as if her mother tongue knows her pain better, can express it more accurately to the world. "I want to see David," she'd said in Czech, delirious from the morphine. She held my hand, blue eyes focused on mine, her face wrinkled and sallow well beyond her sixty years. A dying face. And nothing I could do.

"Matka," I said, my Czech sounding foreign and reluctant as it came out, "David's gone. Remember?" But I'd decided I'd try to find David. Somehow, I would bring him back.

I have to remind myself how he used to be. My brother was the kind of boy who needed to bury any dead thing that he found—overturned beetles, road-kill squirrels, wilted azaleas. After our father died from a sudden heart attack, David had screamed during the entire wake because he wouldn't be able to bury Dad along with the baby robins and drowned earthworms of his backyard cemetery. He was only eight, still too young to be jolted from the illusion that we all live forever and that Dad would come back. Me, I was thirteen and knew better. I spent the whole wake trying to get him to shut up—even threatened him with promises of Dad's ghost coming back to punish him.

"Dad will come after you," he'd snap back. "You're the one not crying."

He was always smart like that. Too smart. Yet even with his IQ of 159, he couldn't have known the real reason I wasn't crying: because I hated the fact that death demanded it of me.

But David had such a huge heart, such sensitivity, that I used to worry about him. Particularly after Dad died. You can't afford to be so sensitive, I'd think. Not with life the way it is—sudden heart attacks. People getting old, dying. I didn't want him to know about any of that. I was determined to keep him innocent, Dad's death his only lesson. And overall, life was good to him. He was the precocious child every parent fantasizes having, extroverted and charming, very much my opposite. My parents had taken out a second mortgage in order to send him to the best private elementary school in the Chicago suburbs, a school "for the gifted" that had a minimum IQ requirement of 130 for its students. David was already well into algebra when my father died, a boy genius for whom everyone had such great expectations. Including me.

"Do you go to Angkor Wat?" the moto driver asks me over the noise of the tiny engine.

"What?" I open my eyes.

He glances over his shoulder at me. "Do you go to Angkor, Miss?"

"I don't know."

He laughs. Why else would I be going to Siem Reap? Why does any foreigner ever come to Siem Reap, if not for Angkor? But my thoughts aren't even in Cambodia anymore, let alone Angkor Wat.

"I give you good price," the young man is saying. "Ten dollar for day. I take you, Angkor Wat."

The driver readjusts my bag on the handlebars, sending us zigzagging across the road.

"You're going to kill us," I yell over the sound of the engine.

"Ten dollar for Angkor Wat, okay for you?"

He's got me thinking about the story on the AP wire about the French woman who was shot here last week. It was in all the papers. Travel advisories against going to Siem Reap. "What about the Khmer Rouge? A woman was shot."

"Yes, but she go too far. Not safe, place she go. I know safe place."

I watch the rice paddies drift by, the sun streaking the water between the new seedlings. The color of young rice plants must be the purest green on earth. An intoxicating green.

"Do you know an American named David?" I ask him. "He lives in town."

"No. I never see this man."

But his answer was too fast, too negligent.

"He's got brown hair, blue eyes," I say. "He's a Buddhist student. I think he lives in a temple somewhere."

"No. I never see this man."

An old woman, hunched and walking by the side of the road, her red sarong torn and stained, stops and gazes somberly at us as we speed by. I look over my shoulder at her. She hasn't moved. Her eyes remind me of my mother's eyes. Eyes that know too much, that can't bear the knowing.

Reminds me that according to Buddhism, life is suffering. My mother had had enough pain by the time my father died, though. She was nine when her own parents, Czech dissidents, had been sent to their deaths in one of the Nazi camps. Her aunt ended up taking her to America after the war, to Cicero, Illinois, the closest to Prague you could get in such a strange and prosperous place. Still, my mother made every effort to grow up an all-

American girl; she had done such a good job that by the time she was an adult, all that remained of the Old Country was the faintest perception of a rough roll to her *R*s. She had, in every other way, reinvented herself. Her life was like one great part to play in the name of normalcy. No more pain. No more suffering. She wanted things to be Good. Thy will be done. A Catholic, she prayed every day, morning, noon, and night, with the fervor of the Jews I've seen nodding before the Western Wall. Thy will be done.

Hard, then, to go on remembering, but I have no choice. I remember. The police cars arriving at our door on that Saturday night. Me, just graduated from Boston University and home for the summer, unpacking clothes and trying to picture myself in New York City and Columbia's graduate program in journalism in the fall. David, eighteen, now a senior in high school, gone with my mother's car. Gone all day, past his evening curfew. Gone well into the night. And so the flashing lights from the cruisers, the firm, unfamiliar knock on the front door. All of these things combined into a single, crushing terror. We pictured blood, hospital beds, horrible talks with funeral home directors feigning sympathy. I heard the slow beeping of a machine monitoring vital signs. The terror crushed into me. As I stumbled from my room to the front door, my mother already stood there, speaking in a low voice with a policeman, an old acquaintance of my father's, standing on the stoop.

"What happened? I asked her.

They were both silent.

I turned to the cop and must have yelled for an explanation. He took a step back. Another policeman looked at me solemnly from one of the squad cars.

"David has had an accident," my mother said.

"What happened? Is he okay?"

The policeman watched me from the stoop, his eyes looking tired. Profoundly tired. So sick of delivering bad news.

"This man has been telling me . . . that David—he just killed someone."

My legs quivered from the adrenaline.

Now the tears rolled down my mother's face. "This man says that David killed a little boy . . . with the car. Killed him."

The little boy was Jeremy Randall Parker. Age four. I can never forget the name: Jeremy Randall Parker. Services for Jeremy Randall Parker. Of 1201 Windhaven Court. David Marzek held for driving while under the influence and manslaughter in the death of Jeremy Randall Parker. About to begin preschool at Manning Elementary, La Grange, Illinois. Jeremy Randall Parker.

According to the papers, it happened this way: David had been driving down an alley behind some houses, well over the posted speed limit of five miles an hour. He had had some beer at a friend's house and his blood-alcohol level had reached the point of illegal intoxication. Little Jeremy had been playing inside a large washing machine box, and David, thinking the box was empty, had accelerated to run it over. When he felt the bumping sensation, he immediately stopped and got out of the car. A moment later he was running to a nearby house to call 911. An ambulance came and the boy was rushed to the hospital. Jeremy died en route. Time of death, 5:38 P.M. CST.

After my mother paid David's bail and took him home from the police station, he'd stopped speaking and eating. That same evening, he'd put a knife to his arms and wrists and carved himself up so thoroughly that by the time my mother had discovered him, he'd been unconscious. He was rushed to the hospital. From that moment on, he took up residence in the state mental ward. They restrained his arms. He was fed intravenously and counseled by psychiatrists. Doctors performed a kind of medicinal alchemy until a concoction was found that doped him up enough to curb his self-mutilation impulses and bring back his voice.

"It was an accident," was their mantra to him. "You didn't mean to do it."

I was there during one of these times, standing just outside the door, listening to one doctor's recitations. David's voice, low, foreign-sounding, snarled out, "What the fuck do you know?"

And silence. Because they didn't know. How could they? All those doctors had gone to school, gotten their Ph.D.s in clinical psychology or psychiatry, thought they were experts in the human soul. But David had killed someone. It wasn't a reparable thing. Jeremy Randall Parker could never come back.

The moped lurches.

"Can you slow down?!" I yell.

He does. For once, he takes it easy.

I breathe deeply, feeling the adrenaline pulsing through my body. I look out again at the incredible space of this part of Cambodia, and the blinding green of the rice paddies. Considering all that's happened to this country, I don't understand how it can be so beautiful.

"What do you think of Pol Pot," I ask the young man's back. "Do you like Pol Pot?"

Over the sound of the engine: "Yes, of course."

I'm not surprised. I push my sunglasses higher up on my nose and stare at the back of his neck, at the slice of dark brown skin above the top of his Bulls T-shirt.

"Why?"

"He kill clever people. Clever people steal from poor people."

"Oh."

"All clever people dead. If people doctor, dead. People teacher, dead. People rich, dead. This is good thing for Kampuchea."

I remember an old Slavic fairy tale my mother used to read to me called "Vasilissa the Beautiful." An evil witch, trying to trick a young girl in order to kill her, discourages the child from asking too many questions. "If you know too much," the witch warns, "you'll grow old too soon."

As we slow down at a crossroads to wait for a truck to pass, I know I can't be near this man anymore. I hop off the moped and grab my bag from the handle bars.

"What is problem?" he demands.

I throw a dollar at him. "Fuck off."

III.

I WALK INTO THE DOWNTOWN AREA of Siem Reap, and I'm relieved to see that it hardly resembles Phnom Phen. Rather, it looks tired to me and ready for sleep. There is no urgency here, no sense of chaos. The air doesn't smell sickly pungent from garbage rotting beside the streets. Instead, it smells fresh, like after a rain. White-washed, mildew-stained buildings languish along the streets. On the side roads, a few colonial-style houses sit as evidence of France's old Indochine empire, shaded by giant trees. Moto drivers wait in groups on the side of the main drag, watching me pass, perhaps hoping I'll hail one of them. But I like the walk. It gives me a pleasant sense of direction, purpose.

I'm not worried yet about finding David—if I can dig up Dinka warlords in the Sudan for interviews, I'm sure I can find Siem Reap's only American Buddhist novice. Yet, I can't figure out how to convince him to come home. You'd think it'd be enough, our mother's dying, but if he were to come home, he'd have to face all the legal responsibilities of his actions. After he was discharged from the hospital, he went to court. My mother spent a fortune of Dad's insurance money on the bond and a decent lawyer for him, and the judge ended up suspending his sentence for manslaughter, heavily fining him and requiring him to stay in the state by putting him on probation for years. David would be able to avoid prison. It seemed a blessing. I started to believe in the miracle of time then, that it could resolve anything if enough hours went by, enough days passed. Each night felt especially auspicious, as if it were proof of my brother's inevitable rescue.

I still ended up going to Columbia University, hoping my journalism classes and the enormity of New York City would distract my attention from my brother and what had happened. I simply couldn't stay home to watch it all unfold. It was making me crazy, and my reaction was to just get away, stay away, for as long as I could.

My mother told me about the continued fallout, though. Shortly after the six-month anniversary of the accident, David had broken the conditions of his probation by driving my mother's car without a license, in order to go to the Fox River. He'd parked, then hiked along the river with a pickax and towel. It had been one of the coldest days on record for the Chicago suburbs, -3°F, wind chill factor in the double digits. I can imagine some of the tree limbs so weighted with ice that they'd broken and were dangling despondently over the river. I can picture David debating all of this, stopping every now and then to feel the river's icy surface with his fingertips. Perhaps he was conscious of the silence of the snow, the sense of a world so deeply caught in winter that the green spring is unimaginable. And here in this place, he stopped finally, something inexplicably correct. He heaved his backpack to the ground, brushed snow from the ice's surface, and started to chop himself a hole.

The hole needed to be large, because he would have to dive into it four times—naked. Four times in, four times out. On the forth plunge, he would have to dive to the bottom and come up with a handful of silt to put in a leather pouch, a sacred pouch.

All of this came out of the shrink's report. I still can't imagine what was going through his mind, though. It's not clear how many times he actually got in and out of that water before conditions became too much for him. I was told that afterward, back in the state hospital, he kept mumbling an old Algonquin phrase for days. A shrink got the translation out of him—"See the great warrior, I will make him rise." Apparently David had dug up some information at the Newberry Library in Chicago about an old Shawnee manhood ritual. Teenage boys wanting to be reborn into men with honor and virtue underwent an arduous sort of baptism by jumping into a river four times in the middle of winter. On the fourth plunge, the boy dived down to the bottom of the river to grab a handful of silt that would be sewn inside his pa-waw-ka pouch, a magical charm of protection that he wore around his neck. Only the bravest, strongest of them attempted it on the very coldest days of winter, achieving a more potent reward. Wearing the pa-waw-ka, the new warrior was blessed and became immune to malign forces. All the evil in the world could no longer hurt him.

David had wanted the hardest test, of course. He would have died if a man hadn't driven by and noticed him, naked and floundering in the river. As it was, he was rushed to the hospital with a severe case of hypothermia and barely a pulse, and they were lucky to have resuscitated him.

When I heard about it, I left grad school and flew back from New York. Someone needed to knock some sense into David, and if the shrinks or my mother couldn't (and obviously they couldn't), then I would. My brother needed me.

I head toward Siem Reap's post office. David's last letter, which arrived a year ago, gave it as a return address. There's a chance someone might remember him, know where he's living. The post office is a small building that resembles a run-down warehouse, a staff of dozing employees seated behind an ancient window stained with fly carcasses and fingerprint smears. I show the employees my press credentials to let them know I'm serious. Using the manager as translator, I tell them I'm looking for an American. Apparently, he's been in here and it's important that I find him. I give his name and physical description.

The woman at the counter shrugs. Another man says many of the Buddhist monks live in the temples by Angkor, but he's not sure if there's a white man among them.

As I head to a guesthouse nearby, I stop in a couple government offices and some stores along the road to make inquiries about David. My Cambodian is terrible; we speak in either French, English, or Japanese—whichever of these tourist languages they've learned. I have to coax the French out of some of the older staff, as they still hesitate to use words that would have sent them, "clever," educated people, straight to the killing fields. They tell me they've seen no foreigners in Buddhist robes. It is the same old story.

I give up. For now. I'll head to Angkor tomorrow. I get a room at a place called the Mahogany Guesthouse and have dinner in the rooftop restaurant. A group of young backpackers sits nearby, an outspoken American man bragging to them that no matter where he's traveled, he's "drunk the water everywhere" and has never gotten sick.

"Only people with weaker constitutions get dysentery and all that," he's saying. "It has to do with the constitution."

Another genius. I order a beer and take out David's letter. I don't open it yet, but study the envelope made of thin, airmail paper. My beer comes and I take a long sip, wondering if David didn't have someone else going into town, mailing his letters for him. I take out the letter now and stare at the handwriting. Small, printed script. Calm script that is barely familiar. Used to be I couldn't read his handwriting at all as it traveled and wound about, looking more like Arabic than anything English.

> *Dear Chris,*
>
> *I finally got your letter about Mom. (The post office in town had it for months.) I know why you're upset. You think I've just run away from everything. And I know you think I need to own up to what you call my "responsibility" for what happened. I can't figure out how to get you to understand that I'm not running from anything anymore. I've thought about what you wrote, how Mom is getting worse and needs to see me. It's not that I don't care about her, or you. Believe me, I wish I could see her but if I return to the States, they'll never let me come back here, and I've found something here that sustains*

me. I've found the virtuous path, the Noble Eightfold Path, and
have entered the Sangha.

I put down the letter and sigh. I've read it over a hundred times, but it
always feels like a first reading. I have trouble knowing where my brother's
sincerity ends and his indoctrination begins. This seems like a milder version of his pa-waw-ka ritual back at the Fox River—yet another attempt to
obliterate the guilt.

I'm starting to think that David is too much of a coward to ever come
home. It must be cowardice. I think he has this illusion that if he stays away
from his problems for long enough, they'll vanish. I've met expatriates like
that living in remote corners of the world, burnt-out, alcoholic men living
in grimy bungalows with local mistresses fussing about them. Sometimes
they're useful if you're following a story, need tips on how to handle a situation, but they've stocked up so much history there's an odorless stench
about them. Maybe they killed someone, made a bad business deal—you
never find out why. I just don't want David to turn out like that, burnt-out,
drugged-out on some West African beach, abandoned by the world.

I sip my beer. An Indian man sets up a microphone in a corner of the
room and starts singing a Bob Dylan song. The backpacker clique next door
passes around a joint and sways to the music. The American man offers it to
me and I shake my head.

"Where are you from?" he asks.

"Chicago."

"Seen Angkor Wat?"

"Tomorrow."

The other backpackers turn their attention to me.

"We're going to try to hire an army escort so we can see Banteay Srei. If
you want to pitch in some money, you can come with."

They're talking about the distant temple where the French woman was
shot last week. The Angkor Wat area is too heavily guarded by government
forces for the Khmer Rouge to ever get close to it, but Banteay Srei, all alone

in the countryside, is fair game. I've never seen any photos of it, but it has always been described to me as "too beautiful for words." And it had better be, for people to risk their lives to see it. It had better be one of the most beautiful places on earth.

"You won't be able to get an escort there," I tell them. "The place is off-limits. The Khmer Rouge are still all over."

"We're going to try. We're hiring some soldiers."

"Look," I say, "I'm a reporter, and they won't even let me near the place. I did some asking around today, and the situation is still bad."

They glance at each other. Why should I care? Let them go, let them try to go. The French woman had herself an armed escort, and she was still shot. But they're so young, like my brother. I somehow feel responsible for them, for what they don't quite know about the world.

"If you end up going somehow," I say, "stay inside the buildings as much as possible. Don't let someone get a fix on you."

"'Get a fix'?" one girl asks.

I feel exhausted. "Snipers."

They glance at each other again. The American remembers about the joint and checks to see whether it needs to be re-lit.

"Cashed," he says.

I turn back to David's letter, to the part that starts to get crazy.

> *I've written to Mom already to tell her how I feel, and I think she understands. It's just you who I can't seem to reach. It's just that for the first time since what happened, I've found peace in the Glorious Root-Guru, the Blessed One, Avalokiteshvara. Every day I pray that I and all sentient beings will reach the Blissful Realm. I pray that the Root and Lineal Gurus will bless me with Resolution in order to reach this end. May they bless me with Emptiness.*
>
> *Chris, I love you and Mom, always.*
> *—David*

"The 'Glorious Root-Guru,'" I say, trying out the words. The back-packers look over at me, thinking I've called to them.

The Indian man starts singing a Steve Winwood song, "Can't Find My Way Home." Figures. It's time to go to bed. I head down to my room on the second floor, opening the door with my key. None of these rooms have windows, and only the tired light from the hallway seeps in beneath my door as I close it behind me. I don't turn on a light. Don't want a light. From one of the rooms down the hall, I can hear the dull pattering of Cambodian voices coming from a radio or TV set. Tonight, I miss silence.

I collapse onto the bed, smelling the dust rising about me from the sheets. It seems amazing that I may actually see my brother tomorrow. I remember the last time I saw him, how they had called him a "critical case" in the hospital, his pa-waw-ka rite an "attempted suicide"—they always had a marvelous way of disguising situations with words. I had understood everything for what it was, though, that he was trying desperately to pay for the death he'd caused, and it seemed inevitable that both my mother and I would also have to pay: we would be forced to watch him suffer, unable to help.

I was finally allowed to visit him a few weeks after the incident at the river. I remember all the security in the hospital and how the visitor's area felt like a prison with a make-over of summer camp: steel doors opening up into a large, unassuming lounge area with wood-paneled walls and fluffy, friendly couches, counselors pumping out obligatory smiles in passing. David was smart, though, would have noticed how all the friendly objects he encountered had been chosen with patients' self-preservation in mind, none of them able to be removed or destroyed.

I waited in the lounge, facing an overhead television with the volume turned off, basketball players running around the screen, in and out of my consciousness. I must have been frowning; a man with glasses and mustache hesitated before coming into the room. He smelled like after-shave lotion, was trim and professional in a button-up blue shirt and tie.

"Christine Marzek?" he asked.

I crossed my legs and nodded. "Chris."

"I'm Dr. Moran, David's doctor." He shook my hand. "You look like you'd rather be somewhere else."

"Yeah." I studied him: in his early thirties, probably fresh out of some doctoral program and in his first real job—David was his first real job. My hands were shaking and I ordered them to stop.

"So you're his big sister?" he asked, smiling. I'd forgotten psychologists' expertise at smiling. Their obsession with gaining trust.

"Yeah." My voice was quaking, and he acknowledged it with a flicker of his eyes. "How is he? When is someone going to help him?"

He sighed and pulled up a chair. "It'll take some time."

"This must be part of it, part of the deal," I said.

"What deal?"

I looked at him. "His deal with the universe. His penance for killing a person."

Dr. Moran studied me for a moment. He had the classic moist shrink eyes, the voyeuristic compassion.

"I'm not sure he's being punished by anyone," he said gently. "He's too busy punishing himself."

"You ought to be a priest," I said.

He blinked in curiosity.

"You're so eager to save people. You know, there's nothing you can do for my brother. How do you reverse what he did? How do you make up for it?"

He watched me intently. "I can see how much this hurts you."

"Can your Prozac bring people back from the dead? My mother goes to church three times a day now. She can't talk about anything without quoting the Bible. All I ever hear about is goddamn redemption and salvation, redemption and salvation. Drives me crazy."

"This must be hard for you."

I sighed and re-crossed my legs, glaring at the TV. Tiny men were throwing a ball back and forth to each other.

"We can talk about it, if you want." He crossed his fingers and waited, but I didn't say anything. "Look—I can't promise any quick fixes. But I do suggest that—"

"My brother's brilliant. He excelled at everything." My voice was too loud. I shut up and stared at the TV again.

"These things take time."

I laughed at that. His silly optimism. If I couldn't get over it, then how was David supposed to?

He studied me in silence. Finally: "Your mother said you'd dropped out of grad school to come back here."

"Yeah."

"She told me that she's worried about you. Do you plan on returning?"

"I don't know."

"You were going to Columbia's School of Journalism, right?"

I nodded.

"It's a prestigious program."

I shrugged. "Matter of opinion."

He leaned forward and looked at me, waiting. When my eyes finally met his, he said, "I'm concerned about you, Chris. I want you to go back to school. How many more lives have to be messed up over this?"

It didn't seem like something a shrink would say. It was too direct, too certain. I rolled my eyes, my hands shaking again. "You don't even know me."

"Okay," he said, leaning back.

"I just want to see David."

They brought him in. To take one look at him was to know that he would never again be the little brother I'd grown up with, whom I'd taught to read and write, to recognize the constellations, the cumulus clouds catching the skirt of Cassiopeia. I realized then that the images I held of people were inaccurate at best, nothing but a desperate composite of choice memories. Five years older than David, I remembered holding his newborn self in my arms. I remembered the delicate vulnerability of his tiny fingers, the softness of his skin. The first time my mother had tried to hand him to me, I'd run off in terror. I hadn't wanted the responsibility of him. What if I dropped him? Ruined him in some way?

David was thin now, pale, with limp, shoulder-length brown hair. In my memories—those intractable memories—he was still athletic-looking, had a runner's sinewy body and broad shoulders. He was still the wrestler who'd won State, the National Merit Scholar, the grinning, mischievous young scientist whose project on electromagnetism had won him first in Nationals.

But I tried to focus on the present: David, wearing a stained white T-shirt and blue sweatpants, smelling moldy like disinfectant soap. He had a dragging walk, like some crazy person's. His eyes wandered about the room as if he were a baby trying to fix on things and understand their purpose. When he sat down in the chair next to mine, the orderly with him—a fairly large, strong man—took a seat in a far corner of the room and locked his gaze on the TV screen. He was here with us because David had been caught with a pen he'd stolen, hurting himself.

I wasn't sure what to say at first. I tried laughing. "This place is a pit, isn't it?"

No response. He was working at the cuticles on his fingers, peeling off pieces of skin. I glanced briefly at the long pinkish scars covering his hands and arms.

We'd never been a hugging kind of family, but I hugged him. I took his heavy body into my arms and held it. He felt bony, frail, his arms remaining at his side. When I caught the orderly glancing at us, I cupped the back of David's head in my hand.

"You have to get over it," I whispered into his ear. "You have to."

No response. I was told that he often refused to speak, that his voice had to be coaxed out of him.

"Talk to me."

Nothing.

Here was something I couldn't solve. David had done this to himself, and I couldn't think of a cure.

Holding David tighter, I looked across the room. The sun was slanting in, lighting up the end of a blue couch. I focused on the light as it hit one landmark after another—the next cushion on the couch, the edge of a floor tile. The onslaught of light was barely perceptible, yet soon the entire end of the room was blinding me.

I motioned to the window and the orderly got up to pull the curtains. Then I heard a sound. From between David's legs, a stream of water rolled off the vinyl chair and trickled to the floor.

I went back to New York. There was nothing I could do, and I couldn't handle seeing him again in that psych ward. My mother called me periodically to tell that he was getting better, that his therapy was working. Finally, after nearly a year in the place, they discharged him under a policy of out-patient supervision. My mother took care of him, making sure that he stayed doped up on his medication and visited his doctors. In the meantime there were more court dates and talk as to whether he should go to prison for breaking the conditions of his probation and driving my mother's car. It seemed as if the craziness would never end.

Yet, he'd gotten out of the hospital. I couldn't believe it until I was actually talking to him over the phone. His voice was soft, hesitant; he sounded like a child keeping secrets. When he asked me for money, I hadn't thought anything of it. All I wanted to do was help him. I had a few thousand dollars saved up, and I sent it all to him, believing—as did his doctors—that he really wanted to get his GED and apply to college. But a few days after he got my check, he disappeared. It was a serious matter, as he had broken the out-patient agreement with the hospital and the courts. The police had a warrant out for his arrest; if they caught him, he'd be going to prison for sure. Then I received a postcard from Mexico. All it said was, "I'm sorry."

I knew David wouldn't be coming back.

IV.

I LEAVE MY GUESTHOUSE as the sun rises, determined to find my brother. The stray cats and dogs claim the mornings here, sniffing about the closed-up food stalls of the central market and the piles of garbage stacked along the streets. The closed stores and empty streets remind me of being in Skopje, Macedonia, on my way to cover Bosnia's war, and how I panicked and wouldn't leave the train station because of the steel shutters pulled down over the storefronts outside. In the Sudan and Mozambique, shuttered stores meant impending chaos: rebel advances, women being raped, male children conscripted into ragtag rebel armies. They meant destruction—with me in the middle of it. Again.

Yet, I'd asked for this life. Originally, I'd been going to school in broadcast journalism, but it had suddenly seemed too quaint and meaningless after all that had happened with my brother. I began studying international affairs with the idea of becoming a foreign correspondent and getting the hell away from home. A year went by, and I didn't hear a thing from David. Then I got a postcard from Varanasi, India, with no message on it. But being from Varanasi told me everything I needed to know. I wondered if the brahmins of that holy city were teaching him anything. I wondered if they'd convince him to go home and deal with the repercussions of his actions.

I ended up graduating from Columbia and accepting a job with the Associated Press. I'd be a stringer, covering international news. They needed people to work in their foreign bureaus, people who didn't care where they went or what they did. Pretty soon I was off on my own, freelancing in places like Khartoum and Mogadishu. As one war photographer once told me, "The shit holes of the world always have the best stories—if you can get yourself out of them." David might have said my karma was good, though he couldn't have known how much I tempted the world. How much I hated it for its senseless parceling of benevolence and pain.

I start walking down a street, taking deep breaths. The moto drivers notice me and materialize from the alleyways to ask me whether I need a driver to take me to Angkor Wat. I look at each person, not knowing who to choose. Whenever possible, people and things need to feel right. Across the street, I see an old man in gray cap and wrinkled white shirt. His face is drawn, somber. He leans against a beat-up blue motor bike, watching the young men swarm around me.

I quickly walk across the street. He looks at me with quiet surprise as I get on the back of his bike.

"Angkor Wat?" he says.

"Yes."

We start driving along the river and through the downtown, building after building shuttered with the dawn. The air is cool, still. Almost cold. Yet, with the rising sun, I can feel the midday heat beginning its offensive.

The driver leans over to tell me his name is Ga. "Muslim," he says, pointing at himself. Then he cuts a finger across his throat. "Pol Pot."

I know what he's telling me. The Cambodian Cham Muslims were Pol Pot's pet project, were among the first people to be slaughtered along with most of the country's Buddhist monks. Ga is a rarity. The last of his kind.

"Mother, father, brother, sister—" He cuts a finger across his throat as he drives, then points ahead toward the Angkor temple complex. "Sras Srang."

The large mass graves of Sras Srang, in the midst of the most popular of the Angkor ruins.

"Me," he says. Then he points at his ankle and pretends there's a chain around it. "Khmer Rouge. Understand?"

"Yes."

We drive on in silence. I don't know what to say. There is nothing I can say.

On the way out of town, I see a small Buddhist temple and ask Ga to stop so I can ask about David. No one is inside when we enter. There is an old stone Buddha without a head, surrounded by brass bowls, prayer flags, rice offerings. A single stick of incense burns from a bowl before the altar, giving off a thick, sweet scent.

I point to the headless Buddha. "Khmer Rouge?" I ask Ga.

He nods emphatically. "Kampuchea is bad, bad country. No good, Kampuchea."

I put my own chin on the neck of the Buddha, linking my hands with those of the statue. Ga stares at me, perplexed.

"Is Banteay Srei beautiful?" I ask him, remembering the temple where the French woman was shot.

"Yes, yes." He looks at me, his eyes moist. "You want see? I can take."

I move away from the Buddha. "You mean, go there?"

"Yes. Go."

"Oh God—it's too dangerous." I laugh.

"No, no." He pulls the red checkered scarf from around his neck and puts it around my hair. "You hide." He tucks my hair under it. "Okay. You Kampuchea girl."

"Too dangerous for you, then."

He shrugs, his face drawn. Perhaps he's not scared of anything anymore.

A monk in an orange robe appears from the back of the temple and slowly approaches us. He winks a hello to me and I bow to him. I ask in French if he's seen a young American man named David, living at any of the temples in town.

He grins and answers in English. "Yes, yes. Yesterday I see him by the Bayon temple. By Angkor."

"Is he all right?"

The monk looks at me, perplexed by my question. "Of course," he says.

WE RETURN TO SIEM REAP, to the French Cultural Center in town so I can make an international phone call. I want to give my mother the good news—that I know where David is, that he's all right and hopefully

I'll be bringing him home. It takes the manager twenty minutes to put the call through, and I keep waiting, hands wringing, wanting to tell Matka that after six years, she'll be seeing David again.

The manager hands me the phone at last, and it's my great-aunt on the other end of the line. Her voice sounds fuzzy from the bad connection, her heavy Czech accent further obscuring her words. I have to ask her to repeat what she says, and when she does, and when I think I understand, I lean back against the wall, closing my eyes.

"Since when?" I say.

"Since yesterday morning."

"Will she come out of it?"

Silence. "They don't think so."

I don't know what a "coma" means, exactly. I've only seen it in the movies, where it usually means death. Coming out of it, then, becomes the convenient act of divine intervention—and I know that real life is never so convenient. I ask my aunt in Czech to tell my mother that I've found David and he's coming home. We lose the connection.

I pay the manager for the call and go to the bathroom. Leaning my head against the mirror, I avoid looking at myself. I know I should have come out here earlier, when Matka was healthier. I shouldn't have waited so damn long. I bang my head against the mirror, shaking my head.

I leave the bathroom to sit on the veranda of the French Cultural Center, and order a glass of scotch. When it comes, I drink it down and order another. A couple of French businessmen, overdressed for Siem Reap in shirt and tie, glance at me as if I were an afterthought.

Maybe I hadn't come out here for Matka. I was the one who wanted to bring David back. Without Matka and David, who do I have left? What connections? What reason to go home? The loneliness of my life can make me go crazy at times. There was that assignment down in Madagascar when I ran into Helmut doing a piece for the *Berliner Zeitung*. We were both down in Toliara where the riots were starting. I forget what those riots were about.

All I really remember are the seashells. Spectacular seashells set up in perfect rows along the sand. Raggedly dressed children sold them by the oceanfront, shells of all colors and varieties. Conches, augers, giant cowries, the shells giving off the undeniable stink of rot. Shake them and you heard a dead thing inside.

I bought some anyway because they were so beautiful, then Helmut and I got a room in a dumpy hotel overlooking the Indian Ocean. We made love while the first shots went off outside, the rickshaw runners leaving their ranks in front of the hotel to dash for cover farther down the road. We made quick, hard love, as if the world were about to end, the ceiling fan wobbling and pumping away at the dusty air over our heads. Afterward, when we discovered to our dismay that the world hadn't vanished, we hired a driver to take us back to the capital, Antananarivo. We wanted to fly out to Nairobi, forget Madagascar had ever existed. During the ride, Helmut and I kept our distance and we talked about mundane things. We both knew what we wouldn't say: we were disappointed by the sudden normalcy of things, our lovemaking trivialized to mere boredom—just a bout in the heat of yet another dumpy hotel room. I forget the rooms faster than anything else. They might have all been the exact same room, somehow transported from one country to the next, mysteriously finding me again and again, like a bad dream.

I finish my scotch and see that Ga is waiting for me across the street, gray cap pulled down. When our eyes meet, he offers me a smile. I try to smile back, but it feels sloppy on me.

I pay for the drinks and walk over to him. I steady my voice as I speak. I want to know if he'll take me to Banteay Srei, after all. I want to see something beautiful.

V.

IT'S A LONG RIDE. Ga dresses me up like a Khmer villager, checkered red scarf hiding my hair, one of his wife's hand-woven silk sarongs around my waist. The rice paddies trail by on either side, sharp, brilliant-colored fields that pass like enormous seas of green. Farmers tend to the tiny seedlings, glancing up as we speed by. Small villages of raised, thatch-roofed huts appear at intervals. I hide my face in the small of Ga's back, taking peeks at them. Even these poorest of families have lotus pools in front of their huts, sacred pink and red flowers spreading out across the surface of the water, their color offering a sanctuary for my gaze.

I remember when David used to talk about going to Brazil just to see the giant macaws, those rainbow-colored parrots. He used to be obsessed with color. I once bought him a New Guinea Birdwing butterfly with wings of blue-green satin, and he hung it up in his room over his bed as if it were a cross, enraptured by it.

"I'm going to go to the Amazon and New Guinea," he'd said to Matka.

She smiled, convinced. We were all convinced.

"I know you will," she said.

But he never did make it there. Probably never will. It doesn't make sense to want anything. Everything is a matter of what you're allowed to have. Thy will be done. Reminds me of being in the Middle East. People unable to speak to me about the future without saying Insha'allah—God willing—their eyes directed toward the sky.

No one has noticed yet that I'm not Cambodian. And this, too, feels like a gift. Something I'm allowed to have. I wonder when the generosity will end. The Khmer Rouge have already collected twelve foreigners' heads in the past three years, each one bringing international notoriety and news coverage. Young aid workers were taken while trying to rid the land of its mines. There were some foolhardy backpackers looking for a good story to tell people back home. And of course the French woman last week, with her army escort and their AK-47s.

None of it enough.

We do about 15 mph now, the road dusty and full of potholes. Ga points ahead. In the distance, in the midst of a large patch of jungle, I can see what looks like a small pyramid. Banteay Srei. We drive closer until we reach a thatch enclosure, some kind of barn. Ga stops and tuns off the engine, parking the bike inside. From a distance, we're only peasants getting out of the sun. I must be content to view the temple from afar or not at all. I understand why Ga insisted on this, on my staying by the road; approaching Banteay Srei, having any obvious interest in it whatsoever, will endanger my life. The only way I can see the beauty is to pretend I don't see it at all.

A few old village men drive a water buffalo toward a nearby village, glancing at us as they pass. Their eyes widen when they see my blue eyes and white skin, and they mutter something to Ga and shake their heads. He quiets them and shoos them on.

Alone, I walk up the road, clutching the scarf beneath my chin and stuffing some stray hairs behind my ears. I take a peek at the temple. It was constructed over one thousand years ago but is so well preserved that it looks as if it had been finished yesterday.

It's made of sandstone, a central tower rising in the middle. I've never seen such a place: the stone is so intricately carved that even from this distance it looks animated. Smiling, full-breasted women gaze out from porticoes guarded by coiling serpents. Flowering filigree wind and trail about columns and cover the walls like vines. On the arches, elephants parade before Shiva, the Destroyer, seated on his throne above all his minions.

Ga whistles to me from the side of the building, telling me I've gone too far, that I should come back.

I head across the moat, toward the entrance to the temple. It's guarded by human-sized men with snarling lion heads. They kneel on one leg before the entrance to the temple, their heads cracked open by the Khmer Rouge.

I pause before them, and wait for a moment. They seem to be daring me on. I head up the stone steps and into a courtyard. Tiny figures flutter about the walls and gaze out at me from the filigreed buttresses and archways, looking curious or perhaps scared. I glance up at the cobra-headed nagas, each scowling at me, then out at the surrounding jungle. I see no one, but that doesn't mean no one is there. In the distance, by the barn, Ga is waving at me, urging me back to him.

I see a spread of dried blood on the stone floor of the courtyard. It must be where the French woman was shot. The rain hasn't come since last week, and there hasn't been anyone brave enough to come by to wash up the blood. I walk over to the spot and wait. I pull off my scarf revealing my blond hair, and wait. This is how it happens. A decision is made. Fate or bad luck. My mother would call it fate. All of it, fate. The will of God.

Ga waves his arms wildly at me.

Shiva, the Destroyer. Vishnu, the Redeemer. They are the reason for this temple.

But no shot is coming.

I head back the way I came, through the courtyard and down the steps past the lion-headed guardians. I slowly make my way across the stone bridge and over the moat to the safety and anonymity of the dirt road. The lion-headed figures now look small and helpless from this distance.

I walk over to Ga, where he is already starting his motorbike. He shakes his head at me.

"Not safe," he says, pointing at Banteay Srei. "Bad place."

I replace my head scarf and get on the back of his bike without a word.

There are tears in his eyes. "Bad place."

VI.

O N T H E W A Y T O the Bayon temple, to find David, I ask Ga to stop. He pulls over without a word, turning off the moped's engine, leaving us in the middle of an ancient bridge bordered by giant, beheaded figures. I walk to the side of the bridge, gazing down at the waters of a wide moat, heavy with algae and duckweed. If I find my brother, I'm not sure what I'll say. Because of how my mother is now, half of me wants to yell at David, demand to know what kind of life he thinks he can have here, deluding himself with his Buddhism.

Ga joins me, gazing down at the murky waters, and I watch him. He was imprisoned, probably tortured, and I wonder what he thinks when he sees these beheaded figures everywhere, all over his country. I want to give this man thousands of dollars, make him a rich man, convince him that there is such a thing as a kind god and a benevolent universe.

Instead, I do nothing.

We look out at the ancient moat, jungle pressing in on both sides. At the end of this bridge stands a giant stone turret topped with four faces of Avalokiteshvara, the Buddha of Compassion. Here is David's "root-guru," his bodhisattva. I turn to stare at the faces, each one looking off in a different direction and smiling serenely. The bodhisattvas intrigue me. According to Buddhism, they were on the verge of reaching nirvana but refused to go to it. They opted to return to the world of suffering so that they might offer their assistance to all beings. For one thousand years, these sublime faces have been gazing down at the world. At the great Khmer civilization rising before them. At the invading Thai hoards. At the abandoned city of Angkor, left to the jungle until a French explorer discovered it again in the 1860s. And then, not so very long ago, directly beneath their gaze, at the soldiers of the Khmer Rouge driving Siem Reap's undesirables over the moat, to mass graves prepared among the temple ruins. Perhaps Ga's father came this way.

Perhaps his brother, or his sisters. The faces would have gazed down with their half-open eyes, blessing all who came before them, judging no one.

"Do you like this place?" I ask Ga.

He shrugs.

"But do you . . . Your family . . ." I cut a finger across my throat and point down the bridge.

He picks up some pebbles from the ground and beckons me to him. Placing them on the stone bridge, he looks at me then throws one off.

"Brother," he says.

He knocks off a second.

"Sister number one." And a third. "Sister number two."

Two more stones leave for his parents. And a few more for other family members and friends. Finally, he holds up what is left of the pile of stones, a small handful now, and these he pockets. "Mine," he says. He taps his pocket. "Mine."

I nod.

But he shakes his head in frustration and points to my shorts. I pull out the empty pocket.

"I haven't really—"

He grabs my wrist and hands me his pocketful of stones. "Yours." He looks me in the eye until I realize I'm supposed to pocket them. "Yours."

THE BAYON IS DIRECTLY AHEAD, at the end of a long road bordered by jungle. At first glance, it looks like a large pile of rubble. Giant carved stones lay haphazardly in the grass, and Cambodian children in ripped T-shirts climb about them. As we approach, little girls lift younger siblings to their hips and run to the road. They surround me, begging for some riel.

As I pass out what bills I have, I see a couple of Buddhist novices in white robes sitting in the ruins, muttering mantras. I'm thinking one of them might be David, and go to them, but they turn out to be Cambodian women. When I give them David's name, say "American," they nod their heads and point at the Bayon temple.

Looking for some way to enter the temple, I climb up a steep stone stairway. It ends at a dim corridor that winds into alcoves where beheaded Buddha statues rest in smoky candlelight. Monks in orange robes sit alone or in pairs before the statues, praying with their alms bowls before them. I search every dark chamber, confronting one headless Buddha after another in the labyrinth-like passageways.

All of the Buddha statues in this temple have been beheaded. I know from being in Phnom Penh that it's almost impossible to find a Buddha anywhere in this country that hasn't been decapitated. There must have been so many heads to take off. Did the Khmer Rouge smash them all? But they must have done something with them. I want to know where they are. I want to find them, put them back on. I swear to God, I could devote my life to putting them back on.

I go up some stairs that are narrow and slippery from the polishing of nearly eight hundred years of passing feet. Light appears, and I find myself in an outside courtyard where gigantic stone faces greet me from all angles, some head on, others in profile. No matter where I walk, there is no way to avoid them. Every approach to this inner sanctuary is guarded by these visages of Avalokiteshvara, the Buddha of Compassion. The architecture is such that they look through entryways at me, through small windows and long corridors. It's impossible to escape their gaze, to be forgotten by them. Always: the wide lips, half-closed eyes, delicately curved nose of the bodhisattva.

David isn't anywhere. There is no one in any white robe. I sit on the stone steps, the giant faces beaming down on me from several angles, some from high above, others great and auspicious before me. I can't stop looking at them—they're whispering and cooing to me. Such kind reassurances, such beautiful words. Secrets about life. Glorious, enigmatic secrets, and all I can do is listen. I tell them I'm afraid to leave this place. I tell them about my brother, and how he killed a young boy. I tell them my father died and my mother is dying. I tell them about the woman I knew in Sarejevo who kept her little girl in a bomb shelter for a year, only to finally let her out and see her get blown apart. So much that I can tell them. The ravaged villages I saw in Mozambique. The anguish in refugees' eyes—I've lost count of it all. So much that I can tell.

The faces know all of this already, and they coo to me, whispering beautiful things though some have pieces of their cheeks missing, their eyes, the crowns on their heads, from Khmer Rouge target practice. They want to guide me into the inner sanctuary, the tower of stone that is at the center of the temple. I walk up the steps, the light growing dim. Incense smoke catches on sunbeams and wafts out through shafts of stone into the sky. In an alcove, a headless Buddha rests among bright red prayer flags, lit by a single candle. A Buddhist monk in an orange robe sits in front in the near-darkness, holding his mala between his hands and counting off one bead after the next, eyes closed, lips flawlessly moving. He doesn't seem to notice me as I walk by him; only the flame of his candle is swept up by the motion of my passage.

There is a faint light in the darkness ahead, and I feel my way along the stones to the spot. It's a tiny patch of light, and when I stand in it and look up, I see that fifty feet above, at the very top of the tower, the sunlight falls in. Smoke spirals up to it past the enormous stones, and I'm certain—I can't explain how—that my mother has just died in this moment, the stone faces still whispering their wisdom.

I hear the mantra of the monk, a low, even humming, and discover that I've been crying for some time. The tears have soaked the front of my shirt, and now the cool air of this inner chamber causes me to shiver. I turn around and glance at the monk, trying to make out his face. His eyebrows and hair are shaved off, and that, along with his placid expression, makes him look innocent, as if he were a child. I'm envious of the radiance of his face, how it resembles the giant faces outside. I watch how effortlessly his lips move.

How gracefully his head bows. And now, as his entire body leans forward, the light illuminates his hands, which hold the prayer beads, and glows on a series of pale pink scars that wind down his arms.

I fall back against the stone wall. Whispers assail me, repeating my brother's name over and over. Kneeling down, I can feel the stones in my pocket pinching my skin. I want to see if his lips will stop moving. I want to know if the mantra will end. Minutes go by. He doesn't stop. An hour. Another hour. The incense smoke finds me, curls about me, its scent lingering on my skin. I can't wait any longer. There must be some way to leave here without disturbing him.

Marie Henry

At the Change of Seasons

ERIC IS GOING BLIND. When he looks out, kelp beds trail down under the surface of murky water. Over the phone line, he says: Tell me about yourself, what you are doing, right now, this minute. Sitting on a chair that looks like a mushroom, looking down from the window, red leaves falling, one pigeon on a roof peak. And I am holding a stone, I tell him. I am trying to connect with the ground.

He tells me about when he was in India, near Burma, during the War. Whenever he became fearful, he would lie on the earth on his belly, he tells me, and the fear would pass through. On his belly, with arms and legs spread out. Like a starfish, I say. More like a grasshopper, he tells me. No, more like one of those bugs that glides across the top of the water without really touching it.

Merry Speece

Fire Sermon

ONE TIME, he said, the barn at the Children's Home down the road toward Flatrock burned.

Barns burning is what we talk about when we are together lying there naked.

And did your folks go to the barn burning? I asked.

Now, what do you think? he said.

Yes, I can see their faces lit up as when in a shopping mall on a Sunday afternoon they look and poke each other and stare at the scorched and twisted hands of the arthritic or stare into the eyes of the blind.

The eyes are on fire and everything the eyes see is on fire.

Barns burn sometimes because wet hay catches on fire. How can I believe it? Spontaneous combustion, yes, I know. Then, if I put a rag in a Ball jar and get some life form, why can't spontaneous generation be true? Yes, if you put a writer alone for long enough in Appalachia in an unfinished house, then all of a sudden one night she'll rise up out of the pile of wadded rag paper—her firetrap—and up and have a baby.

Just like that. No, I burned long for that child. The flames of grassfire come in a wave across the field. The only way to stop it is to cut the earth, but we just keep watching the wave of fire coming toward outbuildings and think someone else will get the plow. Out of the fire of childbirth, I tore off my oxygen mask and gasped for ice. He at my bedside rose up from the fallen ash he was, wasted as he was from my endless flame, the wave of flame, and he, the only person of the many who looked on at my nakedness and suffering, the only one who loved me, brought me ice in a little paper cup and put just enough on my tongue.

And there have been, yes, many times I've brought this good man water myself. When he is on fire, his scrotum hangs down loose. I put my hands on his balls to tell how much he burns. Let me feel again, I want to make sure. He laughs; he just has a little cold and has come home early. He laughs: "Leave me alone." I climb into the waterbed. Those were the good times, brief candles, visions, a flash, lights held up in the diurnal darkness.

But remember the other times I was on fire sick with fever day after day for three years and saw my face shrivel in time's heat and saw one of the thousand furnace doors of death open for me, and I thought every man looked cool to touch, cool as water. Just let me drink a little and lie down. I thought that a man, that love, that passion between two human beings could keep me from disease and death. It is not true. Not first love, not new love, even as strong as they are. Love is kerosene thrown and flesh a chunk of fuel that will hold fire for a long time.

Oh we are the children that cry to touch the fire, to set something on fire and to try to put it out with such a little breath. I have seen in a shopping mall in a toystore a child who could be my child, a child who has been badly burned, trying to stare out from the skin stretched tight around his eyes, trying to go on with his life. My God, my God, how does one learn to breathe again and walk away?

And our earth inside itself burns, and marl burns for years, and shafts mined by human hands burn unchecked. And our whole earth can burn in minutes, each of us with our fingers pausing in an act of undressing on a button that detonates a firestorm out of our own blackened hearts. And how do you stop the earth from burning? There is not water enough for the whole earth, not water that will not rise immediately as steam.

Burns with passion, hatred, infatuation, birth, old age, death, sorrow, lamentation, misery, grief, despair.

And what did they—*you*—do at the barn burning? I asked.

Everybody just stood around and watched, he said, because there is nothing else can be done.

Sharon Cameron

Beautiful Work

AFTER THE FIRST MEDITATION PERIOD of the morning, when the sun was almost overhead, I went outside to the road where there is an oak tree and a maple tree. The road from one tree to the other is flat. In the direction of the town I can see where the hill slopes downward. On the other side of the road is a row of chestnut trees. Wind is blowing chestnut blossoms onto the street. Beneath a chestnut tree, pale yellow butterflies fly in and out of lilac bushes. Blossoms still hang on some of the branches.

My course was thirty paces long. As I walk, the road begins to rise up and crumble under my feet. The pavement is cracking and buckling. Destruction rises from within it and breaks the pavement into dangerous pieces, into volcanic rocks, tossed on top of each other in a ruin. Now the sun is directly overhead. I recognize, at a distance, Louis, my grandfather, coming toward me. He can walk on the heaving pavement easily, even though it collapses under his feet. Louis says as he approaches: "Time *does* this to a road, Annie."

In the middle of my path I stood still. I looked up at the trees. The wind was blowing. The wind was green and blowing. Suddenly I saw into the leaves. They were far above me, but close up. They were magnified, huge, changing color with great speed while I looked. I was looking at leaves rushing toward their own extinction. I saw, through the blowing, the turning of the lush green leaves to red ones. The green ones *contained* the red ones and already were them. The leaves were turning and blowing while I looked. Wind was roaring in the trees at a distance. The wind widened as it approached. I stared into the trees above me. I could barely see. The colors of the world bled into each other. Greens paled into grays and whites. The backs, the underside of the leaves, tossed and blew. Silver glittered coldly in the light. Then the wind quieted. Louis said: "This is death. It will frighten you less and less."

T H A T   A F T E R N O O N   I   W A L K E D to the Meditation Hall past the apple tree and the peonies. A sweet bush, honeysuckle, throws its perfume into one of the back windows of the Hall. By the stone wall at the bottom of the driveway iris blooms. I can see the dark purples on the inside of the flower. Lavender petals curl upward. The silky peonies are cream-colored, with ragged edges where the seams have split, magenta, like blood stains on white fabric. Grass recently cut. The air is dry and light. My body is transparent. Light from the midday sky glints through it at an angle. Joy arises. The joy is outside in the air like the iris's cool lavender rising around the midnight-blues. The edges of the joy are crisp. This was a different sweetness than the grass or honeysuckle. This had evolved from the milky insides of the pain-seed's fruit.

I feel sad. I noted it behind the lids of my eyes. It fell away. Sadness arose in my chest. It fell away. Nothing was left.

I walked to my meditation cushion and sat. What I called "sadness" was a sequence of sensations in the lids of my eyes, in the area of my heart, in this sharpness or that burning, separate, discontinuous sensations that the word "sadness" obscures. Each time the emotion I called "sadness" arose, I lifted it up in my hand and looked at it, turning it this way, and that. I am at work on "sadness." The sensations were discontinuous. This was also true for "impatience," and "tiredness." It was true for "thought." Thought tried to make sadness solid. Thought itself was an arrow in the mind. My body was taken up by a benevolent force. But there was no reason for fear.

Al was lying in a field of corn. He was sleeping. I parted the corn stalks and kneeled beside him. The soil on my knees was damp.

"I am seeing the ending of things," I said.

Al continued sleeping.

"I am speaking to you," I said. But the tassels of the corn blew over his eyes and the long green leaves covered his face. I could tell by looking at it that the corn was almost ripe.

"I have something to tell you," I said. "It can't wait."

Al slept on.

"All right," I said. "Two can play that game." I lay down beside him, and folded my arms against my chest, as if I were dead. Next to me, I could feel Al breathing.

"I have a thing or two to ask you. Are you of the opinion that I can learn to do this by myself? I honestly don't see how," I said.

Across the field I could see through the stalks of corn. The green and straw-colored tassels glittered. Above, the sky had bright stars in it, although it was still day. I looked at the stars. I grew afraid.

"If you won't talk to me, I'll talk to myself," I said. I was silent.

Then I heard a plow at the edge of the field of corn. The plow began to excavate the ground, even though corn was already standing in long gleaming rows, even though stars shone on the corn.

"Stop," I screamed. "Don't you see two people are sleeping here? Or that a crop is fruiting? Any fool could see this is hallowed ground." The plow did not stop. I heard it at the very edge of the field, turning up deep furrows of earth, exposing the roots of the corn.

"We'll be destroyed," I said to Al. I got up on my elbow and looked down on him, but his sleep was deep and dreamless. I could see nothing.

I stood up and took his two feet in my hands and tried to drag the body to the side, away from where I could see the plow would eventually drive its blade through earth, but I could not move him.

"Give me directions," I said, "or tell me how to wake you."

The plow was getting closer. In the sky the stars flashed. Then they burned, cooled to a cloud of ice, broke into pieces, and began to fall.

That night when I tried to sleep, the loud bee-sound arose. It was buzzing and teeming close to my ear. My head turned into space. The bee-sound strengthened. My head disappeared into the space around it. *There was no single consciousness to unify what happened.* There was hearing-consciousness, seeing-consciousness, feeling-consciousness, thinking-consciousness. These states of consciousness were distinct from each other like shiny beads on a string, polished beads set so close to each other I could barely see the beads were separate pieces. But not like that at all. Nothing, no filament, held the beads together. This is why Isaac closed his eyes when I spoke. Isaac knew this.

"If you had the sense you were born with," my grandmother said, "I'm telling you. . . ." She was gardening, forty years ago. A scarf was tied over her head. She wore a gingham sundress. She had beautiful legs. She was comfortable in her body. She knew she looked good. Even bent over the dirt, she looked elegant. Her back and arms were tan. When she wiped her arm across her brow, I saw the arch her body made: lean and tight and hard. When she leaned over farther, light caught the hem of her dress. Now I could see that under the gingham the backs of her legs were brown and smooth. It was summer. She was pulling at the beets. But the beets weren't coming. The greens were breaking off in her hand. When her earrings caught the light, they glittered.

"Telling me what?" I asked. I sat to the side of the garden. She had her back to me, bending over the beet greens. She was impatient, trying to get the plants to come up whole. I loved my grandmother's summer body.

"My Sol died in the war," she said. "He was shot down over Germany the day Germany surrendered. I am making borscht. Even if I can't get the beets out of the ground, I'll make it. They never found his body."

"My mother told me."

My grandmother turned from her digging to look at me. "What does she know?"

"See the dirt under my nails?" she said. "I couldn't bury him. I love you best, after Sol. Pick the dirt off the beets. Can you do this for me?"

"The beets are underground," I said.

"Never mind. I've been digging and digging for years. I want to come to the place where the body is. It must be somewhere. Listen, if I knew I had to die, I'd do it differently." She laid a beet leaf next to me. "I wouldn't have spent twenty years grieving for Sol. I wouldn't have chased your grandfather out of my room, or put rags between my legs so he couldn't enter me. This is what I would have done," she pulled the scarf off her head, and shook her long brown hair out. My grandmother was beautiful.

She sat down on the grass and brushed the dirt off her hands. "I think," she said, "I would have taken a lover." She put her hands along the sides of her bodice and smoothed them downward. I could see the outline of her nipples. She said: "I know I would."

"And when you die, what shall I do?" I asked my grandmother.

"Can you dance?" she asked.

I shook my head, "No."

"Then make me a few words. Tell about the night your grandfather came to me in Russia. We were sixteen. We had our pictures taken under the maple tree. In the early evening we went into the woods and lay in the autumn leaves. We took off all our clothes and he caressed me."

The next morning when I woke, a sharp, burning sensation drove into the arch of my foot. "All right," I said. I stood up.

When I sat in meditation there was "beating" and "humming." "Heat" arose out of the "humming." It moved downward into my feet. I put my right hand to my right foot. I jerked my hand away. My foot was burning. Vertigo. Words arose: "the vertigo is from the extreme disconnection of the sensations." Words fell away. "Is from," "Is from," I repeated. Nothing is holding this together.

The beating quickened. It was wearing a path outward from my throat, through the flesh, to my neck. The disconnectedness—of the beating, the pulse, the pressure, the ripples, the hardness—made this unendurable. My body and this energy imploding had nothing to do with each other. It will go on like that: this pulsing strung through my sentient body.

I was on the verge of seeing. I couldn't see.

In the next meditation period I heard the humming, the sound of life. "What is that? What is that?"

During the "humming" I saw the vast body system. Without my willing anything, cogs of various diameters turned in spite of me. I could hear the metal wheels going around and around at many different velocities. The sound of the whirring wheels became cacophonic. You could see how the whole thing worked, *if* you could *see* the whole thing. I couldn't. In successive moments there was a spasm, a thought, a tightening, an in-breath, aversion, turning. The turning was like a buzzing and humming inside a fermenting vat.

THE MEDITATION INSTRUCTIONS that I follow are the same as they have always been: "Watch the arising and passing away of things. When your attention is not clear, use a mental note to sharpen the mind." The same instructions. But today I *see* differently.

I see the breast bone is broken. The rib cage is turned outward to the world.

I see the entity that is "myself" break up and crumble. Then I see the piece of myself I call "thinking." "Thinking" is independent of any consciousness, which is individual and intentional. "Thinking," "touching," "swallowing," "tasting," "seeing," "hearing" are separate as drops of rain are separate. As geese flying are separate. As leaves from trees of different species lie along the ground and are separate. As the dead are separate from one another and from the living.

In my body, form is broken up by the chaotic dispersal of the buzzing, rippling energy.

The bee-sound of the streaming energy moves from left to right. *I am not solid.*

In the last sitting of the day I heard a *narrow* hum: a different energy, more tunnel-like than the round, expansive buzzing. Eventually another hum from my left ear came to consciousness. It was lower still and concentrated like the sound of a swarm of bees in a lilac bush.

I am telling you the whole thing, as I can see it. There were these three streams of energy: the narrow hum of the universe, the note this body made, and a third mysterious hum. There were no feelings. There was equanimity, and happiness. It was a relief to see nothing but this mechanical process, these sounds at three frequencies.

The beating had thinned out. The energy unknotted and spilled throughout my body.

The bee-sound drenched my head with streaming. It surged under the sitting bones and widened in my groin. It pulsed along my shoulders and down my arms. It was sweet and powerful, not ominous. It was not menacing, only strong. My body burned.

I said to Isaac: "During meditation, impressions register, but not deeply. In meditation, my body is a surface. It has no depth."

Isaac yawned.

"I say they don't register," I continued. "There is nothing for them to register *on* except awareness."

"Why don't you read," Isaac said.

"In a minute. It's disconcerting to see my body permeated by energies, inside and outside of it, more disconcerting than to see space *replace* the body. The body is conserved, but it's disarticulated as material substance, and then made up again of immaterial energies. When space *consumes* my body and there is no more body, I think it is uncanny. But when my body is unmistakably there, I know this is how it ordinarily is, even though it is no longer composed as body, but permeated with light.

"So—I'm telling you—the body is composed of energies, and feelings of different pressures. I had a thought about this, but it vanished."

I looked at Isaac. His eyes were closed. I said: "Won't you tell me anything I want to know?"

"Not a thing," he said.

"And when I go home?"

"Oh, you'll come back," he said. "You'll keep coming back."

I looked at Isaac. His face looked like snow.

I sat in a field of snow. Snow numbed my bare legs, which were stretched in front of me. I had only shorts on and a summer top. Ahead a wild rosebush grew next to a pointed rock. The rock was ochre and blue. The rock and the wild rosebush were far away. Herons flew against the horizon, and the sky— shading to violet and gray in the distance—brightened against the earth rim like a sky that's clearing after a long rain. I thought there might be a rainbow. There was no rainbow.

"We were all expecting it," the voice said. "Don't you think it's balmy?"

"I don't think anything," I said.

"It's time that you begin," the voice said. "Thinking never hurt."

"I can't see," I said. "My legs are frozen. The glare off the snow is terrific. If I close my lids, I feel them against my eyes. They hurt. Open or closed it's the same."

"Make a story of it," the voice said. "Embellish. It helps a little. I'm not saying it helps much. But if for instance there are characters, there must be a plot. So much can happen if you're lost in that."

"You're not an authority," I said. "I have my own views."

"But you can't state them," the voice said. "Of this have I no doubt."

I looked at the snow. It was banked to my left and glittered. Against it there was a glacier and, around it, a cold glacial stream. There was the rock, too, next to which the wild rosebush grew. The edges of the roses fluttered. So there was also wind. "I can't state them," I agreed.

"And so," the voice said, "I make my point. In those conditions, people have been known to freeze. No telling, too, what happens to the mind."

"If I look at the sky," I said, "I will be certain. Either there'll be the light that burns away at my eyes, or there will be the weight of my lids."

"I'm telling you, it's pointless," the voice said.

"Completely pointless," I said.

When I sat that afternoon thinking *arose.* Thinking blotted out awareness. Thinking was the release of certain electrical impulses, like a spasm or a twitch that resulted accidentally in a thought. Thinking came from the firing of neurons. When awareness didn't rise up to meet the thought, the thought was bent by its nature to substitute a false world for a true one.

I saw the mechanical nature of these sensations: sounds, noises, thoughts, waves rising in my chest, moisture and tightness when swallowing. A spasm of energy pulsed through my left foot, cramping the toes. The energy kneaded my foot with its own design and purposes.

I felt affectless. There was no place for affect to be located. In the place where a self *was,* I saw the contraption of the apperceptive mechanism shaking itself to pieces. "Disappointment" when I looked at it with this kind of sight was only this pressure or that burning.

I heard the hum and the bee-sound constantly. And for a few mind-moments, I felt liberated. *Hearing this changed everything.*

Something, right now, prevented me from dying. I was a clear bottomless glass through which there was continuous pouring. I felt it was the pouring that preserved my life.

Now thinking arose again like a glinting blade. Awareness was gone. The serrated blade ripped away at nothing. I can't tell you how long the sawing lasted. After the sawing finished, a film spread over my mind and clouded it up. Awareness arose again. The film lifted. *Thinking and awareness do not exist simultaneously*. And when they do—it seems they sometimes do—awareness is a light that *shines* on thinking, illuminating *what thinking is*.

It was absurd to say "I am" ("I am thinking," "I am happy") about any part of this mechanical process. The thought "This is degrading" rose into my mind. The thought splintered.

Awareness alone is not mechanical. I cannot say what awareness is. Awareness is nothing. *Is no thing*.

Anne Carolyn Klein

The Mantra and the Typist: A Story of East and West

WHEN I WAS FOUR my parents acquired a black Royal typewriter with round shiny metal keys edged in chrome. The clicking keys, the flashing fingers and, in those days, the smacking sound of key against paper commanded all my attention. Words created with such potent sound and swift motion, I surmised, must have compelling power. Power for what I could not yet know.

My parents did not type much, but they spoke exuberantly—German, Slovak, French, and most especially their native Hungarian, along with their more recently acquired and surprisingly adroit English, rolled off their tongues with equal ease. My own words, however, were limited to English, the only language by which they communicated with me. Although I could neither speak nor understand it, Hungarian filled my ears day in and day out, whenever they conversed with each other. Hungarian was the sound of home to me, but not a home I could speak in. To this day it is simultaneously familiar as a mother tongue and altogether foreign.

The frustration of daily, hourly, being exposed to two languages with access only to one and no way of translating between them produced an interesting tension in me, and perhaps for this reason, long before I could read, I was mad to write. Since I could not yet form letters, much less spell words, this was frustrating. Still, I was determined to fashion my one language into as many forms as possible.

Consequently, the gleaming new typewriter pulled me like magnet. But I was not allowed near it until one winter holiday when I was confined to my room to recover from a fever. How was I to amuse myself? My parents' solicitous attitude made me bold. "I want the typewriter," I said.

It was brought in and placed on the desk by my father. My mother pulled out some paper from an old notebook. I left my bed and sat on the chair in my pajamas, with the old-style radiator sending out healing heat under the desk. I began to type. Short words, long words, mere strings of letters really, and thumbing the space bar with assurance whenever the spirit moved me, blissfully free of the need (since so familiar) to constrain myself to the vocabularies of any known tongue.

Was this writing? This happy excitation rushing through my body, pouring out as scrambled words. Mere letters and syllables really, expressing only the inchoate exuberance that prompted them. I had the opposite of writer's block. No need to search for words, a secret moebius movement brought them to me. They rushed in fast and raucously, jumbling together. I didn't care, I was writing wholeness. These words weren't objects to be manipulated, they were friends at my party, the louder, the more sheer drumming exuberance the better. Meaning was in the impulse. Their hum was all.

This hum never faded completely. But once I mastered the alphabet and became literate I never again composed with the sheer physical aplomb and full-bodied confidence of that initiatory authoring. Now words clogged the moebius movement, they stopped swirling and humming together. Noticing this, I outgrew my childish sense that they could all join in for one open and jubilantly careening festival. But my passion to test the power of typing remained, reinvigorated, in fact, as I hobnobbed with romance and other languages. When I finally burst through the English barrier of my childhood, *parlez-vous, parlez-vous,* I was thrilled. Finally, I could translate across systems, first systems of language, and then other systems as well. How I wanted to make the most of this!

I came to excel in typing. I loved learning its patterns: the letters of the left hand, *abcdefg,* and of the right, *hijklmnop.* Then back to the left hand in the upper row, *qrst,* and a quick pass to the right for *u,* flash to the left with *vwx,* swift pass again to *y,* and finish at *z.* The pattern amuses the mind, the speed charges my body. Perhaps it was partly this charge that attracted the first love of my life, someone who on every level spoke my language. His body was my body. Charged with joy, in class I typed my teacher's words on the desk top to see if my fingers could keep pace with them; after a sentence or two I was always behind. Even so, in ninth grade there was a typing contest, which I proudly won, hands down.

For my sweet sixteen, my parents gave me an electric typewriter. In college I earned serious pocket money with it, typing other people's English 101 papers and a dissertation on Wittgenstein. This was definitely work, formed from the play of fingers I continued to love. A decade later, I wrote my own dissertation, on the relationship of hard intellectual work to mystical experience, in a burst of passion and sweat, composing, polishing, and retyping the final chapter in a single day. For typing this dissertation, I bought the kind of magic electric typewriter that erased letters and lines at the touch of a button. The true instrument of my need however, of my still unquenched thirst to test the power of typing, was yet to come.

But even before computers, graduate school was a time of serious typing for me, and an expansion of my linguistic horizons as well. My long-lost first love phoned to say that Tibetans had the last word on language magic. I enrolled in Tibetan class and quickly discovered that learning Tibetan was not like learning French: there were no textbooks for it. But the Dalai Lama's office hand-picked eminent red-robed Lamas to help us out. We looked at texts, and, above all, we tape-recorded every word they said in explanation of those texts. "This is form," a recent arrival from Dharamsala told us, pointing to my tape-recorder. "And here is emptiness," he added, still pointing to the same place.

The Lamas also discussed other things, like the mysterious relationships between sound and meaning, intention and action. Some of the greatest Tibetan scholars of their generation poured the sound of their words into our ears and onto our tapes. But mere sound is insufficient for graduate students smitten with letters. After hearing the Lamas' lectures, everyone wanted to study them in print. It was thus necessary to turn that sound into writing. That meant serious typing. It meant me.

During those years I transferred their sounds into four books of letters. In doing so, I developed a new art form. I became expert in transforming sound into form, and especially unedited speech into edited writing with a seamless flow of flashing finger action. It was my joy to dispel the subtle boundary between sound and letters as quickly as possible, to unite formless sound and letter formation in this very modern manner.

I liked breathing in sound, then physically projecting it onto paper. It created a more interesting interior texture for me than typing notes from printed copy, moving always from form to form. The other graduate students lived constantly with print, reading it, writing it. I lived at least half with sound. Perhaps it is partly to this that I owe certain unusual events.

Westerners understand letters to be form. The shape of an *A* heralds the printed alphabet, not the alphabet song of childhood. Sight trumps sound; we read, we do not listen. But the Lamas felt that letters themselves are sounds, which the inscribed shapes merely represent. Their sounds all emerge from, and dissolve back into, the expansive sound of *Ah*. Intoning this invites inner spaciousness merely by opening the breath and throat for a long, deep *Ah*. I typed and breathed.

As my facility grew, I became more and more able to produce letters the moment their corresponding sounds, English or Tibetan, came forth on tape. I now could type on desktops and keep up with the lecturer. Even better, when it came to transcribing the Lama's speech into letters I no longer paused for tape rewind, spent less time stamping the foot pedal. The moebius was moving again.

An even bigger change occurred when I became an oral translator, directly processing spoken Tibetan sounds into spoken English ones. The former issued from the Lama's mouth, moved through my mind and body, and emerged out my mouth as speech. This speech then entered the ears of other English speakers and then made its way through their minds, bodies, and beings. As a typist I was a reifier of speech; as an oral translator I moved from one species of sound and life energies to another. The constrictions of form applied less and less.

Translating orally is being in trance. Indeed, as a translator I must be so entranced by Tibetan words that my own words, my own thoughts, are hurriedly suppressed. It is like dreaming someone else's dreams, and dreaming them intensely. When the flow is even and strong, my mind becomes an empty vessel, a kind of aural page on which the stream of Lama words is almost simultaneously received and translated. I translate him in other ways as well. Without noticing, I speak forcefully when he throws his voice loud, become softer and slower when he paces down. I repeat his hand gestures. This is not intentional mimicry, but an unconscious flow of transposition. His mind is my mind. In facilitating this flow I stumble into an ancient female role. I dream of Yeshe Tsogyal, luminous lady of the wisdom lake who received Buddhist piths and preserved them. Like sibyls of old, I'm a scaled-down oracle. It is not the god that descends, but words, though these are closely linked both East and West. The Lama's words descend in Tibetan, their sounds and syntax rearrange themselves, rise up my lungs, are shaped by my tongue into English. And, perhaps because I love this process, which is also the hardest work I know, perhaps because of the profoundly female charge of ancient archetypes, something starts being born that is thoroughly my own, although I do not see this until much later.

In this way, fulfilling amorphous childhood dreams, I breathe in one language and breathe out another. Afterward I remember nothing of either. I have to read someone else's notes to find out what's been said. And yet the memory of the sound resides somewhere in my body; days later, when someone touches an elbow, puts a hand on my back, the phrases that have lodged there swirl out and I hear them again.

So it was. I typed, spoke, listened, and mediated between languages, between lives. I moved more and more fluidly between streams of speech, vividly transposing one into the other. Most often these oral translations had to do with meditation. Meditation is, among other things, a deep interweaving of multiple human dimensions that embrace sound, breath, body, and spirit in one glorious, sonorous, multi-tonal hum. *Hum.*

> *Words aren't just tools*
> *For getting things straight*
> *pinning them down,*
> *holding them up*
> *Don't use them like hammers,*
> *Or even as thumbtacks.*
> *Don't merely handle them.*
> *Hold them, melt them to your marrow*
> *From where,*
> *Nourishing your heart,*
> *Loving your soul,*
> *They rise again, aloft from your lungs*
> *Flowing out graciously*
> *Helping the world exist.*

This hummed message, a surprise guest, made me wonder. Could typing shift my surroundings? The answer, it turns out, is all in the translation.

After years, hundreds of hours of listening and translating for Lamas who spoke only Tibetan, I met one who also spoke English. He did not need a translator in the usual sense. But his students were readers who wanted to capture the fleeting words of living speech, the better to reflect on them.

A different kind of trance resulted. Once again, I focused only on sound, but instead of bringing it through my chest and voice into other sounds, it sped from my ears directly to my fingers and out the keyboard, onto the screen, into the disc. My keen aural attentiveness to his words together with my visual focus on the screen contracts my attention, condensing my thoughts into a state beyond any of the languages of my life. Again and again, the sounds of the Lama collapse into my alert open space, and then emerge on the screen in my lap. Light bounces off the screen, instantly connecting sound, screen, outer and inner space. I am typing faster and faster, binding together in yet another way the sound and the form, and the two minds that produce them, until the two arise simultaneously. They flow into each other, they swirl and change places until the words flowing from my fingers are my own words, describing the space in which all this occurs, and now it is my words that issue and are heard as the voice of the Lama.

My simple trance-fixed openness to the words I transmit has revealed something else. What is not said about oracles is this: they do not simply work for others, they become such deep and receptive vessels that they find and give voice to what is profoundly their own. It is an important secret.

After this transformation I am continuously aware of the source within. I return home. I take my own newest instrument, an almost-oval dusky blue computer called an iBook, from my table. I sit on my floor, cushioned by yellow carpeting, my book-tiered wooden desk on my left, colorful shrine on my right. I place the iBook on my lap and begin to write. The words stream through me as a steady coursing from my heart to my hands while the blue writing space softly whirs and stirs, sending the whirs streaming through the open skylight above my head, whir-hri , whir-hri. As I write, I know that a Lama is right now speaking these words that I whir down, while someone somewhere types them into her own space, as I once did, letting it become her story until she is so open to inspiration that she recovers and rewrites a new one. We are all revealers of the texts inside us.

With this revelation I find new sensuality and power in living, languaging and the love of both. "The path is blocked by vowels and consonants" says the wandering muse. But the space bar is a bar no longer. My mouth and ears no longer closed to foreign tones, knowing no longer only outside me, I revel in linking revelatory tongues. Words flow again, they stir and whir freely, *Hr:*

> *Ask the wrong questions*
> *And the road gets longer*
> *Ask none at all*
> *It will disappear*
> *Hang with one answer,*
> *You're stuck at a stop sign.*
> *BHO BHO the clear eyed beacon seer.*

Keith Heller

Memorizing the Buddha

OVER TWO THOUSAND YEARS AGO, on the teardrop island of Lanka just off the southernmost tip of Jambudipa, there lived a man named Deva who had too perfect a memory. He lived alone in a village in the forest that was a minimum of mud walls in an excess of moving green and worked as a tailor and a sandal-maker and sometimes as a barber when his razors happened to be sharp enough. He was alone because he was an only child whose parents had died in his childhood, and he had been raised by a farmer and his wife who themselves had died as soon as they'd finished teaching Deva all they knew. Past thirty years of age in a village where most were lucky to pass twenty or even ten, he was still alone in his life because no sane woman could bear to be in the presence of that boundless memory of his for more than a season or two. She would soon tire of all his interminable reminders and struggle to be released.

Before they died, his foster parents had promised him in marriage to a young woman, a girlish vision in expensive robes and grotesquely arranged hair. All the heavenly signs had been propitious, and the proposed date had even been divined, when one day the bride-to-be happened to make the mistake of asking Deva if he remembered where she had laid an amber comb that she was particularly fond of.

"It's under your pillow in your uncle's house," he informed her.

"No, it can't be," she objected. "I'd never have put it there and, besides, I clearly recall having it in my hair when I came here from Mihintale yesterday. It must have come loose along the way, and now it must be lost forever somewhere along the road."

"Or under your pillow in your uncle's house, my love," Deva repeated with the patience of a monk.

"Don't be absurd! How could it ever be there," cried Sanghamitta, "if I took it from home, kept it in my hair, yet didn't see it still there when I got to Uncle's? It would have had to fly from my head, through the jungle and through his window, into the room that was reserved for me, and then somehow slip under the pillow and have been missed by the maids who fixed up my bed. Are you mad, Deva?" she said to him with an exasperated glare. "Your little village here would have to be filled with magicians and demons for such an impossible chain of events to have taken place."

Deva took her hand and sat down with her on a marble bench near a pool of calming water. Then he explained, "When you came here from Mihintale, my sweet, you were wearing your amber comb in your hair, but I could see that your rough travels had dislodged it and buried it deeply within your lustrous hair. Then at your uncle's I noticed you pat a few stray hairs back into place with that precious gesture that belongs to you and you alone, and that forced the comb to fall backward until its teeth became caught on the rear collar of your blue-and-yellow silk robe. Later," he went on shyly, "I was fortunate enough to see through your bedroom window one of the maids hanging the robe up on a peg, and as she turned to go, the comb tumbled down into one of the creases of the unmade bedclothes. Now I know the woman who tends to the beds in your uncle's household quite well, and she has the peculiar habit of flipping the blankets under the pillows that could easily have resulted in your comb's being flung beneath the pillow so far that no one who wasn't looking for it would have seen it there. So, my treasure," Deva concluded with a gentle stroking of her sculpted hair, "your lovely amber comb now lies under your pillow in your uncle's house. As I said."

When the priceless adornment was found precisely where the tailor had predicted, instead of gratitude and awe, Sanghamitta turned on Deva a look of dread and feminine cautiousness. Perhaps she was imagining their long future together, a future that would be filled with constant reminders and repeated corrections, not to mention his unflagging memory of every other woman he'd ever glimpsed, spied on, or yearned for in his life. The proposed marriage was canceled for suddenly discovered astrological reasons, and Sanghamitta returned to her search for a husband who would remember no more than what she wanted him to remember.

Even Deva's closest friends had little to do with him for this same reason, and his best customers sometimes paled at his comments and felt that he was rummaging unfairly about inside their souls. Every sentence shouted through an open window and every knot on a passing sleeve stayed with him forever, while his fellow villagers grew to resent being reminded of all the crops that had failed on them and the anniversaries of all the deaths their families had ever suffered. Doctor Renu, the local Ayurvedic practitioner who had crossed over to Lanka as a boy with a strange and special knowledge, had once told Deva, "People are always telling me that they'd like to sharpen their memories, and they ask me for herbs to help them do so. But remembering too much must be like living two or three lives at the same time, and who in the world would ever want to do that?" The tailor had understood. He had often found himself yearning for a pure, sublime forgetfulness that would empty him completely, but he knew that this would never be for him, not anywhere on this side of death.

The village in which he lived was called Ratna after the precious stones that in the dim past had once been gathered from its hills. Now it was nothing more than a faded vision of a glory that no one could recall, not even

Deva. Ratna was located midway between the great city of Anuradhapura with its Gold Dust temple and Brazen Palace and the smaller Mihintale with its Kanthaka temple and the caves where Mahinda had lived after he'd come from his father Asoka's court with the Buddha's teachings. But Ratna's only road wound through dense undergrowth, and long ago wild brambles and creepers had been allowed to obscure the passing traffic with a natural latticework of branches. This helped to preserve the village from political upheavals and the various temptations that too much wealth and knowledge often give rise to, yet the isolation also doomed the village to being forever forsaken, its people as ignorant of the world at large as they were of the stars above. Deva could have lived there all his life, if not necessarily in joy, then in a peaceful loneliness, memorizing the daily length of each blade of grass and telling the children that their favorite playing pebbles had been left under the pipal tree next to the water tank.

Still, if Deva never tired of Ratna, the people of Ratna did finally tire of him and of all his continual references to the land they had been cheated out of at their coming of age or the failed vows to reform their ways that they had made only last year. Deva was a shy man and at a loss for words that didn't have something to do with a memory that he had borrowed from someone else. Yet appropriating another man's history was hardly the best way for him to make friends for life.

One day, as he was sitting outside his door, idly chewing on a spear of *mana* grass whose minty freshness tinted the air around him, a fellow villager turned toward his house with a determined step. Deva knew him to be the old man called Bahu who officiated at Ratna's miniature shrine to the Buddha and blessed the townspeople by begging his food and few possessions from them. The tailor was not a follower of any faith himself, having never found enough room in his soul for otherworldly beliefs among all his stockpiled memories. But he had shaved the heads and faces of Bahu's two or three novices from time to time, and he had supplied them with yellow, patchwork robes and sandals, sometimes admiring and even envying them their obvious equanimity.

"You're the tailor and the memorizer, aren't you?" the monk asked him shortly as soon as he came up to him.

"I do sew, and I do remember things pretty well, yes," Deva conceded.

"So what are you doing out here?" Bahu said with a critical glance into the house. "Why aren't you in there working?"

Deva looked uncomfortable. "I'm resting. Besides, it's not quite the right time of the year for repairs or new clothes. People are too busy clearing out their fields and planting."

"Oh, really? Is that why the seed seller hasn't come to ask you to make his daughter's wedding robes? And is that why the wealthy Kuveras have turned to other tailors for their linen? The way I hear it," Bahu teased him, "the whole village is finding different sources for their clothes and sandals, even if they have to travel all the way to Mihintale."

Squirming on his chair, Deva mumbled something about discounted costs and customers settling for inferior dyes and fibers. But, all the while, he couldn't help but blush and look disheartened at the old priest's criticisms of his trade.

"Maybe it's because everyone in Ratna has grown weary of that blasted memory of yours," Bahu suggested as he lowered himself with a groan onto a tree stump. "Maybe they're afraid of hearing too much of the truth at one time. They might even believe you're a shaman of some kind who has magical powers that might harm them. Of course, if you ask me, it's simply a matter of human nature. No one should spend all his time looking backward into the past. That's why we were born with both of our eyes on the front of our heads!"

Deva knew he was right. The stiff uneasiness of his neighbors had been getting worse with every passing day. But for now he could only shrug helplessly and say, "What's the answer, then? If I can't practice my trade in my own hometown, where can I work at it?"

"I'm glad you asked me that," Bahu said briskly, rising and grasping the younger man by the shoulder. "It just so happens that I have a job for you to do, something that requires your peculiar talent for memorizing."

"Where? Here in Ratna?"

"Hardly." The old man waved a flapping sleeve at the road that lay obscured behind a stand of trees. "You'll have to come along with me first to the capital of Anuradhapura where some of my brothers are in need of your services. After that, well . . . "

Bewildered, Deva asked how long he would be gone from his house, though he took scarcely a last glance at it, knowing that he would remember its every wattle and shadow forever, whether he wanted to or not.

"Perhaps just long enough for your neighbors to learn how to appreciate you again," Bahu told him, tugging at his wrist to hurry him along. "You never can tell. By the time you get back, you might even have a whole new set of your own memories to bore them with."

The road to the capital seemed long, but the old man ignored the repeated offers from the cart and bullock drivers who overtook them. He pressed on with a stolid gait that soon had Deva wheezing with effort. They shuffled through the gray dust and stumbled in the wheel ruts as the arching trees dappled their backs with leaf silhouettes and the flickers of sun dried the sweat off their necks. Before long, Deva had reached the furthest point he'd ever been away from Ratna, and the excitement of the journey began to temper his impatience at having been so rudely summoned from his home. He stared about him at the thickening traffic of palanquins and sumptuous cortèges and, for the first time in years, looked forward to beholding scenes that might remind him of absolutely nothing else on earth.

"I've never been to the big city before," Deva finally confessed to Bahu who was walking just ahead of him. "What's it like?"

"You'll love it. It's loud and filled with movement."

"And beauty, too, I suppose."

"All movement is beautiful," mused Bahu, "as is all change and all impermanence. We only suffer from them when we don't recognize them as such."

After a time, Deva gingerly asked the priest, "Isn't that also where the Mahavihara stands, the great monastery that King Devanampiya Tissa built for Mahinda so many years ago? Is that where we're headed now?"

This reminder slowed Bahu down a bit as he tried to describe the place. His voice was raw with age, as harsh as dry sedge in wind, but when he spoke, his affection for the monastery softened his tone. He told Deva of the Mahamegha, the lovely piece of parkland that the past king himself had mapped out by ceremoniously plowing a circular furrow some two hundred years ago. In the rapture of a man who was visiting his version of paradise, Bahu elaborated upon the sights that awaited them. The Mahavihara that Deva had just mentioned, he said, would take their breath away with its solemn, holy glories. The Thuparama temple and its glittering dome, pinnacle, and spire rising above the Buddha's own right collarbone would rob them of all speech until sundown. And to sit beneath the sacred bodhi tree that had been seeded from the original by Mahinda's own sister was, to hear Bahu tell it, nothing short of life-changing. By the time the two men had reached the outskirts of the city, even the tailor was eager to see what lay ahead of them, and he gave only a little thought to the quiet seclusion of his hut back in Ratna.

At the entrance gate into Anuradhapura, Deva got his first taste of the capital when they encountered a makeshift camp of vagabonds, squatting around an overturned cart that was blocking their way.

"What do we do now?" he worried aloud.

"I think I know a short cut," Bahu said, veering uncertainly off to one side.

The monk led him to a flaw in the city wall that admitted them into a neighborhood of silversmiths and goldsmiths where artificial lights glinted from doorways to compete against the sun, and hammer blows rang like thunder. House followed house, each cramped with its shoulders lifted up to its ears, and the maze of lanes and alleys overwhelmed Deva, although Bahu instinctively seemed to know his way well enough. Because they came into the capital by a side door, as it were, Anuradhapura appeared to the tailor as what every great metropolis really is, an assemblage of discrete, village-like communities. He passed beneath arches where bast weavers, chandlers, and rope or candle makers scented the air with their oils and the grease of their metal tools. Fortune tellers and astrologers shouted at him, promising to tell him all about his future and even his present and his past, when in truth Deva knew more about the last two than any other man alive. Closer to the center of town, guilds of herbists and apothecaries advertised immortality, while further still armorers and swordmakers proclaimed how easy it was to kill or be killed. At first, Deva felt his old apprehension coming back to him, the dread of how many fretful nights he would have to pay for all these new, indelible sights. But then he realized that now he'd had the privilege of seeing almost everything there was in all of Lanka in a single afternoon.

When they turned the final corner and the expanse of the Mahavihara monastery stood before them, the strain in Bahu's body relaxed, as if he had suddenly settled into a warm pool.

"We're here," he murmured happily. "We've made it through."

They were welcomed by a trio of young *bhikkhus,* hardly more than boys, who greeted them respectfully, then clapped their hands with joy at meeting strangers. The novices directed them through a long series of corridors and halls—living, meeting, and worshiping quarters from which issued a serene impression of well-scrubbed wooden floors, simple food, neatly rolled sleeping mats, and blank walls. As astonished as Deva was by all the new spectacles surrounding him, it took him some time to identify the low, constant reverberations that filled the monastery. They were, it turned out, only human voices, chanting or reciting or merely mumbling, though there seemed to be no cul-de-sac, no closet, that was free of their endless rustling, steadier than water.

"What's that noise?" he asked Bahu in a hush as they followed the three boys. "It sounds like praying."

"It isn't. It's memorizing."

Eventually, the guests were ushered into a dark chamber and into the presence of the monastery's abbot. Mahathera Sali was not, at first, a particularly imposing figure. He was thin and of middle age, sitting rather casually on a reed platform that was raised only slightly above the floor. His robes hung loose upon him, and his bony wrists lay idly in his lap as if he lacked the strength to lift them. As such, Deva thought him no more distinguished than any farmer in Ratna of above-average holdings. Yet, when the abbot turned to look at him and took the tailor's measure in a single, probing glance, he knew he was in the presence of a mind that was probably as all-encompassing as his own.

Poor old Bahu, in a fit of piety, tried to prostrate himself before his master, but the Mahathera would have none of it.

"My father and even my grandfather used to speak of you with love," he said, leaning down and helping the visiting monk to his feet again. "Do you still repeat the *Mahasamaya Sutta* over to yourself every day in its entirety?"

"From morning until night."

"Admirable, admirable." Returning to his mat, Sali nodded kindly toward the younger man. "And here we must have the renowned Deva of Ratna, the famous rememberer, the never-forgetter, the one man in all of Lanka who is destined to save us from oblivion. Come closer, my friend, and show us what you're capable of!"

At these words—half jesting and half demanding—Deva hesitated, unsure what exactly was being expected of him. But then he took a deep breath, stepped forward, and recited, "You're the tailor and the memorizer, aren't you?" After that, he went on to repeat, word for word, every single sentence that had passed between him and his traveling companion ever since they'd left Ratna.

"Amazing," the Mahathera sighed after Deva's performance had been confirmed by an astounded Bahu. "We're forever in your debt," he said to the old priest, "for bringing such a living treasure to our aid."

Sali soon had a frugal meal of rice with ghee and pulses prepared for the visitors, and then over tea he explained why Deva had been summoned here.

"We'd like to hire you," he began with a boy's teasing smile. "Or, rather, we'd like to hire your memory."

"Sir?"

Sali set down his cup and seemed to consider. Then he went on, "I take it that you, too, are a servant of the Conqueror?"

"Our King Vattagamani?" Deva replied patriotically. "Aren't we all?"

"No, I meant our Lord Buddha." The Mahathera traced a graceful gesture with his hand at the room around them, the hallway outside the door, the whole monastery, the city, the island, the world. "I was only thinking that you, like so many of us and so many of your neighbors, might also have taken the Buddha, the Dhamma or the Teachings, and the Sangha or the Order as your three refuges, the Triple Gem."

"Well . . ."

Faced with the faintly imperious stares of the monks, Deva could think of nothing better to do than nod at Bahu and say that he'd always meant to ask the old man about the faith, but had never quite gotten around to it.

"And a most outstanding teacher he would have proved to be," Sali said. "Yet, given the extent of the Dhamma—some eighty-four thousand sections in all—it would be impossible for any one man to grasp or understand it all. What you may not yet know," he added, "is that, during the four-and-a-half centuries since the Master's passing, not a word of these Teachings has been written down in any language, or very, very few. Instead, all has been committed to memory by the thousands and thousands of faithful *bhikkhus—*

and, yes, the female *bhikkhunis* as well and even some lay followers—who have held to the discipline as we do here. Each of us remembers whatever we can, our own small plot of garden to tend, if you will. But the five thousand different *suttas* or discourses are simply too much for any one normal man to remember all by himself.

"And now," sighed the Mahathera disconsolately, "after King Vattagamani's fifteen years of exile and the droughts and famines that have cost us some twenty-four thousand monks, we've lost so many of our reciters that we're in peril of losing the Dhamma altogether. Do you remember," he asked his fellows, "how that old man from Sigiriya was for a while there the last of us who knew any of the *Mahaniddesa Sutta?*" They grumbled in recollection, then Sali fixed Deva with an urgent stare. "That's why," he implored him, "we're in such sore need of your services now—if, that is, your talents are all they've been claimed to be!"

Without warning, Sali quickly recited in a single breath, "*Yatha agaram ducchannam vutthi samativijjhati evam abhavitam cittam rago samativijjhati.*" The words of the strange language leapt and sang in the Mahathera's mouth like a bird held barely captive by a string, while the wonderful echoes of it seemed to fill the air. "Now you," Sali ordered with a hard look at the tailor from Ratna.

Yet Deva was more than equal to the task, not only repeating the sentence syllable for syllable both backward and forward, but also adding all the facial expressions and bodily movements that he'd seen the abbot make over the past few minutes. It was a stunning feat, and old Bahu shone with pride as he regarded his protégé. Only much later, when Deva's heart was in danger of being lost to love, did he understand how prescient Sali had been in choosing the passage that read, "As rain breaks through a badly thatched house, so passion breaks through a badly tended mind."

"You'll do," the Mahathera pronounced shortly, then he turned and left the room, and the interview was over for the day. All around him, Deva could feel the tension in the monastery begin to soften and ease, like a lotus flower settling upon a lake, and he congratulated himself on overcoming the first hurdle. Yet he couldn't help wondering what might come next.

The Order's plan was clever enough. "We think it's time," Sali explained the following morning, "for safety's sake, that the Dhamma be set down permanently in writing. To that end, five hundred of us are to convene in the cave temples at Aluvihara with our best scribes to copy out what we've memorized onto the dried *ola* leaves of the talipot palm tree. And we propose that you should come along with us to help."

"But I can't even read," Deva stammered in shame, "or write. And certainly not in this Pali language that you've been telling me about."

"There'll be no need for you to do either. All that will be required of you will be to listen and remember. We'll teach you the sounds of the language," the Mahathera assured him, "so you can hear it and repeat it correctly, and then we'll have you sitting off to one side during each of the copying sessions. You, Tailor, shall be our final stopgap, our final recourse, in case of any disagreements or disasters. We Lankans, you understand, have never been very confident about book learning. We've known too many men with big libraries in their homes, but nothing at all in their heads. In this way, we'll have the best of both methods." Sali smiled and reached across the table to grasp Deva's forearm in a grip as soft as a baby's. "And who knows?" he finished mysteriously. "By the time we're done, you might understand our Lord Buddha far better than any of us."

So, over the next few weeks, after old Bahu had returned home to resume his post, Deva spent most of his days squatting in a stuffy room with a panel of teachers who instructed him in the sounds of the Pali tongue. He soon grew to appreciate its rounded, sibilant music and the snaking length of its words. The masters would recite representative sections of the Dhamma, and Deva would repeat them back to them, not always with the best rhythm or enunciation, but usually free from error. No one ever asked him if he understood the meaning behind any of the sounds, but eventually he managed to piece together enough clues to construct his own version of the language.

For a memory like his, such a task wasn't hard. He remembered everything he was told, including the occasional mispronunciation, and added it to the growing store of particles and connectives, forms of address and circumlocutions, whose echoes often kept him sleepless at night. By the end of the first month, he had become a breathing encyclopedia that included thousands of proper names and locations that even Sali himself didn't know, not to mention Deva's becoming the first person in the monastery to ask where a water strainer had been mislaid or which alms bowl belonged to whom. The only problem he ever encountered was one of surfeit. Sometimes he thought of so many words that could be substituted for another that he disputed his teachers' interpretations of the texts, an impertinence that none of them tolerated very well.

In the end, though, what pleased and astounded Deva more than anything else was this same magnitude. The proportions of the Teachings rose before him like an approaching mountain or like a cloud whose mass sailed ponderously across the sky, dragging a city-wide shadow beneath it. Early on in his lessons, he had chafed at the stock phrases that recurred so frequently that they lost most of their meaning. He had grown bored with the tiresome lists and categories and irritated by the wasteful theorizing that obscured such elementary human emotions as doubt and fear. But then he began to marvel at this complex, organic edifice that had originated with a single man. The personal Jataka anecdotes from the Buddha's last and previous lives, the contrast between the use of dialectics and everyday examples, his infinite patience with all classes of people, even his scattered instances of humor and playfulness—everything combined to create, not so much a new religion, as a new way of living. Even after nearly half a millennium, the insights gained by that one man during that one night of total awakening at Bodh Gaya in northern Jambudipa apparently still had the power to animate whole nations.

And yet, Deva wondered, how simple it all was, how self-evident! How many times would a new convert exclaim, "Whatever is born and begins, decays and dies," a wisdom that any common farmer in Ratna would agree with? How often was spiritual awakening likened to the most mundane, "as if someone were to set up what had been knocked over, or to point out the way to one who was lost, or to bring a lamp into a dark place, so that those with eyes could see what was there"? These and hundreds of other, similar everyday expressions pleased Deva immensely and transformed what could have become dry, academic lessons into examples that might have been witnessed in any village in Lanka. The Buddha's sending a bereaved mother to look for magical mustard seeds in every house that had never suffered a death was the most compassionate reminder of mortality that Deva had ever heard of.

The only one who didn't seem to be very impressed by the tailor's progress was the Mahathera himself. He supervised the lessons from a distance, watching out of the corner of his eye with a disappointed look on his face. At times, he even shook his head in despair and walked away, and these were usually the times when Deva had just finished repeating a particularly long and complicated passage. What more he was hoping for from the tailor was difficult to see, but Sali continued to keep his own counsel and refused to give the slightest encouragement to the project that he himself had begun.

In an effort to speed things up a bit, he assigned a young nun, Rohini, to teach Deva the *Therigatha,* an ancient collection of nuns' poetry from which she had taken her name. When she first came into Deva's room, he could hardly respond to her greeting. Small and fragile, yet still solid in the strength of her figure, she stood with a slight lean to one side, not unlike some bean pods as they droop earthward at the tip of a branch. Her cropped head was regular in shape, and her eyes flitted teasingly about the room in the darkness, while the jute scent from her clothes wafted over Deva like freshly poured wine. She was so much more attractive than any of the women back in Ratna that he couldn't look directly at her face. But she only laughed good-naturedly at his awkwardness and sat down across from him.

"Are you ready?" she asked.

"Ready?"

"To hear the poetry," she said with a patient smirk. "There are seventy-three poems and five hundred and twenty-two verses in all, so we'd better get started, don't you think?"

Deva and Rohini shared a wonderful afternoon together, listening to the melody of the old songs and easing some of the loneliness that both of them felt. After the lesson was finished, Rohini stayed on to talk about herself and gossip about the monastery. As it turned out, she was not altogether happy with the way the Order was being run.

"Why shouldn't some of us *bhikkhunis* be allowed to travel down to Aluvihara with the rest of you?" she demanded loudly. "There are quite a few of us—myself included—who can read and write, and we're no less devout or sincere than the men, more so than some I could name. Don't we suffer from enough special restrictions as it is?"

"What kind of restrictions?" Deva prompted her so as to keep her near him longer.

"Well, we're already prohibited from so many little things, from failing to salute even the youngest *bhikkhus,* or from spending a rainy season in any place where there are no monks, or from ever criticizing them, even though they can criticize us. We all understand," she conceded, "that it was the Master himself who made these rules and that he must have had his own good reasons for doing so. But didn't he also say that his Discipline would last only five hundred years instead of a thousand, if women were allowed to enter, and aren't we all still here? Yet it still hurts that, after all this time, we're so little trusted by our own abbot and brothers."

"That's horrible," Deva declared without knowing if it really was or not. As far as he had heard, the Mahavihara monastery was a model establishment in the capital. But the way Rohini looked at him when he expressed his sympathy encouraged him, so he went on, "Isn't there anyone who could convince the Mahathera to change the regulations or bend them a little?

From what I've learned of the Teachings so far, equality seems to be at their very foundation. Couldn't anyone go and remind him of that?"

"Only you," Rohini answered quietly and then walked out of his room.

When Deva broached the subject with Sali the next day, the abbot was more receptive to the idea than might have been expected. "You've made a good point there," he said with an appreciative look at Deva, "and I promise you that I'll give it my most serious consideration. We'll have to leave for the Aluvihara caves before the rains begin to fall, but I'm not sure you'll have finished learning all that you need to learn from Rohini by then. And, believe me, her presence would be viewed very seriously by our rival monasteries, so I'll need to balance the danger of a schism with the benefits of her participation.

"Tell me, though, do you happen to have any favorites among the Teachings yet?" the Mahathera wanted to know. "Have any of them stood out in your mind, whether you can understand them completely or not?"

Deva was prepared to mention two or three of the discourses that had especially struck him. There was the touching *Mahaparinibbana Sutta* that described the Buddha's passing and the *Vatthupama Sutta* whose similes of dyes and cleansing wells made him feel homesick. Yet, for some reason, he found himself reverting to the more emotional viewpoints of Rohini's special *Therigatha* poetry.

"Ah, so our young nun has already made quite an impression on you," Sali cried with a note of triumph in his voice. "She is one of our best scholars, not to mention a dear, sweet girl in her own right. It's only too bad that . . ."

His hesitation frightened Deva, who quickly asked, "Too bad? What's too bad?"

"Her disfigurement and her past," the Mahathera explained, never taking his eyes off the tailor. "She bears some scars on her throat from a terrible attack in her youth, when her betrothed went mad and tried to strangle her, and she had to kill him in her own defense. They're quite unsightly, and her story is infamous throughout this part of Lanka, which is why she sought sanctuary here among us in the first place, though now both make it harder for her to win the goodwill of the townspeople to our cause. Didn't you discuss any of this during all your time with her? Don't you at least remember the scars?" he challenged the tailor. "I was under the impression that you never overlooked or forgot anything."

Yet Deva had no memory of the scars, and the news of her scandal hardly fazed him. All he could think of was of Rohini's soothing voice, her devotion to the poetry of long-dead nuns, and her righteous anger at being excluded from equal membership in the Order. After a lifetime of remembering every meaningless, inconsequential detail of his surroundings, now Deva couldn't even recall what was probably her most distinctive feature.

"Perhaps," he said as he turned defeated toward the door, "you should find yourself a new and better memorizer. It seems that I've failed you before we've even started."

Sali let him almost leave the room before he called out after him, "Or passed your final and most difficult test."

Deva stopped and said, "Sir?"

The Mahathera waved him back and had him sit at his right side. "The Buddha," he told him, "was a common man who had an uncommon insight that was so strong that it profoundly changed him for the last forty-five years of his life. But the Dhamma that he taught during that time had nothing to do with gods and saints, but rather with men and women and their human lives here on this earth. He didn't want to promise us some perfect afterlife in some perfect heaven, but wanted instead to wake us up to the life that we're all living right here and right now. How did the Master answer the brahman Dona in the *Anguttara Nikaya* when he asked him if he were a god, an angel, or a spirit?"

Deva knew the answer to this. "He said he wasn't any of them. He was simply awake."

"And that's all those of us here will ever expect of you," Sali said with a kind look. "We expect you to be a real man with a real heart and a real mind. You don't remember Rohini's scars, and you aren't bothered by her history, because you're a man with passions and illusions that still blind him. But that may pass with time. That may pass."

Satisfied at last, the Mahathera dismissed him with a friendly nod, and Deva walked out into the clear air of the monastery compound once again. He still despaired about the hard work that lay ahead of him, and he wondered if he were truly prepared for the long journey through the jungle or the weeks and weeks of droning word-checking that would follow. But he was encouraged by a passage that he recalled from near the end of the *Udumbarika-Sihanada Sutta* where the Buddha claimed to be able to bring any man to awakening in a period as short as seven days or as long as seven years. It seemed that Deva had plenty of time left.

Still, for all his growing enthusiasm for the Sangha's grand project, he couldn't keep his eyes from straying now and then toward the seductive shadows of the women's building across the way. Whether Deva would become a full-fledged follower of the Buddha or not was something he needed more time to decide. But, as he turned back to his own room, he felt oddly thankful that his vast and bloated memory had not yet clung to either Rohini's perfections or her imperfections. Now he had only that many more excuses to see her again and again, and always as if for the very first time.

Diana Winston

Mi Mi May

I N CALIFORNIA WE WOULD SAY she had no boundaries. The concept probably doesn't translate into Burmese, but you get the picture. Her name was Mi Mi May and she was one of the wealthy Burmese people practicing at the monastery. She was in her late twenties, about my age at the time, with long hair that always seemed perfectly combed and styled. She must have spent hours on her hair, which could explain why she was never in the meditation hall. She wore silk brown longyis—the Burmese skirts worn by both women and men—and detailed white cotton blouses. Under the pretense of failing at meditation and trying to occupy her time, she was always in everyone's business, especially mine. She took a special interest in me, the American nun. I tried to avoid her, but after seven months of intensive meditation, when my practice began its downward spiral and I stopped looking so concentrated, she pounced on me. One day on the path by the lake, once we were well out of the way of the watchful eyes of the Sayadaw (our teacher), she crept up behind me and whispered loudly:

"Your boyfriend, he is leaving soon."

"He's not my boyfriend."

"Yes he is, everyone says he is."

"I am a nun, he is a monk, how could he be my boyfriend?"

"Well, you won't be one forever. You came to the monastery together. He is very handsome, a very good boyfriend to have."

"He's not my boyfriend!"

"Yes he is. Su will be so jealous."

"Who?"

"Su, the Taiwanese yogini who stopped practicing because of—how you say?—hemorrhoids. Su is jealous of you because she is in love with your boyfriend."

"She's married."

"Doesn't matter, she is in love with him."

"Aren't you supposed to be meditating? Why are you looking around so much? You notice everything."

"I cannot help it. My meditation is so bad. I cannot practice, but I do not want to leave. So I have to look around."

"What's wrong with your practice?"

"I cannot attain nibbana."

"Oh?"

"I am very close, very very close, but I keep falling backward and now I cannot even reach 'arising and passing away.' I am a terrible yogi, but I cannot leave the monastery either, maybe it will happen another day."

"Not if you keep talking so much."

A FEW DAYS LATER she cornered me in the shoe room outside the meditation hall.

"Here, Sayalee (Sister). Here is some ramen for you. And some Nescafé." She stood there, hands outstretched with a neon packet of ramen. I chose to ignore the smug smile. I glanced around to make sure no one was watching and then furtively shoved them into my bag.

"Sayalee, do you like fried chicken and burgers?"

"Well, not hamburgers."

"No, no, chicken burgers. On buns."

"Yes, of course I do." God . . . I started to fantasize. I hadn't had something even remotely American-tasting in seven months. "Why?"

"My mother will come this week, and I can ask her to stop at the best burger joint in Yangon (Rangoon) to get chicken and burgers for me and you. What else do you want?"

"Um . . ." I was well aware that as a nun I wasn't supposed to express wants. Then the words came tumbling out of my mouth. "Chocolate. I'm dying for chocolate."

"No problem. Come to my room on Wednesday after lunch."

W E D N E S D A Y   I   A T E   L I G H T L Y and knocked equally lightly on her door.

"Mi Mi? Are you there?"

"Oh, my mother did not come today. But please come in, I will give you some Nescafé. I saw you didn't eat much, and you clinked your spoons so loudly as you ate. Do you know everyone laughs at you? They think it is very funny, because you eat slow and mindful but when you put down your spoon and fork on the side of your plate it goes *ping-ping! pong! ding! ping!*"

I turned bright red. "Why hasn't anyone told me this?"

"Oh, I told Sayadaw to tell you, but he said he cannot tell the foreign yogis what to do. I think he is afraid foreigners will not give money when they leave, so he will not be strict with them. He is not very strict with me either. The other day I say, 'Sayadaw, why do you not give me more strict instruction? If you gave me more strict instruction then I could reach nibbana. Instead you just say, Please keep trying.' He got very angry, he say, 'Mi Mi May, you are not a baby, I am not your father, if you want strict teacher, go see Sayadaw U Dhammajiva.' I cry and cry when he say that, how can he be so mean to me? Maybe my parents will stop giving him *dana*, or take me home."

"Mi Mi, why don't you leave? You are barely meditating, you are talking all the time, and you hate it here."

"Because if I leave, then I won't be able to reach nibbana. If I don't reach nibbana I may go to the hell realms, and I scare! I scare!"

"But nibbana could take lifetimes, we don't know how long it will take. We can't make nibbana happen."

"No, I am close. You see, Sayalee, six months ago I came to the monastery to get better concentration to pass my accounting exams. I had never meditated before. I meditate for ten days and at the end of nine days I reached *uddhyabhaya* [first stage on the progress of insight: "arising and passing away"]. I was very surprise and very happy. Then Sayadaw-ji, he told me now I have reached *uddhya,* I can reach nibbana, guaranteed. So I work very hard and go through all the stages of insight and then I could not go past *sankara upekkha* [stage before nibbana]. Every time I almost get there, *I scare!!* So I cannot. Then I realize it is not my fault, it is too hard to practice in Yangon. I tell Sayadaw-ji I want to leave the city monastery because there are too many old ladies gossiping all day there. I know I can reach nibbana better in the country. In the city I must sleep in one room with snoring old ladies. How can I reach nibbana with all those busybodies talking and snoring instead of meditating? So I asked for my own *kuti* [meditation hut] in the country and Sayadaw-ji let me come. Now I have very nice, very private *kuti*. But I have been here four months and still no nibbana. So I feel so bad and I cannot practice well, so now I talk a little."

"A little?"

"Okay, a lot. But what else can I do?"

"Close your mouth and practice."

"You talk too. See, right now you talk to me."

"I know, but my practice is bad too."

"Why?"

I was silent.

"Come on, Sayalee, why is your practice bad?"

I sighed, relieved to have someone to confide in, despite my better judgment. Finally I said, "I have been here seven months and I am also stuck and I cannot reach nibbana, and now I hate myself so much."

"Me too, I hate myself."

"We are terrible yogis."

"Cheer up, Sayalee. My mother will bring burgers on Friday."

FRIDAY BEFORE LUNCH Mi Mi May walked pseudo-mindfully past me and slipped a note into my nun's sash. "Be at your *kuti* at eleven-thirty. Don't eat too much."

I picked through my lunchtime bowl of the usual greasy vegetables and white rice, my mind hardly present but deeply engrossed in speculations of what a Burmese burger would look like.

11:25. I abandoned all pretense of mindfulness and walked briskly to my *kuti*.

11:30 . . . 35 . . . 40. No mother. I knew she was lying. She just wanted to get me to talk to her and be her friend. Aversion, aversion. I was seething.

11:45. I heard rustling outside and voices. I opened my door to four Burmese ladies, all who looked faintly like Mi Mi May, with their bad teeth and fine long dark hair.

"Sayalee Diana?" they inquired.

"Yes, that's me, please come in."

They entered my *kuti* and immediately bowed down three times.

"Mi Mi has told us so much about you. You are from America. You are from which city? We are from Yangon. These are my two sisters, I am Mi Mi's mother, and this is my niece who does not speak English, and . . ."

Barely listening, I stared at the white paper bags in front of her and the wafting smell of the promised fried food. And the clock that was rapidly ticking toward noon. At noon the nun's no-food vow began. I could eat anything I liked between sunrise and noon, but afterward, for seventeen hours, I would be relegated to hard sucking candy and fruit drinks with no pulp, usually the orange-colored sugar water a British friend had nicknamed "Agent Orange."

Hmm, I wondered, will I get to eat the burgers before noon? Oh God, please, I just have to get rid of these people. What do they want? A blessing? A photo?

"Umm . . ." I ventured, "Your daughter is very friendly. Her English is quite good."

"We want her to come home and finish her accounting exams, but Sayadaw-ji says we must let her stay. She may reach nibbana soon, so we must listen to him."

"Oh, I see." 11:55.

"Do you miss America, Sayalee?"

11:56. "Sometimes. But I feel very happy to practice in your country. The Burmese people have been very kind to me."

11:57. "Our uncle U Maung Thin once went to Dutch. He saw many sights and many—how you say?—windmills. We hope to travel, but our government does not give visas easily. Oh dear, it is getting late and we must go, and you must want to eat your burgers and chicken."

I smiled weakly. The clock said twelve o'clock. I was sunk.

"Well, thank you, Sayalee, for being friends with our daughter and practicing in our country. When you leave the monastery you must come visit us and stay in our home. We will cook you many delicious meals like noodles and fish soup, and we can go into Yangon to a very special donut shop. And you can meet our cousins and aunties and uncle who has also gone abroad. Do you like windmills? Please consider us your family here in Burma. You are our new daughter. Anything you need, please do not hesitate. Well, we must go now. Please do not forget us. Here is our address."

In their tiny curved handwriting they painstakingly wrote out their address. They bowed three times upon leaving, and my face flushed. It was well past noon.

A S I W A V E D G O O D B Y E to them from my deck, my next thoughts turned to the bags. Unmindfully, I rushed inside and tore them open. Next to two giant bars of already melting chocolate were what had to be the scrawniest looking fried chicken drumsticks I had ever seen, jammed onto a stick like a corn dog. Repulsed, I ripped open the other bag and unwrapped the sandwiches and burst into tears. In my hand I held a facsimile of the West: a chicken "burger" on a "sesame-seed bun," topped with what passed for cheese, lettuce, tomatoes, onions, mustard, mayo, and cucumbers masquerading as pickles. Screw the vow, I announced to no one in particular. Tears streamed down my cheeks. I bit into the burger. The taste of the nearly familiar slid down my throat as I devoured the chunks. I had never before broken my food vow. As I chewed in great greedy bites I sobbed for missing my country and ordinary food and for wanting to be normal again. I cried, thinking I'll never reach nibbana at this rate, I can barely keep my nun's vows, I'm a horrible failure and a horrible nun. Well, I consoled myself, maybe I'll just quit practicing and stay with Mi Mi's family, then at least I'd get nice things to eat. Except, of course, the government arrests people who bring foreigners into their homes. Oh my God, I'm so self-centered; here I am in the middle of Burma with its draconian military dictatorship and all I can think about is how miserable I am. This started a fresh spate of crying. Suddenly my stomach lurched. I rushed into the bathroom, began retching, and threw it all up. Afterward, as I rinsed my mouth out, I wondered whether since I had vomited it meant I hadn't broken the food vow.

I H U N G T H E R E M A I N I N G chicken burgers from the rafters so the ants and rats wouldn't eat them. Within a day they were moldy and I had to throw them out. The chocolate melted immediately in the heat. And as for the chicken dogs, I gave them to a ten-year-old boy who worked at the monastery.

Francesca Hampton

Greyhound Bodhisattva

CASH OR CHARGE?" The ticket clerk behind the Greyhound counter stifled a yawn and looked up from writing the destination Kunsang had given him.

"Cash," Kunsang murmured. He rummaged in his wallet, extracting a rumpled twenty and two tens. His Mastercard had been canceled two weeks previously, and because of this he avoided the man's eyes. The small shame must be plain on his face, there for the man to see. Though perhaps, since he had so many shames now, no stranger would be able to divine them all at a single glance. By now his sins must obscure another like the clouds of a great storm.

"The bus for L.A. leaves through Gate four, seven P.M.," the man informed him. He was already looking over Kunsang's shoulder at the customer waiting behind.

The Tibetan felt a scurry of relief. No strangers cared for his sins in this place. He hoisted the small suitcase he had not checked and went to settle himself on a faded pink plastic couch with metal arms that discouraged sleepers. Just as well. He could easily have slept himself after the long afternoon of coffee and cigarettes and newspapers in Denny's restaurant. If the metal arms had not warned him, he would not have known the bus station managers would be unhappy with this. In India everyone slept as they wished, even setting up small households of matting and luggage if the wait were long.

Kunsang yawned and looked about him. There was a group of teenagers in line now, wealthy from the look of them. Their white Adidas running shoes gleamed softly in the gloom of the bus station. One boy wore a fine red European ski jacket above Calvin Klein jeans. Kunsang listened for an accent as they bought tickets and caught the growl of German. Idly he imagined himself in such a lustrous red jacket. There would be secret pockets for documents and there was an embroidered logo. He tried to imagine how he would look in such a jacket.

He scanned the other things the tourists carried. Two carried camera bags. Leicas perhaps? Or Nikon? Kunsang sat up straighter. He had always had an interest in photography. How had those young men purchased such expensive things? Were their parents rich? Had they already embarked on budding careers as accountants or architects? It was hard to imagine how much money such a person would have, how much he could buy whenever the wish to buy came to him, without borrowing, without facing the bright sting of humiliation when the money came due.

Kunsang sighed and rubbed his tired eyes. He didn't know why these thoughts kept coming to him, why these material things seemed so attractive, so very desirable. All his life, the great Rinpoche had pointed out their worthlessness in arguments of crystalline logic that none had been able to dispute. Tossing his red robe over his shoulder on the grassy debating courts of the monastery like a general settling in for war, he would pull his *mala* up his arm like the string of a bow, and release his arrows of wisdom upon the upturned face of his debating partner and the circle of watchers seated on the ground. Would he ever see the great Rinpoche again? Or, if seen, would his lama ever speak with him? Surely no disciple had ever disappointed quite so fully as himself.

A young woman had entered the lighted foyer. Her chopped blonde hair blazed in the fluorescent light, and a tattoo, carved in her upper arm, shaped the words "Biker's Whore" above a small, delicately wrought green dragon. She looked as if she had been ill, a fine long-boned Nordic skeleton plain beneath skin that had a bluish cast. There was no fat on her and little muscle left. Her tie-dye T-shirt and a metal-studded leather vest hung loose. Her blue jeans were torn and her feet clad in scuffed knee-high black boots. A small clinking cluster of earrings weighted one ear while the other carried only a single carved ivory death's head. But her face had the oblivious contentment of a freshly supplied heroin addict. She threw down a tattered black leather bag and draped herself upon the seat across from Kunsang.

For a while she gazed about the bus station, her eyes at half-mast. Gradually her long neck curled back until she gazed only at the ceiling, dreaming. Kunsang stared at her, fascinated. Her face had taken on a look of immense sadness; her hands had released her purse and lay limply in her lap, pale hands with long, graceful fingers. How innocent women's hands looked, how tender, though the nails of this woman were broken and dirty, and one finger appeared to have been badly bruised. Kunsang wondered if it hurt her. It seemed never to have been tended. Her breasts were still generous on her wasted body, set high above her frail ribs. Kunsang imagined himself rising and going to sit next to her. He would take her damaged hand in his and kiss it. He would put his hand at the back of her head and pull her dreaming face to his and kiss her lips. So gently, he would run his other hand across her lovely breasts until she responded. Together, they would go to find some private place, and there he would lay her down and enter her, filling her with the soft slow passion that moved in him. And when they had finished he would hold her, surround her with such heart warming joy that she could never possibly feel lost or afraid again ...

The woman lifted her head up and spoke to him, "Got some smokes?" Kunsang snapped his mind free of the fantasy, his face hot with embarrassment, and searched his jacket pockets. He held out the half-empty box of Marlboros. "Take them all," he said.

She looked surprised, but did as he requested, stuffing the carton into the top of her boot after she had extracted one for smoking. She lit it herself, watching him warily. "Thanks," she said. She inhaled, seeming to savor the sensation, and then rose abruptly, shouldered her purse, and headed off in the direction of the ladies' room with a slight stagger.

Kunsang sat back, chastising himself. He had no limits. He had let his mind run in the channels of desire without thought, without control, and now the woman was offended. The Rinpoche had taught him through so many years, so many lessons, to control his mind. "Without morality, the gross obscurations of mind can never be subdued. Without subduing the gross obscurations, one can never hope to remove the subtle obscurations, and without doing that, it is certain, one will never perceive the true nature of reality or be free from the cycle of birth and death."

Now, at the age of twenty-seven, he had abandoned self-control all together. Was there any doubt, as the lama had warned him, that his rebellious choices in this strange country of America were taking him toward a rebirth in hell? He searched his mind for evil. He was no longer sure he was even able to distinguish the good and evil thoughts in his mind. Something gave out when he tried. Something deep inside him gave a whoosh like an old tire leaking air, and he lost focus.

The Rinpoche had come to America five months before, come just to see him, using up funds that would have supported a dozen monks for half a year. The Rinpoche had come to take him home, but he would not go.

The students of the Buddhist center were gathered so tightly in the two-bedroom San Francisco apartment that even the floor space had begun to fill in. He had arrived when they had almost given up that he would come. They opened the door, and he stood rooted in the door frame with Gilda clutching his arm, her red-blonde hair hiding her face buried in his sleeve. His stomach was so tense it felt as if it had become a plate of iron. He looked around at the sin-cere people he had betrayed. It was their money that had brought him to America, their money, and their invitation and their yearning faith in his title, in his mysterious legacy as a reincarnated high lama of Tibet. In the end it was their telephones he had run up such bills on, their generosity that had made so easy all those monstrous debts he could never repay. The door to the bedroom had opened slowly, held by a Tibetan attendant, and the Rinpoche had beckoned. Stepping over cross-legged knees, he went in and closed it behind him.

The Rinpoche looked at him for long minutes without speaking, letting the beads of his mala, clicking softly between strong fingers, speak for him. Grateful for silence, Kunsang had prostrated thrice. Then sat, gazing at the hem of the lama's robe.

"Is the American girl pregnant?" It was the only question the lama asked.
"No."

The soft knock of bead against bead continued. "Then you may return home if you wish." The voice was so soft, so unexpectedly gentle, Kunsang looked up amazed. Where was the wrathful teacher of his childhood, who had cracked his head with a heavy wooden bowl for even a small moment of inattention. The pain had been so sharp he rubbed his head ruefully now, just in memory.

"I cannot," he said.

For just a moment, the beads stopped. Then starting slowly, they resumed, picking up speed. "Many in India and Tibet depend on you," the Rinpoche re-minded him. "You are the twelfth incarnation of the Pawoling Lama."

"How can I be?" the forbidden words had left his mouth at last. "How can you be sure?"

"The signs were clear," the lama answered quietly.

"What signs?" Kunsang challenged, astonished at his own rebellion. "Two lamas had dreams; a child chose the correct bell and mala; you tossed the dice to make a divination. What about the sign of my mind, of my actions? All can

see now that what I truly am is a thief, a breaker of vows, a monk who sleeps with women and thinks only of money."

"It was the Dalai Lama himself who verified your recognition," the Rinpoche countered. "It may be that you suffer still the stains of illusion, but there was no doubt who you are. You have not broken the vows of monkhood. You gave back your ordination before leaving with the woman. You have debts, this is true. But surely you made your debts intending to repay them. You will repay them. We will help you."

"No!" He had stood as if his body owned his will and rushed out of the little room. The shocked devotees in the foyer had not stopped him. The Rinpoche had not called him back. Later he learned the old lama had made arrangements to send another teacher to the Western Dharma students, had paid his debts, and had returned to India two days later.

The girl was coming back, her walk now was smoother, self-controlled, as if, having left the room and returned to it, she more confidently belonged among them. Heavy eyeliner had been applied to the lower lid of her eyes and blue mascara liberally applied. She strolled to the ticket counter, and most of the men in the station followed the deliberate roll of her hips.

But Kunsang's attention had left her for another woman sitting nearby. This woman had neither beauty nor dare in her eyes. She was a tiny brown woman, fully into middle age, with her waist gone to roundness and a long oiled black braid down her back like a Tibetan. What riveted Kunsang's attention was her distress, for a child of four or five was laid across her lap, his eyes closed and his face flushed with fever. His mother was murmuring urgent endearments in soft, barely audible Spanish.

Kunsang shifted his seat, settling himself beside her. The woman looked up at him, startled, when he spoke. *"Cómo está el niño?* How is the boy?" In a string of cheap motels across Nevada and Colorado, Gilda had taught him many phrases in Spanish before her father had traced them and come to claim her back.

The woman erupted in a small wail, *"Ay, Dios mío."* And, seeing his dark face, the Tibetan features so like an Indian's, she began to tell him. Her trickle of Spanish became a torrent as she poured out her story. Kunsang sat back in the cascade of unknown words, intent on the woman's face, understanding, through her shifting tone and expression, much of what language could not tell him. He understood that the woman was alone, facing a long journey home to Mexico with the sick child, frightened. He reached out a tentative hand and placed it on the child's forehead. The smooth skin was hot but not dangerously hot. The long-lashed black eyes opened, and the child regarded him.

Kunsang dug in his bag for a packet of lifesavers. Finding it, with a prayer for the child's good health, he said the mantra of the Medicine Buddha and blew the sacred words on the wrapped pack. The little boy sat up and gravely took the yellow and green flavors offered to him. He said nothing, but he continued to look fixedly at the next flavor, red, so Kunsang gave him that too. A small sigh of satisfaction escaped the child as he placed the red lifesaver in his mouth. He solemnly pushed the other two deep into his shirt pocket and lay back against his mother. She rocked him, crooning again, and pushed the damp hair back from his face. *"De dónde eres?"* she asked Kunsang. "Where are you from?" The vibration of hysteria had gone from her voice.

He had no time to answer. An argument was erupting at the ticket counter. The blonde girl had arrived at the window. The ticket clerk's voice had risen in frustration, "The fare's thirty-eight-fifty lady, take it or leave it!"

"You asshole, all I'm short is a dollar fifty!" the girl howled. She banged her small rhinestone handbag against the window as the clerk slammed it shut. She whirled on the staring crowd daring them not to come up with the money. People looked away. Two teenage boys in gang-banger oversize shirts and reversed baseball caps laughed openly.

Kunsang felt for his wallet. He had ten dollars left. He could afford a dollar fifty. But his wallet stuck in his tight jeans pocket and refused to come out at once, and the girl stalked past the bystanders and out to the sidewalk before he wrested it loose. Through the glass windows, they all stared as she pulled up her shirt and stood brazenly on the curb, chest held high with breasts exposed until a red Chevy Lumina slammed to a stop and a back door swung open for her.

Kunsang stood watching long after the girl had disappeared. The ten dollars was in his hand.

The Los Angeles Express Bus pulled in right on schedule twenty-five minutes later. As the passenger line shuffled forward between the iron guide rails, the Mexican woman chattered to him in Spanish. Her little boy, much revived, walked beside her. Kunsang caught a word here and there and nodded, smiling. They mounted the cramped steps, struggled past other passengers stowing gear in the overhead racks. Kunsang found himself separated from the woman in the confusion, and ended sitting at the window several seats away next to a heavy-faced man with dark skin and a pocked nose.

There was a faint commotion among the few passengers outside. The bus driver had returned, bearing a large coffee and a chilidog. Behind him, almost hidden by his oversize middle and formidable height, was the blonde girl, ticket in hand.

Kunsang smiled radiantly at her as she brushed past, only barely restraining himself from speaking. Such a beautiful girl, who had gone through so much to get on this bus. How much he would have liked to offer her something, his lap to lay her head on, his leather jacket to put over her. But the girl pushed on and on until she found an empty seat near the back of the bus.

There was a decisive thunk as the door closed, and a great wheeze of air brakes. The motor started with a roar. Kunsang's companion in the other seat shut his eyes and spoke with great relief, "We leave, at last."

"Someone waits for you in L.A.?" Kunsang asked.

"I am not going so far as L.A., only a job in Bakersfield. They pay good money for truck mechanics in Bakersfield!" He reached in his pocket and hefted a large wallet. When I have enough I will be able to leave this empty-hearted country and go back to New Guinea."

New Guinea! Kunsang eyed the man with new curiosity. He had heard there were cannibals in New Guinea. But this man seemed warm and hearty, unlikely to eat anyone. He watched as the man shoved the wallet into the overcrowded carryall. A thick wad of twenties protruded over the lip. There must easily be many hundreds of dollars in the wallet. It made him happy to think of the man returning to his family with all that money. Ruefully he though of the ten dollars still remaining in his own wallet. His numbed mind refused to think what he would do when that small sum was gone if no one helped him. His plan was to go to a Dharma center in L.A. where he was not known and where, Gilda had said, a friend of hers might find him a job. Failing that, the center might give him room and board to translate for while—*might*. In India he had never dealt with money. The monastery steward had paid the bills. It was his function only to study the sacred texts, and to prepare for the debating courts and the rituals of the *puja*. Each afternoon he had meditated for an hour on bodhicitta, the Great Wish to benefit all beings, and then received visits of humble peasant refugees from the area of his lost monastery in Tibet who came to seek his blessing. He had been a minor king in a sheltered universe.

But then the videos had been shown in the dining room of the Tibetan Culture Center. He had been invited, with other young monks, to sit and marvel at the strange and alien lives of people in the West. There were fabulous glittering cities and fast cars, daring men with guns who killed other human beings and went on living without pause or consideration. There were beautiful women dressed so scantily it made his heart push at his throat and his face grow hot with shame for looking. In Indian films men and women did not so much as kiss, but in these American movies, the men took the women in intercourse, pulling them onto beds and disrobing them in a tangle of flesh and cloth and confused lust. And he had looked, all the way to the end of each movie, as had the other monks, stumbling out into the sharp clear nights of the Himalayan foothills, his clear intentions shattered, and his body humming.

Over many weeks the poisoned seed thus planted in him had grown, hidden he prayed, from the keen eyes of his lama. It had flowered at last into the secret desire to see that life in the films for himself, to look in a mirror and see on his own body those vivid fine-cut clothes, to look down from the high windows of one of those great buildings onto a city that glittered like diamonds, to run his fingers across the smooth warm body of a woman and learn for himself what the forbidden mystery of sex might be. And suddenly he desired to own things, to hold money in his hands and purchase things, as he had never been permitted to do before, stereos and videos and cars and fine clothes. What was it to own so much? He had to know.

"What will you do in New Guinea?" he asked his seatmate in sudden curiosity.

The man grunted with vehemence. "I'll go out into the trees alone and strip myself naked and stay there until I am clean again."

Kunsang was puzzled. "You have made much money in America. Why don't you stay here?"

The dark eyes in the long pocked face regarded him sadly. "I paid too much for this money. I will stay three months more for the job in Bakersfield, working twelve-hour shifts and staying alone in a small ugly room, and then I will go home and give the money to my family as I promised five years ago. I think it will be a long time before I fill my heart with life again."

Kunsang stared at him, "I don't understand. Everyone is rich here. You could bring your family to America!"

The big man smiled at him and shook his head. He looked out the window and didn't answer.

The bus was on the freeway now, circling out of San Francisco. The busy arc of the Bay Bridge was visible out the window, carrying its thousands of speeding lives. The islands called Angel and Alcatraz swam in an azure bay dotted with white yachts, and the glass monoliths of the financial dis-

trict glittered in the end-of-day sunlight. Just a little, Kunsang had begun
to feel at home in this forbiddingly beautiful alien city. Now he must leave
it for another, unknown, with a fearsome reputation for vastness and vio-
lence. Kunsang closed his eyes and, ever so softly, allowed his head to rest
on the big New Guinean's shoulder as the bus surged through the endless
rushing metal of the traffic and everything familiar fell away from him. In
the quiet certainty of his conclusions the big dark man reminded him of
his lama. Each night of his childhood he had been accustomed to visualize,
as the lama instructed, that he laid his head in the lap of the lama. He would
fall to sleep within this visualization, thus comforted and protected. Oddly,
the New Guinean did not protest the soft pressure of a stranger's head on
his shoulder. As the light faded and the pressure grew more assured, he
even took Kunsang's hand in his, as men often did in his country, and held
it with comradely affection.

Kunsang woke with a start as the bus motor died. He looked out the
window, startled to see that night had fallen and harsh floodlights lit the unfamiliar back lot of the Bakersfield bus station. The New Guinean had already
eased past him while he slept, and now was struggling to pull loose a bedroll
from the overhead luggage.

"Travel safe, man," he said in rumbling farewell, "and don't stay too
long away from your own country." Kunsang stood awkwardly between the
seats as the good man left, and bowed his head over closed palms in respect
and gratitude.

He sat down in the seat the man had vacated and watched as other passengers pushed through to the front after his friend and thumped down
the metal stairs and into the terminal for the break the bus driver had announced. Kunsang craned his neck to see if the blond girl had left while he
slept. No, she was now three seats behind him and across the aisle, gazing
at the dim reflection of her own face in the window glass or the empty big
city streets beyond; he could not tell which. She looked edgier than she
had in the San Francisco terminal. There was a gaunt, haunted look to the

high-boned face that had seemed plumped and young before, and he felt a stab of concern for her.

Her gaze slid over to Kunsang, and she regarded him without expression. She reached below the seat to snatch up her long-strapped shoulder bag, made her way with it to the bathroom at the back of the bus, and jerked the door shut behind her.

Less than ten minutes more and the bus driver was in his seat again. The last of the passengers was climbing the stairs when Kunsang saw the wallet. It had slipped onto the floor as the New Guinean hoisted his bag and turned sideways to the aisle. Kunsang's heart beat fast as he picked it up. He had never before held so much cash in his hands. Feathering the bills with his thumb, he tried to estimate the number of twenties. There were even several hundred-dollar bills. The bus door shut with a hiss and Kunsang stood up. "Stop!" he cried.

He rushed to the front, frantic for the door to be opened again. When the bus driver at last grasped the meaning of his fevered message, he sighed and released the door handle. "Make it fast, " he snapped. "We've got a schedule to keep."

Kunsang hit the double doors running, shoving them aside with his shoulder and holding the wallet above his head for all to see as if he were a drowning man signaling for help. The big New Guinean was standing in a phone booth and turned to gape at him with the rest until Kunsang placed the wallet in his hand. He clutched it to his chest with a kind of sob. For a long moment the two men looked at each other. A long blast of the bus's horn wrenched Kunsang away. No word had been spoken.

The city lights fell behind quickly this time, to be replaced with long stretches of darkness, broken only by fluorescent floodlights over a storage warehouse here and there, or a bare light bulb burning on the porch of a distant farmhouse. There was a hot wind blowing outside, more than just the passage of the bus, and Kunsang watched the great eucalyptus trees, planted in long utilitarian lines to protect the lettuce fields, wrestle with the night as they passed.

The passengers, those he knew and those that had gotten on at the last stop, settled down for the late-night run into L.A., their conversations drifting down to silence. Several seats behind him, Kunsang heard the Mexican child wake and whimper and say something to his mother in Spanish, and he heard her murmured answer. The blonde girl had not emerged from the small bathroom. As he closed his eyes, resting his head against the glass, Kunsang wondered why.

The steady vibration of the bus engine lulled him, and as he fell more deeply asleep the question faded from his mind and a dream of the Himalayas replaced it. He was walking, as he had many times as a child, near his monastery in Tibet in a vast meadow above the tree line where blue mountain crocus edged the dark waters of the high lakes and a golden eagle rode the updrafts off the valley floor. Behind him were the whitewashed walls of a holy *chorten* surrounded by stones carved with the sacred mantra *Om Mani Padme Hung*. In front of him reared the first rank of peaks, vast and white with snow that would not melt even in summer, the granite ridges along their flanks as sharp as teeth.

There was a faint path among the stones, leading higher, and on the path there was a young woman, dressed in Indian garb, with vermilion silk pantaloons and an over-dress of forest green sashed with bright blue. She laughed merrily at his amazement at seeing her there, for he knew at once who she was. Surely this was an emanation of Buddha Tara, she who removes obstacles from the path and seeks the lasting happiness of all that lives. When he had stood too long, staring, she took his hand and, with a gay smile tossed back over her shoulder, led him upward, running.

The path followed a chuckling creek, then crossed a bridge and entered a dark forest. Shafts of sunlight filtered through the branches and a soft carpet of pine needles rustled as they passed. They seemed to cover miles in a few steps, as if they glided rather than walked. The path ended at last at the base of a sheer cliff and a small dwelling nestled against the rock. Night was falling now, and a cold wind coursed the shadows and touched the back of Kunsang's neck. Tara crouched low to enter a door half sunk in earth, and he followed.

He found himself in an underground circular room, warm and lit by many candles. There was a low bench going the full circuit of the room and on the bench many lamas, cross-legged in their red robes, talking quietly among themselves. He stood where he was, very still. As his eyes adjusted to the light, he could see that one space only was empty. One of the red-robed figures, seated higher than the others, gestured to this empty space. With a start, he realized that the man on the throne was his own lama, and that far from being angry, he was smiling at him with greatest happiness. Tara was nowhere to be seen.

Self-conscious in his jeans and Gore-Tex jacket, he took his place among the others and looked about him. The other monks did not stare. They went on with their murmured discussions, and only his own lama spoke to him. "You have found your way to us at last," he said.

"No no," Kunsang protested. "I cannot stay. I was walking on the path outside. This is only a visit. Still," he added with feeling, "it is very good to see you."

"Do you know who these lamas are?" his own lama asked gently.

Kunsang looked intently at the faces around him. Some were very old, some younger. One had the marks of smallpox; one looked mischievous and handsome. Another had a long grey goatee that reached almost to his waist and tattered robes that barely covered his nakedness.

"No, Rinpoche, I know none of these men," he confessed at last.

"Count them," his lama urged.

Kunsang craned his neck to see the full extent of the round, low room, trying to make out all the figures in the dim light of the butter lamps. "Eleven," he said at last." Is that correct?"

His lama sat back with a satisfied sigh. "That is correct. Can you guess who they are?"

Kunsang became aware that the other monks had ceased talking among themselves and were now waiting expectantly. He was puzzled. He had already told the lama that he did not know them. He looked again around the faces in the room. He did not know them, yet he felt their familiarity, like an old memory long out of reach that leaves a sweetness of nostalgia but not the reason. In these faces he sensed a host of memories.

"These are the reincarnations of Pawoling," his lama said quietly. "These are the faces of your own mind, taken birth in eleven generations since you first gained control of the bardo's passage, since you learned to pick your way between a life and a life for the sake of helping others."

Kunsang gasped. The monks around him were rising to stand on the floor at the hut's center. They jostled together with good humor, sorting themselves out on the circular floor, linking arms shoulder to shoulder, until he saw they had made the pattern of an eight-spoked wheel. Only the hub remained empty, and this, they urged with gestures and smiles, was the place Kunsang himself should occupy. When he had taken that place, all the spokes reached out to make connection to him, and the wheel began slowly to turn.

It was a stately dance they made. In the golden light of the butter lamps, brown skins were made bronze, red robes flowed into an earthen wreath of color, and felt-booted feet, stamping the clay floor, raised a haze of golden dust. The monks chanted in deep resonant lines of melody, the notes rising and speeding up as the dance grew faster, until the chanters exploded in laughter and with a wild flourish spun loose from each other and whirled individually. In the center of the room, his arms still extended and his head thrown back in delight, Kunsang spun until he had to stop, panting. When he straightened he saw that all the others, even his lama, had vanished, though no door had seen them go.

He went to the throne where the Rinpoche had sat. The maroon cushion was still warm beneath his hand. Desolate, he laid his forehead upon it. "What does this mean, Rinpoche? What should I do?"

There was no answer, but gradually, he became aware that there was more light in the room than that which came from the butter lamps on the altar. There was an opening into the rock wall that formed the back of the house, and a curtain covered it imperfectly. From the bottom and sides, a dim light was visible from something beyond. Curious, Kunsang pulled aside the curtain and found himself in a rock passage leading deep into the cliff he had seen outside.

The passage was not straight; it wound through the mountain for seeming miles, and the light, he discovered, came from diamond crystals embedded at intervals in the rock with an even brighter light somewhere ahead. He ran his fingers in awe over the crystals as he passed. They were so beautiful, so valuable. In America they would be worth so much money. Yet he was more curious about what lay beyond. He followed the corridor. The floor was of the finest white sand, shimmering in the faint light, as if it were dust from the diamonds themselves. Side corridors branched off the main one, and he peered into them cautiously. Sometimes he thought he heard a faint cry in the distance, a voice weeping somewhere in the dark, but then it seemed only his imagination. Had the other lamas passed this way?

Ahead the light grew and he quickened his pace. There was an end to the long tunnel, and the light from beyond was pouring through, a wash of golden sunlight. At last he stood on the lip of the great cavern and his heart was filled with the sight beyond. A great valley opened there, of rarest beauty. Waterfalls were visible miles away in the crystalline air. They descended from cliffs below a range of sheer snow mountains and gathered in a sparkling emerald river that coiled through the center of the valley. Next to the river, in the shade of enormous trees, amid a meadow bright with flowers, was a palace.

It was a palace like nothing he had ever seen, made, or so it seemed, of the sunlight itself, for the walls were translucent, tinged with colors of turquoise and aquamarine, fiery red, vermilion and saffron yellow, sculpted into a vast fourfold design of curves and arches with elegant chambers all opening on a central hall. He recognized there the mandala home of the Buddha Vajrapani. "Oh, Vajrapani," he murmured in homage, "you whose omniscient mind of power shears though the bonds of confusion and grasping and all their miseries." He knew this Buddha well, for the practice of Vajrapani had been the principal focus of his efforts in the monastery and a reputed practice of all his lama forebears. To find himself now in front of the palace of this sacred deity, a short walk down the path from the cavern mouth to the meadow, was to him the culmination of all his lifetimes of meditation. In the palace, perhaps now he could become one with the deity. He could realize once and for all the nature of his own mind and move forever beyond the reach of birth and death. The absurdity of coins for diamonds, of which department-store items of clothing he should wear or whether this or that woman would find him handsome was a merry joke. He remembered now, and wondered how he could have forgotten.

He started forward.

He had reached halfway on the path. The luminous articulated splendor of the palace before him was clarifying in his sight like the rising of the full moon. The arched doorway was rising above him when he heard the cry. At first it was only a whine, barely distinguishable from the normal sounds of wind through trees or water over rocks. But the whine rose quickly to a scream, and it came from the cave passage behind him.

The sound of another's terror stopped him as abruptly as if he had come to the end of a staked chain. He turned, and without hesitation, sprinted back toward the cave's opening. Where was the person? He listened tensely at the cave mouth. There it was again. A long moan, rising to hysteria, and then a choking, gulping after-sound. To the left.

He ran at a low crouch, straining in the low light, running his hand along the dim wall in case he missed the passive darkness of a true opening. Here it was! The screams rang loud, the sounds of choking terrified him. Whoever was in trouble must be very near the point of death. A small rut at the side of the path grew into a gully as he ran, then turned abruptly away, opening into a low side recess of the cavern. The sound was coming from here.

Incautious, he stumbled into the room. There was only one faint crystal lighting this chamber, but by its dim light, he could just make out the source of the terrible cries. The young blonde woman from the bus wrestled on the floor, a grasping furry unnameable creature like a small ape at her throat, which tightened its legs about her chest and its fingers about her windpipe as it struggled to throttle her.

"Stop!" Kunsang commanded.

Amazingly, the thing stopped, never releasing its grip, and looked around at him with a sly evil little face. A demon.

"Who says stop?" the thing asked.

"I say it, Kunsang Namgyal, twelfth incarnation of Pawoling."

The thing laughed, a horrible rasping screech that echoed off the walls of the dark cavern and down the endless passageways beyond. Beneath its relentless fingers the girl fought and panted for air, listening with wild eyes.

Kunsang forced his shaking legs to lower him into the meditation posture, and gathered his concentration. He focused his mind on his breath, letting it slow and deepen, and then, with the facility of long practice, dissolved his temporal body into emptiness and took in its place the ferocious blue form of the Buddha Vajrapani.

As Vajrapani, he stood up slowly in the circular cavern, gathering power to him in a great wind of rage and clarity, right leg bent and left leg outstretched. His hair billowed behind him as fire. His face was more wrathful than the most awful of demons. His three eyes bulged and glared; his mouth was a black hollow of fangs. Around his waist was the skin of a tiger, and from his translucent blue body light radiated, filling the low cave with the color of hottest flame.

"I repeat. What do you want with this woman?" His voice was a hollow roar.

The demon's death grip on the girl's throat slackened. He looked at the apparition before him in awe, yet answered, "What I want is what she wants."

"You speak in riddles," Vajrapani accused him. "What does she want?"

"She wants revenge," came the sly answer.

"Revenge for what?" roared the Buddha, "Revenge on whom?

"Revenge for the failure of trust, revenge for the paltriness of love, revenge for being born and then forgotten. She seeks to make her parents sorry, and after them the whole world, and I oblige her."

"What is your name, demon?"

"My name is Heroin, holiness. You cannot harm me." The creature's sly look had hardened. Its fingers on the throat grew imperceptibly tighter.

"Can I not? You shall see, demon!"

Buddha Vajrapani began the slow rumbling recitation of his mantra, the blue light radiating from his body now intensifying onto the prostrate form of the girl at his feet. The stone walls shook with his power as he rocked back and forth, his feet burning deep imprints into the rock surface. When he was ready, the Tibetan syllables of the mantra uncoiled from his heart in a long blue translucent stream and entered the mouth of the agonized woman, sinking deep into her consciousness.

Slowly her glazed eyes grew calm as she regarded the terrifying appearances in front of her. Her disordered thoughts became clear and her will regained its strength, and with power easily equal to the task now, ripped the furry creature away from her throat and flung it across the chamber.

A low rumbling filled the passageways leading to their chamber. The rumbling became a roar that shook the walls and then ceased abruptly to leave a ringing silence. Kunsang opened his eyes and found that the bus driver had turned off the engine and had risen to adjust the wording on the destination sign in front of the bus.

"Los Angeles Central," the man announced. He crooked an arm around to scratch between his shoulder blades and exited the open door without a further glance at his passengers.

Kunsang shook his head and rubbed his face to clear it of lingering images. Sometimes the gap between his old life and his new was too great. He became disoriented and stunned for hours at a time. Pulling his meager belongings from the overhead rack he shuffled after the line of departing bus riders, yawning and scratching his short hair vigorously to bring himself back to the present more quickly.

The Los Angeles station at 5 A.M. opened before him in a vista of hightech dreariness. The floor was being wet-mopped by an African-American youth who showed not a flicker of interest in the passenger's presence as they passed, his eyes fixed on the damp squares of green linoleum. There were black vinyl seats separated by sturdy chrome bars to inhibit sleeping here as well. They were occupied, nevertheless, by many sleepers, who arched rib cages and necks into positions of crimped abandon as they slumbered. From the belongings piled nearby, most appeared to be homeless. Already the passengers from his journey had dispersed. There was no face here that was familiar.

Kunsang went into the all-night McDonald's outlet and ordered a Coca-Cola from the tired young Hispanic woman on duty. He sipped it as he stood in front of a stand of magazines and still empty newspaper racks, trying to gather his thoughts and his courage for the day to come. The images on the covers always startled him. On one there was a raven-haired woman in a small black bikini who had developed her chest and arm muscles to the size of a man's. On another, there was a gigantic motorcycle, bulging with chrome implements, parked between the sleek thighs of another bikinied woman, red-haired this time. There was a magazine for stylish men who favored cashmere turtlenecks and Porsches. Kunsang tried to imagine himself in a cream turtleneck with a dark grey collarless seersucker suit and a blonde woman waiting for him in a shiny red Porsche. All around would be the shining lights of large hotels. An avenue leading to a large city would beckon. He closed his eyes and put the cold, beaded surface of the Coca-Cola cup against his suddenly aching forehead. Deep in his mind a heavy guttural voice was laughing, a mocking monster.

He turned away from the magazines and saw the ambulance. There had been no siren. The white county hospital truck with its flashing yellow and red lights had steered into the bus parking compound in silence, pulling up next to the central space where his own bus had just parked.

Curious, Kunsang downed the rest of the Coke in a swallow and dumped the cup in a trash canister. He followed a gathering crowd of onlookers back out to the loading area, waiting to see who might need an ambulance.

He heard her before he saw her. The blond girl, pried out of the bus lavatory, being carried on a gurney between two husky paramedics. There was no doubt that she was conscious. She was screaming her protests at the men. "Where is he? You can't take me yet! Where is he?"

Awkwardly the ambulance attendants worked to negotiate the turn by the door, lifting the gurney over the stair rail and pushing the head far over the driver's seat before they could lower it.

"No!" the girl shrieked. "I have to see him first!" Her chest was heaving, and her face had turned an ashen grey.

The bus driver, weary from the long drive but interested, stood next to the ambulance driver. "Where's who? She got on alone. What the hell's she talking about?"

"Oh they get all worked up about all kinds of things on a drug overdose," the ambulance man reassured him. "If she's this lively, she'll most likely be okay by morning. We get a hundred of these every night in L.A."

"She was unconscious when the woman in the back came up to tell me about her, curled up on the floor in that little space. I couldn't wake her up. That's why we called."

The ambulance man looked startled. "Really? Well that is a little unusual. Generally if they go under it can get real serious. Maybe she was just asleep." He took hold of the end of the gurney as it came close to the ambulance doors and helped hoist the end over the bumper.

"Wait!" The girl screamed her demand this time. "I see him!"

Fighting to sit up amid hands that pressed her down, her eyes met Kunsang's. "Let me talk to him!" She reached out.

Kunsang, self-consciousness forgotten, pushed past the people around him and accepted her grasping hand.

"Thank you," she said simply.

Kunsang's eyes widened. "You saw?" He had believed it was only another dream. He had many.

She looked at him dazedly, as if she had only half understood even her own words and now was losing consciousness again. No acknowledging smile cracked the drug-racked tension of her face.

He reached out shyly, touching her cheek. "Then don't forget," he whispered.

The ambulance men shoved the gurney home. The white doors closed behind them. In the parking lot of the Greyhound terminal the twelfth incarnation of the High Lama of Pawoling, Tibet, watched as it turned on lights and sirens, waited for traffic to give way, and then turned a corner to carry away his first disciple into the unknown pre-dawn streets of L.A.

Easton Waller

The War Against the Lawns

HERE COME THE FOUR HORSEMEN!" Jerry said out loud to himself.

It was his favorite time of the day. It didn't last long, and he couldn't explain exactly why he liked it, but turning onto the unpaved street where Suchai lives always gave him a surge of adrenaline. The sound of gravel grinding under the weight of his rig would shatter the early morning silence of Suchai's tired, blue-collar neighborhood, filling Jerry with an inexplicable feeling of power. It was a merciless sound—savage yet deliberate, sudden yet calculated, a terrifying blend of primal power and mechanical coldness. Jerry imagined it was the sound of the Apocalypse, and it thrilled him to think of himself as the driver of such an awesome machine.

The rig consisted of two parts. The front half was a jacked-up, four-wheel-drive pickup with magnetic signs centered perfectly on the doors and reading, "Jerry Mistretta's Touch-of-Class Lawn Service." The back half was a trailer full of landscaping equipment—rakes, brooms, clippers, an

edger, two mowers, a trimmer, and a leaf blower. Both halves were remarkably clean, especially considering their owner's line of business. Jerry washed
and waxed them twice a week and was unabashedly proud of his equipment maintenance standards. "I'm a detail person," he often told Suchai.
"When a customer sees how good I keep my truck, they know I'm gonna take
just as good care of their lawn."

The immaculate rig stopped in front of Suchai's small, cinderblock house,
and the sound of Jerry's imaginary Apocalypse stopped with it. Through a cur-
tainless living room window, Jerry could see that Suchai was not yet ready.
Worse than that, he was not in any evident hurry. And this bothered Jerry.

After all, he thought, I'm doing the guy a pretty big favor. How many
other bosses out there would bother to employ an unskilled immigrant—
let alone pick him up for work every morning?

Jerry grew more anxious with each passing second. It had rained almost the whole day yesterday, and he and Suchai had managed to mow only
five yards. Normally, they would service twenty customers a day, but the
rain had severely hampered their ability to work. As a matter of policy,
Jerry was committed to finishing all of yesterday's business today. As a matter of principle, he was also determined to service all of today's regularly
scheduled customers. This meant that Touch-of-Class would have to work
faster and longer than ever before. An early start was imperative, and Suchai
was already foiling the plan with his lack of preparedness.

Jerry fidgeted in his seat. He wanted to blast his horn but remembered
that one of his customers lives on Suchai's block. An irritated honk would
likely appear unprofessional, and, so, for the sake of preserving Touch-of-
Class's public image, he controlled himself.

He tried hard not to be mad at Suchai. After all, when it came right down
to it, Suchai was a good worker. Apart from lacking a car and needing to be
picked up every morning, he was an ideal employee—certainly better than
the other partners Jerry had hired over the years. Most of them lasted only
a few weeks and complained relentlessly. Suchai was nearly twice the age

of his average predecessor, but he had already been with Jerry nearly two months and showed promise of staying indefinitely. He never asked for breaks and never complained about the heat or the pace. In fact, he never said much of anything at all. He just did his job and minded his own business.

At long last, Suchai emerged from his house with a lunchbox in his hand.

"Good mornin', Spunky!" Jerry bellowed as Suchai stepped into the truck.

"What does it mean, 'spunky'?" Suchai asked innocently.

"It means someone with a lot of energy and enthusiasm," explained Jerry. "And that's exactly what I'm gonna call you until you put a little pep in your step, Mister Spunky."

"Okay," said Suchai, confused. Jerry wondered if Cambodians were simply incapable of understanding sarcasm.

The rig lurched into motion. Once again, there was the sound of big wheels crushing tiny pieces of gravel. It lasted only to the corner and then disappeared as Jerry turned onto a smooth asphalt road. He concentrated on his mirrors during the turn then redirected his gaze to the road ahead of him. From the corner of his eye, he could see that Suchai was meditating.

Or at least Jerry assumed he was meditating. He was not sitting Indian-style or humming or holding his hands in unusual positions, but he sat perfectly still with his gaze locked, neither smiling nor frowning. Just sitting. His eyes never moved. Even if the rig turned suddenly and sharply, they remained fixed on an invisible and never-budging spot in space.

Jerry had seen Suchai do this on a number of occasions and had always been uneasy with it. He liked the fact that Suchai never complained but was uncomfortable with his employee's tendency to avoid conversation altogether. Jerry liked to talk. Or hum. Or blast the radio. Or run an edger. Or fill neighborhoods with the sound of crushing gravel. Anything but silence.

"Whatcha thinkin' about?" asked Jerry. He spoke forcefully, feigning the need to speak over the din of the truck's engine.

"What?" asked Suchai, somewhat startled.

"I said, whatcha thinkin' about?"

Suchai paused for a moment.

"Nothing," he said, finally.

"None of my business, eh?" asked Jerry, clearly offended but trying to project an air of righteous self-control. "I can take a hint."

"No, no," said Suchai, worried about the effects of insulting his sometimes volatile boss. "I am not meaning this."

"Well, then, what *are* you meaning?" asked Jerry.

"I am meaning I am thinking nothing," responded Suchai. "That's all. Just nothing."

Jerry quivered. He had never before questioned Suchai about his intense stares, and now he wished he had let the topic remain unbroached. The thought of mental stillness—or any other kind of stillness—frightened him.

"Ha!" he laughed. "For your information, it's impossible to think about nothing. Even in your sleep, you're still dreamin'. It's a well-known scientific fact. You can't just turn your brain off, ya know. That's just part of bein' alive. So, unless you're tellin' me you're brain dead, then you gotta be thinkin' about somethin'."

Without waiting for a response from Suchai, he turned on the radio and pumped the volume as loud as it would go. The streets of Holiday, Florida, seemed unusually open at the moment. It was bad enough that the small Gulf Coast retirement town was normally quiet and subdued, but this morning it seemed especially desolate. Jerry attempted to fill the lonesome gap between Suchai's house and the day's first lawn by driving as fast as his public image would allow. As the wheels of his cherished rig spun faster on the pavement, the sound they made grew louder. The blaring music and the roar of the tires made Jerry feel once again like he was a master of the Apocalypse—indestructible and immortal. By the time they had reached the home of their first customer, he had nearly forgotten about Suchai's eerie staring and the unscientific notion that human beings can think about nothing.

"Here we are," he declared loudly, checking off a name on his clipboard. "This is Estelle Nehr. She only has one eye, and she takes care of her husband who's a double amputee. No legs."

Most of Touch-of-Class's customers were septuagenarians. Some were older. And many had visible physical impairments. Jerry had a peculiar habit of reminding Suchai—or perhaps forewarning him—every time they were about to encounter such a condition. Suchai could never tell for certain why Jerry did this. It seemed as if Jerry thought this information would be somehow useful—or maybe interesting. But Suchai found nothing especially informative or entertaining about injury, amputation, illness, or loss. He wondered if Jerry knew anything at all about the atrocities that Cambodia had suffered during the reign of the Khmer Rouge. He wondered if Jerry had even the faintest idea that Cambodians find nothing rare or amusing about missing limbs.

Suchai unlatched the trailer's tailgate, unloaded the nearest lawnmower, and made sure there was a full tank of gas. It was a routine that had become quite familiar to him over the past two months. In fact, it was solely his responsibility. In the entire time that he had worked for Jerry, he had never seen his boss touch the tailgate or lay a hand on a lawnmower. Touch-of-Class had a strict division of labor, and that's just the way Jerry liked it. He had told Suchai that businesses run most efficiently when each worker knows exactly what is expected of him and sticks with his job. Specialization is the key. Productivity is highest when each person acts in accordance with his talents and abilities. "Take me, for example," he had explained to Suchai. "I'm what you call a 'detail person.' I've always been creative like that. So it only makes sense for me to do the more artistic stuff—the finishing touches."

Jerry's primary responsibility was to follow Suchai with a trimmer, leveling out the corners and edges that could not be reached by a mower. He also worked the edger and cleared the clippings off driveways and sidewalks with a blower. He seemed to enjoy his work and often proclaimed that it gave him a chance to express himself artistically. "This is my medium," he had told Suchai. "I'm like a master painter."

The analogy was not entirely unfounded. Jerry was undeniably precise in his work and unmistakably serious. Suchai would often look up from his mower to see Jerry scrutinizing a shrub, trying to decide if another snip was required, or squinting at the line he had just made with the edger, determining its straightness and gauging whether it still needed a little trimming here or there.

Meanwhile, Suchai followed the self-propelled, seven-and-a-half-horsepower Briggs and Stratton mower, row after row, yard after yard, day after day, always keeping *its* pace and not his own. His job required no scrutiny. Aesthetic discernment was a luxury he could not afford. His sole responsibility was to keep up with a fast and unwieldy machine, constantly wrestling it back into alignment and preventing it from wreaking havoc on the customers' flowerbeds.

Jerry and Suchai finished the first five lawns in good time, but on the sixth lawn, Jerry noticed that Suchai's pace had diminished significantly. Although he would never admit it out loud, he knew that Suchai's job was far more strenuous than his own. So, he decided to be gentle about encouraging Suchai to work faster. After all, it was hotter than usual today—and stuffier, since yesterday's rain had taken the form of today's humidity. With all this in mind, Jerry determined that Suchai's current slowness was understandable. A reprimand would not be appropriate, but a pep talk would be just fine.

"Okay," he said as the rig stopped in front of the seventh lawn of the day. "Things are goin' pretty good, but they could go better. I know it's hot and muggy as hell, but we missed a lotta work yesterday. We only got twenty-nine more yards to go if we wanna be caught up by the time the sun goes down. So just suck it in, get tough, and let's get the job done!"

"Jerry," Suchai said, calmly. "Please, do you know? Machine is broken."

"What do you mean?" asked Jerry.

"It's no go by itself," explained Suchai. "It's pushing only."

"Damn!" shouted Jerry. He leapt from the truck and, for the first time since Suchai had been working for him, let the tailgate down. He yanked the lawnmower down from the flatbed and inspected its self-propel mechanism.

"Damn!" he repeated. "Damn thing's stripped balder than a nail! Do you have any idea how much it costs to get these damn things fixed?"

"No," replied Suchai, frankly.

Jerry wondered if Cambodians were simply incapable of understanding rhetorical questions.

"Well, we don't have time to get it fixed today," Jerry declared. "We can't afford to take two days off in a row. We're just gonna hafta keep goin,' as is."

"Maybe can use spare?" Suchai asked, hopefully.

"Nah," said Jerry, "the damn spare doesn't have a self-propel either. Never did. I keep it just in case the engine goes out on the main unit. I hate to tell you this, Mr. Spunky, but it looks like we're just gonna hafta sweat it out for the day."

"Okay," said Suchai, resigned.

Without ado, he took the main unit in hand, pulled the start cord, and began mowing. Jerry began to feel guilty. He refueled his weed trimmer and began tidying the edges and corners of the day's seventh lawn. He tried not to look at Suchai, for fear of the misery he might see on his employee's face. When Suchai was mowing on the south side of the house, Jerry made a point of trimming on the north side of the house. When Suchai was mowing on the east side, Jerry made a point of pruning shrubs on the west side. The few times that Suchai managed to enter his boss's field of vision, Jerry would immediately cast his gaze downward.

He managed to avoid eye contact with Suchai for three more lawns. Finally, on the eleventh lawn, he could no longer control himself. From the corner of his eye, he could see that Suchai's posture had changed dramatically. Normally, Suchai walked upright, with perfect posture. But, now, his torso was slumped sharply forward. Jerry looked more closely, overcome by a morbid sense of curiosity. What kind of misery would he see on Suchai's face? How much sweat would be rolling off his forehead? How close would he be to passing out? Jerry knew he would feel guilty about whatever agony Suchai was suffering, but, somehow, he could not keep himself from looking at his employee more closely.

To his surprise, what he saw was not quite agony. Suchai was slumped, but not from exhaustion. He had discovered that the pressure of his stomach on the handlebar of the mower helped push the machine forward. It was a simple, practical solution to a painful problem. And the look on his face was not one of abject misery. It was the same blank expression that had been annoying Jerry for months. Suchai was meditating while he mowed.

Jerry felt a surge of anger run through his body. He had not wanted to see agony on Suchai's face but felt that a look of agony would have been preferable to that haunting meditative gaze. He resolved to change Suchai's facial expression once and for all.

As soon as they had finished the eleventh yard, Jerry declared a lunch break. Normally, he refused to take such an early lunch. "Full bellies make sluggish workers," he had once told Suchai. "To eat before two is to put a curse on your whole day." But today was different. The humidity was unbearable, and Jerry wanted desperately to give himself a break from Suchai's vexing meditation. His plan was to distract his employee with lunchtime conversation. If he could keep Suchai talking, he could prevent him from making that horrible face.

They drove to a small park overlooking the Gulf of Mexico. Jerry stopped the rig and turned the radio off. As he opened his lunchbox, he saw Suchai reach for the door handle.

"Where ya goin'?" asked Jerry, anxiously.

"Go bathroom," said Suchai.

Fine, thought Jerry, this will give me time to plan a conversation. As he watched Suchai make his way to the tiny latrine on the other side of the playground, Jerry wondered how he would engage such a quiet man in conversation. What topics would Suchai find irresistible? Terrorism? Sex? Scandals in the British monarchy? How rude young people are these days? Jerry suddenly realized he was unaccustomed to making conversation with his partners. Mostly, he teased them, or lectured them, or talked about himself. And now that he really wanted to make one of them talk, he had no idea how to do it.

Suchai emerged from the latrine and began walking toward the rig. Jerry drew a deep breath and mustered all his conversational charm. Then, to Jerry's surprise, Suchai changed his trajectory, headed toward the edge of the playground, and sat underneath a live oak that overlooked the Gulf. Jerry could not see Suchai's face but knew what he was doing.

Jerry's plan to get away from Suchai's meditation had failed, and now he was miffed. He leapt out of the truck and stormed toward Suchai. He did not know what he would say when he reached the live oak, but he knew he had to end this silence as quickly as possible.

"Hey," he said, making sure he spoke loudly enough to foil Suchai's concentration, "aren't you gonna eat?"

"No," said Suchai. "Too early."

"I got an apple, if you want it. It wouldn't fill you up. Just a light snack before we get back to work."

"No," said Suchai. "Thank you."

"I don't blame you for not wanting to eat," said Jerry, desperately trying to fill the empty air with conversation, "what with all them lawns we gotta do this afternoon. You probably don't wanna weigh yourself down, huh? Besides which, lotsa people don't like to eat in this kinda heat. Just kinda makes you feel all heavy, dudn't it?"

Suchai nodded but did not say a word. Jerry felt defeated.

"All right," he said, his tone quickly turning to anger, "I'm just gonna level with you. I'm not the kinda guy to go around tellin' people what they can and can't do with themselves, but you gotta stop spacin' out like you been doin'.' I mean, what if you blank out, and you're not watchin' where you're goin'? A lawnmower's not a toy, ya know. We're talkin' about seven and a half horses worth of power. One second in outer space, and, Wham!, there goes a rosebush. Or, *Wham!*, there goes something worse. I don't even like to think about it?"

"What does it mean, 'spacing out'?" asked Suchai.

"It means not payin' attention," answered Jerry, "and that's exactly what you're doin' when you go into that trance, or whatever it is you do."

"No, no," said Suchai, "Is not true. I am pay attention."

"Come off it," replied Jerry. "You said it yourself; whenever you get like that you're not thinking about anything."

"No, no," said Suchai, "you don't understand. In my country, everybody meditate. It's not mean no pay attention. It's mean pay attention to *everything*. Why? Imagine maybe you have pain. If you think about one thing only, you think about *pain* only. Everything is pain. But if you think about everything, then, pain, it's not the only thing. There is other things, too. You see all of them at same time. This is why I am saying I am thinking sometimes about nothing. You see? I am thinking many things. It's mean I am not thinking one thing. It's mean I am thinking no thing. No thing same as nothing. You see?"

"Not really," said Jerry.

"Okay, no problem," said Suchai. "I explain to you different. If a thought come to my mind, maybe I am hold onto it. Maybe I am not want to let go. It's no good. It's mean I am thinking one thing only. But if a thought come to my mind, maybe I let it go. Maybe I release it. You see? It's good thing. It's mean I am not thinking one thing only. It's mean I am thinking no thing. It's mean I am thinking nothing. You see?"

Jerry had never heard Suchai speak so much before. On the one hand, he was glad that the silence was broken. On the other hand, he was uncomfortable with the content of Suchai's speech, because Suchai had broken the silence only to justify it. This impressed Jerry as a masterfully crafted paradox. In fact, everything Suchai had said sounded like a paradox to Jerry, and the incongruity of it was more than he was willing to tolerate.

"Listen," Jerry said, "this ain't about your theology. This is about the customers."

"What do you mean?" asked Suchai.

Jerry broke eye contact, because he was about to lie and feared that Suchai would be able to see through his dishonesty.

"I mean the customers don't like it when you space out like that," said Jerry. "Whether or not you're payin' attention, they *think* you're in some kinda crazed trance or somethin'. And that's what matters. You gotta remember, these are very old people we're talkin' about. They're very set in their ways. They're not like me, ya know. They got no tolerance for crap like that."

"How do you know?" asked Suchai.

"'Cuz they tell me," answered Jerry, still avoiding eye contact. "They think you're on drugs or somethin.' They're afraid you're gonna rob 'em. And I, for one, happen to care about how they feel. That's the whole reason I'm in this business. Because I like helpin' people. Think about it. Most of these people are knockin' on heaven's door. Their bodies are fallin' apart, and they got no beauty in their lives. Then, I come along, and I tell 'em, 'You may be fallin' apart, but I can make your lawn beautiful.' It gives 'em somethin' to live for. And I'm not about to throw all that away just cuz you like spacin' out on the job. These customers want beauty—not weird expressions. They're very temperamental, you know. Any change in their environment could send 'em over the edge."

Suchai nodded, took a deep breath, and thought about what Jerry had said. Finally, he responded, "Maybe we switch today, yes?"

"What?" asked Jerry, taken by surprise.

"Maybe you mow," said Suchai. "I do detail work. Little while only. Maybe give me short break. "

"What makes you think trimmin' and edgin's gonna be any easier than mowin'?" responded Jerry, defensively. He regretted the words as soon as they left his mouth. Suchai's job was obviously far more strenuous than his own, and any suggestion to the contrary was patently absurd.

"Okay," Jerry continued, trying to salvage the implication that his job is just as difficult as Suchai's, "maybe it's not as *physically* strenuous, but it takes a lotta outa your brain, ya know. Believe me, at the end of the day, I'm exhausted. Mentally, that is. All that detail work requires a lotta expertise. You gotta be thinkin' all the time, and you can only really do it if you've got an eye for art. It's creative work, ya know. It's not just for anybody."

"Jerry," said Suchai, sympathetically, "today is very hot. Very wet. Twice as much work. Twice as fast. Have to push mower myself. Very tired. Very much pain. I must to take my mind off pain. If I meditate, okay. If we switch job, okay. But if we don't switch, if not allow to meditate, impossible."

"Fine," said Jerry. "You win. You get to meditate. But only for today. After that, you're gonna hafta find some other way to control yourself."

Jerry stomped back to the truck and turned on the radio full blast. Suchai sat still beneath the live oak for a few more minutes then returned to the rig with a subtle beatific smile. Jerry wasn't sure if the smile was a smug look of victory or an expression of spiritual bliss. And he wasn't sure which possibility made him angrier. A victorious smile would have been an intentional taunt, and Jerry wanted no reminders that he had just lost a verbal battle to a man who barely speaks English. A blissful smile would have been comparatively innocent but no less a reminder that Suchai was not the one-dimensional peasant that Jerry secretly wanted him to be.

As the big rig headed off for the twelfth lawn of the day, Jerry became more resentful. He refused to speak or make eye contact with his impudent partner. When they arrived at the twelfth lawn, he broke his silence only to announce the name and most obvious physical impairment of the lawn's owner.

"This is Harold Dodge," he said. "He's the guy with the colostomy bag and the dog with the smelly skin condition."

It was one o'clock, and the sun had finally reached its zenith. It was not yet as hot as it would soon become, but it was clearly no longer morning. As Jerry trimmed and edged, he carefully monitored the sound of the lawnmower, determining Suchai's location, and staying as far away from him as possible.

Harold Dodge lived in Crestridge Gardens, an especially low-income subdivision with unusually small yards. Since the next three customers also lived in Crestridge Gardens and had similarly tiny yards, Jerry and Suchai serviced the twelfth through fifteenth yards in less than an hour. Jerry was happy with this pace, but he also realized that they would have to go faster if they were to meet their goal. The Crestridge Gardens clients were the last of the customers that should have been serviced yesterday. It was two o'clock, and Touch-of-Class was only now beginning today's regularly scheduled work.

The temperature had reached its hottest point when Jerry and Suchai arrived at the first lawn of the new business day. Yesterday's rain was thick in the air, and both men were drenched in sweat from shoulder to toe.

Jerry made his announcement. "This is Doris Lynch. She's bug-eyed and has a goatee that'd put Colonel Sanders to shame. I gotta hand it to her, though. She's got one helluva yard."

"I remember," said Suchai.

Doris Lynch's yard was much grander than the ones they had just serviced in Crestridge Gardens. Not only was it much larger, it was much more ornate. There were flowerbeds under every window, each one an explosion of color. There were hibiscus trees, oleanders, a Japanese rock garden, a loquat tree, and a small ornamental pond with a miniature footbridge. The grass itself was thick, lush Floratam, as dark and as green as a Christmas tree.

"She's a beauty, eh?" asked Jerry. "I put in almost everything you see. You might call it my masterpiece,"

Suchai noticed that the grass was glistening and asked, "Why the grass is wet?"

"She's a lawn nut," explained Jerry. "She don't give a damn about water restrictions. She just keeps them sprinklers runnin' day and night. It may be a waste of water, but it's the only way to make a lawn look this good."

Suchai drew a deep breath and unlatched the tailgate. He knew that wet grass meant heavier bags of clippings, harder pushing, and frequent stops to unclog the chute. Floratam was especially difficult because it was a heavy grass and grew very densely.

Since Suchai began his mowing in the backyard, Jerry decided to work in the front. He grabbed the edger and began re-establishing the boundaries between the grass and the concrete. He started with the sidewalk line. The sound of the edger was so loud that Jerry could hear nothing else—not even the lawnmower. It was an ambient noise, so steady that, after a few minutes, it began to sound like no sound at all. The paradox made Jerry think of Suchai's irritatingly paradoxical philosophy. He replayed their lunchtime conversation in his head. He remembered vividly his claim that he is an artist and began to feel self-conscious. As he watched the edger's blade slice through the thick, rich Floratam, hurling blades of grass in all directions, it suddenly occurred to him that his beloved detail work is not really creative. Literally speaking, the grass is creative, because it produces more and more of itself all the time. But Jerry's job was to eliminate the effects of that creativity—to eradicate growth. His job—quite literally—was to destroy nature's progress.

Jerry edged his way up Mrs. Lynch's driveway. There was a thermometer on the porch that read 101 degrees, Fahrenheit. As he turned away from it and redirected his attention toward the edger, his eyes latched onto a sight that startled him. It was Mrs. Lynch herself, standing at her living room window with her bug-eyes bulging more than usual. Jerry gasped. She waved and smiled a big, yellow grin. He was horrified, but he waved back politely, even though he knew he was not concealing his repulsion very well. It was then that he realized he had no real sympathy for any of his customers. His claim to want to bring beauty into their lives was absurd. His enterprise was not so much a service for them as it was a reaction against their twisted faces and bodies. It was *he*—not the customers—who needed beauty.

He crossed the driveway and edged his way down its other side. If lawn maintenance is not a form of art, he wondered, then what is it? The ambient hum of the edger combined with the sight of the rapidly swirling blade to create a hypnotic effect on Jerry's increasingly bewildered mind. He thought of the blade as a furious soldier, deployed to a hostile land and commissioned to kill its enemies without hesitation or remorse. Yes, thought Jerry, that's it! This isn't an art form. It's a war. It's the Apocalypse. Beauty isn't creation, it's destruction. It's cutting back and lopping off. It's looking at the lawn and seeing not the chaotic shape that nature gave it but the rigid shape that I myself gave it through my hacking and slashing.

The blades of grass looked like millions of tiny green fingers to Jerry. They were the greedy, little fingers of Doris Lynch's ancestors, reaching up through their earthen graves and onto the sidewalk. They were always hungry, always grasping. And even if they managed to consume the sidewalk, they would not be satisfied. They would go on to claim Mrs. Lynch, who was their spawn, after all. She was one of theirs, and she already was heading rapidly for the grave. But they wouldn't stop there. They would go on to pull the entire world down to their cold and filthy domain.

This is war, thought Jerry. I cannot give up, because my enemies will never give up. No matter how brutally I butcher them, they will always come back. And so I must fight my fight, no matter how endless or thankless it may be. I will sever and slice and poison and uproot. I will do whatever it takes to keep their selfish little fingers off my perfect, linear beauty.

Just then, Suchai came into Jerry's field of vision. He was toting a catcher full of heavy, wet grass, which he intended to empty into the bed of Jerry's pickup. The very sight of Suchai reminded Jerry of the major battle that had been lost during the lunch break, and his blood began to boil. Jerry no longer thought of himself as the same person who had recently failed in his pathetic attempt to convince Suchai that lawn maintenance is charity and detail work is art. The new Jerry looked back at that lunchtime loser with disdain. He was a killer now, and he was determined to avenge himself.

As Suchai hoisted the grass catcher over the side of the pickup, Jerry grabbed it and wrestled it out of his hands.

"What's going on?" asked Suchai, worried.

"You wanted to switch jobs, didn't you?" snarled Jerry. "Well, let's do it now."

"I don't think it's good idea now," protested Suchai.

"Listen," said Jerry, pointing his finger in Suchai's face, "I'm the one who's runnin' this show. Got it? And I say it's time for a change!"

"Jerry," pleaded Suchai. "Please. Wait. Let's talk."

"So now you wanna talk, huh?" said Jerry. "Well, I'm not payin' you to talk. There's a weed trimmer on the trailer. Now get to work!"

Jerry made his way to Mrs. Lynch's back yard. He attached the catcher to the mower, pulled the starter cord, and began to mow. It had been quite some time since he had operated the old Briggs and Stratton, but it felt great. An edger could only sever a couple dozen ancestor fingers per second, but a thirty-two- inch lawnmower blade could do a hundred times more damage.

Jerry was crazed. Underneath all his middle-aged flab was a fire that had burned up all his braggadocio and wanted to eat something more substantial. He pushed the mower faster than even the self-propel mechanism could have moved it. It seemed the fire was melting his fat, because his body was secreting liquid at an unprecedented rate. Sweat poured off his forehead and into his eyes, but he would not wipe his brow. No matter how badly his eyes stung, he would not take his hands off the grips—not even for a second. This was war, and in war there is no rest. Jerry was happy to have all that power back in his hands. He wondered why he had not commandeered the old Briggs and Stratton years ago. It was the perfect weapon for his war against the ancestors.

After a few minutes of frantic mowing, Jerry noticed that the mighty Briggs and Stratton was leaving large clumps of grass in its wake—a sure sign that wet clippings had clogged the chute. Under normal circumstances, Jerry would have taken the time to stop the engine before unclogging the chute. That was the safe thing to do. But today was no ordinary day. There was a sense of urgency that seemed to hang in the air like yesterday's rain. Stopping the engine and restarting it once the chute had been unclogged would have taken more time than Jerry was willing to spare.

With the engine still roaring, Jerry took the grass catcher off the mower and stuck his hand in the chute. He pulled out a large clot of wet grass, but it was not enough to unclog the chute. So he stuck his hand in the chute a second time—this time even further.

Strangely, the first pain hit him between his shoulders. He thought he might have been stung by a bee. But then he felt a second pain at the knuckles of his right hand. At first it was faint, like a pinprick. Then he realized what had happened, and it became unbearable. He quickly pulled his hand out of the chute. The last thing he remembered before passing out was looking at his mangled hand in disbelief.

J E R R Y   A W O K E   S L O W L Y . The feeling of unprecedented relaxation and the bright whiteness before his eyes made him wonder if he had died and gone to heaven. But then he became aware of a throbbing at the knuckles of his right hand and remembered what had happened. The whiteness was not death's corridor but the ceiling of a hospital room. Jerry looked down at his heavily bandaged hand and marveled at its peculiar new shape. He found himself strangely unable to be horrified by it. Instead, he chuckled at the irony. He had spent his entire professional life setting himself apart from the infirm, and now he was one of them.

As he regained more of his senses, he became aware that Suchai was at his bedside. Struggling to engage the part of his brain that forms words, he stammered and then spoke.

"S . . . Su . . . Suchai," he finally said. "I . . . I'm sorry I called you Spunky. That wasn't very nice of me."

"Okay," said Suchai, "no problem."

"How long have I been here?" asked Jerry.

"You sleep long time," answered Suchai. "But now is morning."

Jerry closed his eyes and felt no compulsion to fill the air between himself and Suchai with noise. He remained silent for what may have been a few seconds or several minutes. Time no longer seemed to matter. In fact, many of Jerry's old preoccupations now seemed unimportant. The customers were waiting for service, and that was all right. The grass was steadily growing, and that was all right. The work schedule to which Jerry had always adhered with unwavering diligence now seemed like the futile invention of a desperate mind. And that was all right, too.

When Jerry re-opened his eyes, a young woman in a white lab coat was standing where Suchai had been. "Good morning, Mister Mistretta," she said, looking at her clipboard. "How are we feeling today?"

"Surprisingly well," answered Jerry.

"That *is* surprising," said the young clinician. "All things considered."

"The war is over," explained Jerry. "And I'm still alive."

"I see," said the scientist, making a new notation on her clipboard. She left the room without saying another word, and Jerry got the distinct impression that she thought he was still too medicated to be rational. But Jerry knew better. Whatever drugs he may have ingested had completely worn off. In fact, he was thinking more clearly than ever before. He drew a deep breath and sat perfectly still. A strange new peace came upon him, as—for the first time in his life—he sat and thought about nothing in particular.

Jan Hodgman

Tanuki

THE BUDDHIST NUN HAD LIVED on Black Bamboo Mountain for over twenty years. She shaved her head after leaving a marriage she could only describe as tasteless. The priest who ordained her thought it might be convenient to have a live-in disciple for various chores and delights, but Koen had other aspirations. After a few wranglings and gropings through morning and evening sutra services, she convinced her ordination master to find a position for her in a remote village temple. And so she had come to Black Bamboo Mountain to live alone and perform the occasional funeral and memorial rites needed by the villagers at the foot of the mountain. In return they brought yen notes in red-bordered envelopes and wheelbarrows with vegetables and sacks of rice eked out from a life on rocky soil. When Koen was off in the mountains gathering wild herbs or meditating up in the stone hut next to the temple graveyard, they would leave their offerings just inside the entryway.

The temple had been abandoned for over forty years before Koen came. The villagers held Black Bamboo Mountain in awe. They found some solace now in having their own village priestess living there, consecrating by her presence a haunted, ominous place full of poisonous *mamushi* snakes and damp clinging spirits. They sensed that the physical placement of the temple buildings, a stone and wood enclave nestled up against a cliff face where a spring charged from underground, somehow gripped unhealthy vapors and unresolved spirits close to earth, a dank torpor invading the grounds. Tales of the exceptional fervor of long-past abbots had been passed down and embellished through generations; village mythology had transformed ardent misanthropes into revered ascetics. The village could only offer meager subsistence to the temple priest and before Koen there had been no one willing to give up the more lucrative congregations farther down the valley, where the rocky soil eroded into broad fertile rice paddies and lush vegetable gardens.

Every morning at four Koen rose from her bedding on the straw-matted floor, dressed in her black monk's robes, lit a stick of incense in front of the memorial plaque dedicated to her aborted baby (her husband had convinced her that the threat of deformity was great since she had contracted mumps during her pregnancy), whispered a short sutra, and climbed the rocky path to the meditation hut. Her feet knew the bumps and turns of the trail even on the darkest of nights, though others found the leaf and moss-covered rocks treacherous.

At the top of the path, the meditation hut nestled at the end of a small well-tended graveyard. Lofty cedars cast perpetual shadows on the five monuments marking the remains of the temple's previous abbots. Koen tended the graves with care, sweeping the leaves daily, changing the water in the bamboo vases every other day, and replacing the *shikimi* greenery and flowers of the season weekly. She gathered the greenery herself from the surrounding woods and grew some of the flowers—chrysanthemums, godetia, peonies—in pots in the few spots of the temple yard that received sufficient sunlight.

Koen lit a candle and a stick of incense in front of the serene Buddha on the tiny hut's altar, then bowed and seated herself in lotus position on her meditation cushion. She gazed out the screen door at the neatly swept moss carpet of the graveyard before beginning her meditation. A sense of profound settledness engulfed her, a feeling of place and connectedness, roots reaching deep into the moss-covered soil and branches reaching high up toward the sunlight and beyond. She struck a brass bell three times to invite the beginning of meditation, each ring of the bell fading into the soulful silence of Black Bamboo Mountain at dawn.

After dinner throughout the harsh winter months Koen gathered up leftover rice and vegetables stewed in soy sauce and scooped them into a tin pan. She pushed open the kitchen door with her elbow and with a loud rising and falling whistle and a clicking of her tongue, called to the tanuki and other needy creatures. Setting the pan at the base of a cliff of red soil, she walked back to the kitchen, slipped her wooden *geta* off outside the door, and took up her post over a sink doing dishes and watching for evening visitors.

Sometimes a greedy gargling and oily flapping of wings would signal that the ravens had caught the scent, their inky shapes almost indiscernible in the waning light. But most often a pair of tanuki, badgerlike animals, would cautiously wend their way toward the pan, one of them making a nervous pass at the food before the smaller tanuki would steal from the shadows and join her mate. Any unexpected noise or disturbance would send the two of them skittering back into the blackness, sometimes attempting to drag the pan with them.

The tanuki of Black Bamboo Mountain lacked the distended stomach of the typical pottery version, like the one appealing to guests in front of the village inn. In the depths of winter, though, their rust and chestnut coats grew thick and fluffy, their earnestness in gulping down the treats Koen left betraying their inability to gather sufficient food on their own. The tanuki so popular in folklore often clutch a jug of *sake* and wear a hat fashioned from a lotus leaf. Dressed in priest's robes, the tanuki is seen as the essence of gratitude, while stories abound of the tanuki as a trickster, a fool, a grateful friend or a malicious nuisance.

Koen knew that most villagers considered tanuki troublesome or even malevolent. Farmers cited examples of raided chicken coops and dug-up sweet potatoes as evidence of their wayward ways. Koen was careful to wait until dark to set out her offerings, knowing that the villagers' uneasiness with the spirits of Black Bamboo Mountain increased with deepening nightfall. Only when there was an unexpected death among the parishioners was it customary for anyone to ascend the darkened steps of the temple gate.

One evening as Koen turned back toward the house after placing a pan of treats in the usual place, she caught the sound of someone walking on the gravel path leading from the temple gate. As she debated whether to hide the pan of food, old widow Kinoshita with the toothless grin waved and called out, "Abbess! Good evening! I've just finished my pickled turnips for New Year's and here's a jar for you!"

Kinoshita-san's husband had been a hard-working farmer, with an un-quenchable thirst for *sake*. He died in a fiery car crash and left a widow of forty-three and two sons. There were many good-natured jokes about widow Kinoshita's husband hunting, even in her present toothless state. She was one of the more frequent visitors to Black Bamboo Mountain, bringing bunches of long white radishes from her garden or a freshly cooked delicacy like the pickled turnips. On her way back down to the village, she'd en-counter other women, shake her head and say with a mixture of satisfac-tion and puzzlement, "Such a lonely life in such a desolate place. A little hair and she'd still have a chance."

Koen usually enjoyed these visits, but this night she was concerned about what widow Kinoshita would say when she saw her feeding the tanuki. "Pardon me, I had some scraps and thought I'd leave them for the 'hungry ghosts,'" Koen said.

Widow Kinoshita clucked disapprovingly, and said, "Everyone knows you feed those damn tanuki. If you ever saw what they can do to a field of sweet potatoes, you'd think twice, but I guess I can't blame you for want-ing some company. They're a little furry for my tastes, but Lord Buddha knows I wouldn't mind a pal of my own. Eeeee-heeeee!" Widow Kinoshita gave a wide-mouthed cackle and bent over in two with her own joke. Koen enjoyed a laugh, too, and the matter was forgotten.

When the winter winds abated and there was no longer a threat of snow, Koen ceased the nightly ritual, fearful that the animals would become completely dependent on her offerings and forget how to fend for themselves. For the first couple of nights that she left off feeding them, she thought she caught a glimpse of the larger tanuki hanging around her kitchen door, and once at dawn she had seen him again scrambling up the path to the hut behind her, but now it had been several weeks since she had seen a sign of them.

On a moonlit dawn in April Koen rose and threw open the shutters to her sleeping room window. For a moment she thought it had snowed during the night, the flash of white on the ground dazzling her eyes. Then she remembered a breeze insinuating itself into her dreams, rattling the shutters, and realized she was gazing on a carpet of freshly fallen cherry blossoms. The dark silhouette of the immense branching cherry tree stood in stark contrast to its blossom-illuminated splendor just the day before. Koen put on her meditation robes, tied the cording around her waist, and, upon lighting the stick of incense in front of the memorial plaque for her lost baby, was filled with a perplexity of anguish and gratitude, a deep recognition of the evanescence of life.

The moon was sinking into the pine-topped hill as she ascended the stone path. The hut seemed to embrace her in her state of deep sensitivity, and lighting another stick of incense before the simple altar, the wafting smoke again spoke to her of impermanence. She thought of a great Japanese Zen master who made the vow to become a monk upon seeing the curl of incense smoke at his mother's funeral. As she bowed toward her cushion, she glanced outside and noticed that even in this season there were needles and leaves and a few twigs scattered over the graveyard moss. She sensed her meditation practice as just this—sweeping, sweeping, sweeping. She sat and breathed deeply, inhaling the smoke and the smell of the woods.

At the first striking of the bell, she thought she heard an answering squeak, an almost imperceptible animal sound from somewhere that felt like deep inside her. With the second ring, there was most certainly a louder high-pitched whimper, a muffled answer to the bell. Koen deepened her concentration and hesitated before the final strike of the bell. Her hand strained in midmotion over the brass bowl, she drew in a breath scented with cloves and sandalwood and expectation. As she tapped the bell for the final ring, quieter than usual, she felt her breath enveloping the little hut. Immediately a jumble of squeakings and squawkings broke out from somewhere under the hut's floor, and Koen joined the clamor with a tumble of merry laughter.

So that's what her tanuki friends had been up to lately! The tiny voices were silenced with a lower growl, and Koen, too, feeling chastised, returned to the source of her sitting with renewed vigor. She intuited rather than felt the motion beneath her, could sense the huddle of warm bodies settle into a collective calm that she, too, was part of.

Sliding the heavy wooden door to the hut closed a couple hours later, she walked to the far side of the structure and noticed a crude tunnel dug precisely under the spot where her meditation cushion sat. Koen squatted to peer into the dark cave and a low growl issued from the indistinct depth. She gave a *sotto voce* version of her rising and falling whistle to reassure the mama, and again sensed rather than saw a relaxing of the brood. Making a mental note to bring an offering of food the next time she came to the hut, Koen started downward toward the temple yard.

Each day of the following week the tanuki under the hut seemed to grow more comfortable with her presence, no longer shushing when she was on her cushion. She followed in her mind's eye the tumblings and cavortings of the little ones beneath her and saw the mama coming and going out the tunnel a few times. One day after an especially deep meditation session, Koen felt a presence over her right shoulder. Upon opening her eyes and turning her head to glance out the screen door, she saw five furry pups crowded around the doorway peering in at the candle on the altar. One of the tanuki shifted its gaze to hers and with two high-pitched squeaks alerted the others, who stumbled over each other toward their tunnel. Koen laughed aloud and clapped her hands in joy, delighted with her new friends.

When she left the hut that morning she saw a few furry faces peeping out of their hole and she bowed respectfully toward them and said in a quiet voice, "Tanuki-sama! Welcome to the celebration!" She reached the bottom of the stairs and looked back up to see a pile of fur rollicking about in the graveyard with squeaks and squawks, like little kittens. The thought came to her that these were the previous abbots revisiting Black Bamboo Mountain in tanuki guise, expressing their gratitude toward the mountain's sanctuary for lives well lived.

That evening as Koen was finishing up the dishes, the bell announcing a visitor in the entryway jangled. She wondered if widow Kinoshita could have died. She had complained of a bad cough around New Year's and each successive report indicated that she hadn't recovered. Just as she thought this, Koen heard the dry hacking of the woman, and for a moment she thought she might be perceiving her from the other side. This kind of event wasn't unusual for Koen, who experienced the boundaries between life and death as permeable. As the coughing subsided, Koen dried her hands and removed her apron, and when she came into the hall to see the old woman standing in the entryway, she blinked hard and then gave a laugh of relief.

"Abbess," the widow addressed Koen, "the villagers are having a meeting at the village hall and asked me to come invite you."

"Maaaaaa, such trouble for an aged woman. I'm sorry to put you out," Koen replied in a formalized manner, wondering what the meeting could be about, requiring her presence at this hour.

"No, no, no, no trouble. Please, come as you are and we'll walk together," said the widow.

Koen took her priest's vestment off a hook near the hallway and draped it around her neck, tossed a shawl around her shoulders and slipped on her outdoor shoes, still wondering what this meeting could be. She hoped the old woman would clue her in along the way, though she didn't feel she could inquire directly. But the old woman chattered on about the moon that morning, the state of her garden, how the village kids were growing so quickly, and Koen couldn't catch any sign of what this was about.

When they arrived at the village hall, the widow pushed Koen through the door ahead of her, and Koen took in the village elders kneeling around the glossy lacquer table, chatting amiably while the women scurried about filling *sake* and beer glasses. Koen bowed formally with her palms together, and in one voice the villagers cried, "Abbotess, welcome!"

The men scooted together making a place of honor for Koen and she said, "Maaaaaaa, such trouble you go to! Don't let me interrupt your fun!"

Upon being seated, the village head placed an empty glass in Koen's hand and gestured for a bottle of beer. "Just a sip among friends," he said, as he poured the glass halfway full. Koen was swept along with the scene and forgot to protest as she nodded in greeting to several of the villagers.

Putting the beer bottle down, the village head shouted, *"Kampai!* Cheers! To our illustrious abbotess, guardian of Black Bamboo Mountain!" and all the villagers shouted, *"Kampai!"* while several of the women rushed to pour themselves a swallow to join in the toast. Koen felt the flush immediately as she sipped the beer, a physical reaction to the concentration of attention fixed on her. The village head cleared his voice in the manner of beginning a formal, memorized speech and said, "Koen-sama. Indeed we are all indebted to you for your years of service as abbotess and protector of Black Bamboo Mountain."

Koen shifted uneasily on her heels, sensing there was something more than just gratitude motivating this meeting and speech.

"For twenty-five years you have faithfully served as our spiritual mentor, performing our memorial rites and funerals in a worthy Buddhist manner, helping our ancestors cross over to the other shore. You have tended Black Bamboo Mountain impeccably, serving the spirits of our departed abbots in an exemplary way, and indeed, have provided us all with a model of Buddhist virtue." The grizzled man lowered his voice to a conspiratorial tone and continued, "I might say I was one of those who was somewhat skeptical of having a woman assume the position of abbot, but I have nothing but words of praise and gratitude to offer you after your fine service."

"'After' my service?" Koen thought. So there is some dissatisfaction, some desire to replace me? This thought came to her not with panic or anger, but with a deep sadness. Black Bamboo Mountain was indeed a part of her, and she a part of it. She sensed how the contentment she had striven for in her earlier days had indeed settled upon her in her solitary life on the mountain. But how could she think of leaving? Above the boom of the village head's voice and the hush of the assembly, Koen strained her ears to catch a curious scratching sound from underneath the floor. No one else seemed to notice.

"We of the village have conferred, and, knowing what a great amount of work it is to keep the grounds of the temple to the extent that you have, we feel that at your stage of life it is only right that you be provided with relief from such an onerous task. We therefore have drawn up a design for a small cottage for your retirement, and Tanaka-san," he nodded with an ingratiating grin toward one of the village elders, a wealthy widower retired from his *sake* and wine delivery business, " . . . has graciously offered a building site at the corner of his property." Again the curious scrabbling of claws on wood focused Koen's attention, a noise that she alone could readily interpret.

"Maaaaa, it has been my duty and, I may say, delight to be a part of Black Bamboo Mountain these twenty years and I most certainly am not complaining about the work involved . . ." Many of the villagers present also saw through the village head's words immediately, knowing how Koen still roamed the forests each spring digging bamboo shoots, and continued to rise earlier than most of the farmers. "But if it is the village's will to have me step down, well . . . I don't know what to say. It's certainly a most generous offer and I will consider it carefully . . ." Her voice became more distant, as if even now she was drifting away from the village. The scratching on the floor had ceased and Koen strained to follow the actions of her invisible companions. What were they up to?

At this point, the broad-shouldered president of the farmer's alliance stood and said, "As a matter of fact, we've consulted with the temple authorities, and it's been arranged for my son, Kazuhiro, to obtain his priest's papers and succeed you as our next abbot. As you may know, the abbot of Tachitani, the next village, plans to step down from his position and Kazuhiro will be taking over the duties of that congregation also."

Koen knew she should be concerned, even alarmed at this turn of events, but even now her attention was concentrated more closely on her five furry companions outside than on the unexpected proceedings unfolding before her. The old woman who had escorted her to the meeting gave her a nudge, and she realized the villagers were awaiting her response.

"Well, I thank all of you for giving me the opportunity to . . ." and at this, a great clatter of glasses shattering on the kitchen floor diverted everyone and the village head's wife appeared in the doorway brandishing a broom.

"Tanuki!" she shouted, and everyone laughed and poked each other, some of the farmers vociferously shaking their heads and launching into tales of other furry encounters. Koen, taking advantage of the pandemonium, stood and excused herself, mumbling something about "her children," and the women nearby giggled and made way for her to leave the hall.

Outside in the chilly evening, Koen gave her whistle then clapped her hands in annoyance, shooing the tanuki on home ahead of her. She was joined by widow Kinoshita, who said, "Abbess, I know it's a surprise but the cottage will really be quite fine. Any one of us would be proud of it. You can do your gardening there, join us for our teatimes . . ." she left off in mid-sentence as she watched Koen hurry toward the temple steps, realizing that though she may have taken her vows out of necessity, the abbess had really been quite content with her life on the mountain. This came as a shock, for it had been Kinoshita who had suggested the plan to the farmers' alliance president when his son lost his job in the nearby town.

"Goodnight, grandmother," Koen called down from the gate of the temple. "Take care in the dark."

"Goodnight, abbess. Think about it. Tomorrow you will see it's a good plan," said the old lady, though she knew now her words were false.

The following day when widow Kinoshita returned to the temple to confess her role in the plan, carrying an offering of bamboo shoots dug by her grandchildren, the abbess was nowhere about. She pushed open the door to the entryway, calling, "Abbess? Koen-sama?" She noticed the place tidied up even more than usual, and in the corner of the entryway was a bundle tied up in a purple scarf with the temple's insignia on it. Resting on top were Koen's vestments. The smell of incense suffused the air and Kinoshita-san, rather than feeling a sense of unease, became aware of a supreme serenity. It was not a new feeling; it was just that her preconceived dread of Black Bamboo Mountain fell away and for once she could appreciate the soulful stillness of the place.

Placing the bamboo shoots next to the bundle clad in purple, widow Kinoshita turned to contemplate ascending the dilapidated steps leading to the meditation hut. Somehow she knew there would be no answer to her calls, and as she closed the door of the entryway and glanced up toward the temple graveyard, she saw amid the gravestones six tanuki pups peering down at her.

Dinty W. Moore

No Kingdom of the Eyes

WHAT MULARKEY SAW to be a tan-robed monk bending over in the fog-hidden field, in the darkness beyond the monastery, by the dim light of an August moon, turned out to be a horse.

But first he saw "monk." He registered for a fleeting moment the oddity that this man wore a tan robe, not the usual gray or black, but he saw the monk nonetheless, on the side of the gentle hill, bending down as if inspecting the soil.

Mularkey hiked toward the distant shape, to say a brief hello, perhaps ask a question. He wanted human connection, some acknowledgement after five days of enforced silence, now that sesshin had officially ended.

He was ten feet from the stooped-over meditator before he realized his mistake. The horse, a tan horse, must have escaped from a nearby farm.

Mularkey hadn't expected the horse, or the fog, or much of anything that had happened. On his meditation pillow just hours earlier he had clearly heard the rattling of a large wooden rosary behind him, and then, as if he had eyes in the back of his head, he saw a nun, a Sister of St. Joseph, walking the aisle of Zen Mountain Monastery. It was a monk, of course, not a nun—it was Anzan with the kyosaku stick—but he heard what he heard, and saw what he saw, even with closed eyes.

Now he struggles to balance this second misapprehension: the horse, or monk, or what. He is no longer even sure which is the illusion, or which is real.

Something is eating the thick grass.

Something snorts, the heated air turning briefly to steam as it escapes the thick nostrils.

Something stirs inside of Mularkey, a giggle. Then a laugh.

He bows to the horse.

"Thank you," he offers.

Jake Lorfing

Old Horse

T SHOCKED HIM, hearing the gunshot echoing back from the hills. Pulling the trigger and feeling the blast had blinded him, emptied his head, stopped his heart. And then, hearing the sigh of the wind, he watched Petunia's once great chest deflate and her sleek brown head relax into the dirt. Oh my, he thought, oh my.

That morning had been no different, an old man going through his rituals. Putting on pants and shoes, peeing, feeding the cat as his coffee dripped. Out the screen door off the kitchen, kicking it shut behind him. Thirty steps, maybe, to the shed—he called it the barn, though the real barn had long since fallen in on itself—this was just a lean-to, really, with a small pen opening to the pasture. Cool for July, and clear, thirty steps maybe, coffee carefully in hand and cat at his heels, out to say hi to Petunia. She was old, twenty-something, not good for much anymore. Didn't follow him on walks like she used to, and she'd never been much to ride. But she liked to be scratched, and she seemed to appreciate him, and she'd been the witness to his getting old. We've gone downhill together, he thought, stepping through the gate.

That morning she beat him to the bottom. Finding her on her side, at first he thought she was dead. Then she jerked in a breath, twitched a front hoof, and turned her head to look at him. He knew. He knew, and unable to meet her eyes, he looked through the fence at the western mountains. Hazy, maybe rain later. He had to touch her ears before he could meet her eyes and the heaviness they shared. She knows. She knows, he thought. Oh my. It all stretched out in front of him, the quiet, the isolation, the loneliness, the sureness of it all, the way it was. Stretching out beside Petunia, feeling her breath through his thin pants, he sipped his coffee. Well, Petunia. . . .

His wife had named her. His first choice was Betsy, but he lost that argument. Lost most of them, he remembered. It had been his wife's idea to move out here, it was her late uncle's place. And buying the colt from a neighbor seemed a good idea, if they were going to call it a farm. And then his wife died, went to the doctor's and never came home.

He heaved himself up, thinking it would be something if the shoes were reversed, if he was the one down and couldn't get up. Petunia couldn't get the pistol for him.

That's what he did, got down the pistol from the back closet. Older than the horse, and used a lot less. He sat at the kitchen table, taking it out of its box, cold, heavier than he remembered, watching his hand shake. It was easier to watch his hand than the pistol. Loaded, no reason why it shouldn't work. He thought about staying at the table, he thought about shooting himself, he noticed the dust balls under the stove and the cobwebs above the door and heard his teeth grinding, and he walked back to the barn. No cat this time; he didn't notice.

Still here, he said to Petunia, getting down and touching his head to her neck. Bones, skin and bones. Surprised you made it this long. So "when's" is the question, he thought. The vet had been out, a while back, and said it would be like this, just one day she wouldn't get up. He'd said he could come out and take care of it, but there really wasn't much to do before then. Once she's down like that, said the vet, you'll need to put her down for good, and they'd talked about how to do it.

And this time he said it out loud. When, Miss Petunia, when do we do this? You and me, girl, you and me. He'd set the pistol down behind Petunia, and now he picked it up and showed it to her, thinking she should know. Her eyes flared wide, she tried to lift her head, and he set the pistol aside. Was it the smell or did she really know, he wondered, her short breaths wetting his hand.

It's time, he said softly, can't stand this any longer. Picking up the pistol, he remembered helping his mother kill chickens, and it shocked him that he couldn't remember killing anything else. He decided on the back of her head, knowing he couldn't look her in the eyes, knowing it would be too much to have her look at him. Petunia tried to lift her head to watch, wild eyed again. Easy girl, easy, easy. Ancient dust danced around her ears on sunlight through the cracks. He smelled manure and urine, gun oil, old horse and fresh hay. He stood, held the pistol a few inches behind her right ear, later remembering the terrible pressure from the trigger, and fired.

That afternoon he didn't feel so bad. He put the pistol away—he didn't remember how to clean it but he tried. And he went out to sit with Petunia, several times. She looked so small, so bony, so decrepit. Are you different, he wanted to know, or am I just now really seeing you? He even lay down against her flank, feeling her, her skin and bones. Smelling her, thinking maybe she was changing already. He'd glance at her head, it didn't really look too bad, but mostly he stayed at her hindquarters.

By mid-afternoon the flies were getting fierce, so he soaked an old towel in some kerosene and put it over her head. It was the best he could think of, and it seemed to help some. Later, the temperature would drop—that'd help, too.

That evening, breaking his routine with a second cup of coffee—he didn't feel like eating—thinking, well, this day's sure been different, the thought that had been at the back of his mind all day slowly worked its way around to the front. There's a dead horse in the barn. Now what? Now what?

There were answers, of course, about what to do with Petunia, but he didn't like any of them, and really didn't want to think about it, just then. Tomorrow. Tomorrow, he thought. Oh my, tomorrow will be a mess.

And in the dimming light he walked to the barn, this time the cat trailing along, and sat down across from Petunia and started to cry.

Victor Pelevin

The Guest at the Feast of Bon

Translated from the Russian by Andrew Bromfield

THERE ARE SEVERAL small, red spheres suspended in mid-air close in front of my eyes. Their color is pure, their form is perfect. They are very beautiful. As I gaze at them I recall what came before.

All of my life I have striven to understand what beauty is. It was everywhere—in a flower and a cloud, in a symbol traced out by a brush, in youthful faces drifting by in a crowd and the fearlessness of a warrior prepared to die. Every time beauty deceived me, pretending to be something new. But then I would recognize it, as one recognizes a familiar melody played on a different instrument. I could sense that the perfection in the flexure of a bird's wing, a sword-blade and an eyelash manifested one and the same inexpressible principle. But I could not grasp its substance. When I thought about this, my mind would begin wandering aimlessly or founder on its own stupidity. And if I did manage to hold this question in my mind, instead of becoming comprehensible, beauty simply disappeared and it was as though I were left contemplating the black mirror-surface of a lake on which only a moment before the sun had been shining.

I would not have been able to explain intelligibly to another person what beauty is, and I doubted that anyone else might be able to do so. The definitions that I had encountered in books on philosophy and art could be discounted. Their awkward and unwieldy logical constructions were entirely devoid of the very quality they attempted to define, and for me that was clear testimony to their pointlessness. But I knew very well that words, which are incapable of explaining beauty, are capable of retaining it and even creating it.

I see several small coins scattered across the red pile of the carpet. They are very close. In my vision they are slightly blurred, and so their gleam seems very gentle and soothing, and yet it retains the chill menace that emanates from metal even in its most peaceful incarnations. But the menace radiating from gleaming steel has always seemed to me quite trivial in comparison with the horror of everyday life, that very thing which from time immemorial has made people bury in books the finest pieces of stone that they have succeeded in mining from the barren quarries of their souls. In the same way people used to bury coins in the ground in times of discord and strife. But disturbances which make it necessary to hoard money happen only rarely in the world, while that endless catastrophe from which people attempt to preserve beauty by hiding it in books is a constant occurrence. This catastrophe is everyday life. And in reality it is impossible to preserve anything—it is exactly the same as attempting to save a man who has been condemned to death by taking his photograph just before his execution. I have only ever known one book that succeeded in doing something of the sort. That was *Hagakure*.

"I discovered that the Way of the Samurai is death." Everything else in the book was simply a commentary on these words, a secondary meaning derived from the application of the cardinal principle to various aspects of life. It was by correlating them with beauty that I first began to understand where its mystery should be sought. On all the roads that led to it the final tollgate was death. And since there was nothing beyond that, death and beauty proved to be essentially one and the same.

The coins on the carpet also remind me of another thing: the most perfect of forms, the circle, is also death, for its beginning and its end are fused into one. And so the perfect life had to be a circle that would be completed and closed if even a single point were added to it. The perfect life is a perpetual vigil at the very point of death, I thought, an anticipation of that second when the gates that conceal the most important thing of all will be flung open. It is not possible to stray from this point without losing sight of that most important thing; one must rather strive constantly to attain it in the face of all the delusions of the world, so that the gleam of beauty may even be reflected in life, and if not endow it with meaning, then at least render it less hideous than it is for the majority. That was how I understood the words of *Hagakure:* "In an 'either/or' situation choose death without hesitation."

Unlike what is hidden in the ground, that which is concealed in words is intended for others or—in the case of the finest of books—for nobody at all. *Hagakure* was precisely one of those books for nobody—Jocho ordered that all of his words that had been recorded on paper should be consigned to the flames. The beauty of this book was perfect because it was not meant to have any reader; it was like a flower blooming on a mountaintop, not intended for human eyes. Its fate was like the fate of Jocho himself, who had intended to follow his lord out of this life, but carried on living at his bidding; to liken books to men, *Hagakure* was a samurai among books, just as Jocho was a samurai among men.

What else was this book? Strange as it may seem, I think it was an expression of love. It was not love of men or of the world. It does not seem to have had any specific object. Or if it did, we cannot discover what it was—Jocho believed that love attains its ideal state when a man takes its secret with him to the grave. That was how he wished to act with the book he had dictated; he is not to blame that this secret was discovered by others.

Not only am I thinking about books, but I can see their spines on a shelf. I shall have no time now to discover what they are about, but that does not distress me. There are too many unnecessary books in the world, and very few that are worth remembering, let alone keeping. Therefore Jocho said that it is best to discard a scroll or a book after reading it. That life is also a book is a comparison as banal as life itself. But what point is there in reading it to the end if all that is important has been stated in the initial pages? And once you have realized this, what point is there in rummaging through the small print of endless footnotes? The best possible thing is for a man to die young, while he is still pure and beautiful, but I did not realize this until my own youth was already over. The only thing left to do was to prepare myself in a fitting manner by altering as much as nature would permit. Admittedly there was something artificial in this, but it was nonetheless better than insulting death, as most do, with the hideous deformity of old age.

Death could be genuinely beautiful. I could spend hours in contemplating images of St. Sebastian, and I wanted to die like him. Of course, I was not inspired by the idea of literally repeating another's experience; I understood only too well what difficulties would be encountered by the organizer of such a bold artistic experiment. I also knew that in reality Sebastian survived being shot with arrows and was beaten to death with sticks (there were no pictures on this subject, the reason being, I suspected, that the rich homosexuals of the Middle Ages and the Renaissance who commissioned the images of the youth in torment might consider the second type of death too literal a metaphor). In any case, the thread of life had to be snapped by my own hands, otherwise death would be transformed into a trite social procedure. Having decided therefore that I myself would loose the arrow that would kill me, I nonetheless trod the path to my ideal as far as possible, by making my body perfect—even more perfect than what I had seen in the pictures.

My obsession with St. Sebastian was not, however, the product of a perverse and sadistic sensuality. What interested me in the story of the praetorian tribune was its spiritual aspect. The blood flowing down over the tree to which he was bound for execution was the blood of a saint, and that endowed the event with special meaning. What I found moving about this death was that it fused beauty with something more sublime.

Sebastian was a saint. He was a vessel inhabited by God, the absolute master of the entire theater of life. Therefore his murder was in reality the murder of God—it was not by chance that in my fantasies Sebastian appealed to the One God on the morning before his execution, after he had risen from his bed that smelled of seaweed and arrayed himself in creaking armor (strange that in my childhood I should imagine the Roman officer's bed in that way—as exhaling a faint aroma of dried seaweed). And how could anything stir the soul more profoundly than the death of the very source of beauty?

The sight of the youth transfixed with arrows affected the sensual side of my soul less than the mystical, although I cannot say that I felt reverence for the European God. We call God that which we are not yet capable of killing, but once we have killed it, the matter is closed. In other words, God exists, but only within certain limits. Nietzsche transgressed these limits with boorish frankness; de Sade acted with a more vile elegance—but even that free intellect could scarcely have imagined Saint Sebastian killing himself with his own hands.

When we kill ourselves, I thought, it is an attempt to kill the God dwelling within us. We are punishing him for condemning us to torment, we are attempting to match him in omnipotence, we may even usurp his function by putting a sudden end to the puppet show he began. He may create the world, but it is within our power to dissolve it into nothingness; insofar as God is simply one of our ideas, suicide is by definition the murder of God. And moreover it can be repeated an endless number of times, as many times as there are people capable of resolving to take this step, and each time God ceases to be God, vanishing forever into the darkness. How many gods whose names people do not even remember have already vanished into that nothingness! But to save your God—and yourself with him—is in any case impossible, no matter how many times you click the camera-shutter before the execution.

I was once photographed touching my lips to a rose. When I saw that picture I realized that no more pre-execution photographs needed to be taken; there was no longer anything to restrain me from taking the final step.

And yet for some reason I waited. Of course, I had no need to nurture my will to die—it was like a wild beast that had been living in my soul since I was a child. But this beast had previously been on good terms with the other tenants: in addition to death, I had many other passions. Death was an obliging odd-job man—he could be the co-author of a book, the theoretician of an aesthetic credo and even the invisible witness to an orgy of love. I suppose we were friends. But I had not planned to appear as a client in his ghastly barbers shop until a certain apparently unremarkable event occurred.

It was the thirteenth of July several years ago. I am quite certain of the date because I remember it was the first day of the Feast of Bon. The mountain road along which I had been walking led me to a small village. At the gates of the village were the dying remnants of pyres, which had been built, as always on that day, so that the spirits of the people's ancestors might find their way home. It was already evening: there was a smell of burnt hemp in the air. I remember some bird calling loudly several times. Strangely enough, there were no people at all around—the only person I saw was a little girl clutching an armful of flowers, whom I met on the road beside the village. She walked straight past without giving any sign that she could see me. I halted and gazed for a long time at the smoke rising from the pyres. Gradually peace descended upon me; everything I had been thinking about was forgotten. And then a page of *Hagakure* rose to the surface of my memory. I saw it as clearly as though some invisible hand had opened the book in front of my eyes:

"Is man not like a mechanical doll? He is made most skilfully—he can walk, run, and jump, even speak, although he has no spring inside him. But next year he may easily find himself a guest at the Feast of Bon. Truly, in this world all is vanity. People invariably forget this . . ."

People do not visit each other's houses during the Feast of Bon; the text referred to spirits. Its meaning was that we are all fated to die and become spirits.

"But who am I in reality?" I thought, and a shiver ran down my spine. "Here I am standing in front of these locked and bolted houses. I have come here along the road, attracted by the smoke of the pyres. Did I think last year that I would find myself here at this time? No one is expecting me here, but nonetheless I am a guest of this mountain village. I am a guest at the Feast of Bon. At this very moment. Then is there any difference between the living and the dead?"

A window that had long been nailed shut in my mind swung open and I suddenly recalled a ceremonial procession that I had seen as a little boy.

This was a very important memory for me. It marked the boundary that separated me from my childhood. Something strange and frightening occurred in my soul as the procession was moving past our house, bearing along an altar on a litter. The older I became, the less I understood what had happened on that day. The event itself lived on, vivid and colourful, in my memory, but its imprint was entirely devoid of any content and meaning that might allow me to explain what could have produced such an indelible impression on me. Although I could remember the cords on the altar and even the copper rings on the priest's staff, it was essentially a memory about nothing. All that was left of it was the outer casing, like the chitinous shell of a long-dead wasp—externally the form, color and line had been preserved, but inside it there was nothing but emptiness. "Probably," I thought, "there never was anything else, it is simply that in childhood every one of us is something of a magician, and we know how to fill this emptiness with our own fantasies, and they become reality for us."

But in that moment of clarity and peace as I stood beside a dying pyre I experienced once again what had affected me so profoundly many years before. And then afterward I forgot it again—probably because I was not able to express the essence of this experience, and we can only retain in consciousness those things that we have managed to deck out in words. When the moment had passed, all that remained in my memory was the phrase "a guest at the Feast of Bon," everything else had vanished or faded away. The memory had become shallow and empty once again, but I knew that something very important would return to me at the moment of death.

Looking back, I can see it was on that day that my desire to die became simple and sincere. Although there is a somewhat comical ring to the words "looking back" in the present situation.

The Way, said Jocho, is something superior to righteousness. I had assumed that these words referred to the most famous line in *Hagakure,* the one that children learn in school even in our inferior times: "I have discovered that the Way of the Samurai is death." To die was a very righteous act, this much was clear at least from the fact that all the holy men and saints without exception had acted in this way, even the Buddha himself. But how was it possible to traverse the Way in a single moment? I pondered over this at length. The nub of the matter was that in any case there was no other possibility: together with life, death is contained within the single moment that is all that exists; it is its authentic goal. It is death that consummates the present instant of time, no matter how many tens of years its incessant self-transmutation might continue. This was a cold and rational explanation, resembling the proof of a mathematical theorem.

But death was also the Way in another, poetic sense. Perhaps because I had spent my life trying on and wearing various masks, there was nothing I valued so highly as sincerity. If a man treads the Way of Sincerity, said the ancient verses, the gods will never turn their faces away from him. But what was the Way of Sincerity? I knew of no answer better than the verse by the unknown samurai in the tenth volume of *Hagakure*:

> *Since everything in this world*
> *Is no more than a puppet show,*
> *The Way of Sincerity is death!*

To follow the Way of Sincerity meant to live every day as though you were already dead, said Jocho. I had lived the greater part of my life the wrong way around—I had been like a dead man who believed that he was still alive. But what I experienced in that mountain village at the Feast of Bon gave me the strength to embark on the Way of Sincerity, which consists of a single step. Following that Way I have arrived at my final rendezvous with beauty and death. It is not possible to be closer to death than I am at this moment. But I do not see beauty. Or rather, I do not see that beauty which I expected to find.

I see a shoe and a blood-spattered trouser-leg, foreshortened as they would be if a football had eyes and saw the leg of a player. Behind them is a bookcase with four empty shelves; together with the leg, they form a shape that resembles the hieroglyph for "Way." So this is what the Way of the Samurai looks like in reality. It might have made one laugh. Or cry. But all that is left to me is to drift on along the level shoreline of this relentless thought, gazing at the lightning-flash of the blade frozen in midair and the distorted faces of the people who have just—at the second attempt—severed my neck.

Hakagure says that a man whose head has been cut off can commit one final act. When I was alive I regarded this statement as rumor from the realm of stories of the miraculous, like the stories of Ueda Akinari that I used to read as a little boy in the bomb shelter during the nighttime raids. Now I know that it is true. As I slashed open my belly, I thought of *Hagakure,* and this memory has stretched out to fill the whole of my long journey toward death, becoming my final act—which can perfectly well be a thought.

But it is not like the ordinary thoughts of an ordinary man. It is not like anything else at all. It is as though a spectral rosebush has blossomed in empty space, only to drop its leaves and disappear forever the very next instant—like lungs that have come into being for a single breath. This bush is my mind. It is also my final thought. I can see the point at which all the threads supporting my life converge. How strange, it was there in plain view, and yet when I was alive I did not notice it. But now that this rose has appeared on my vanishing bush, I shall not be able to press my lips to it. Strangest of all is the fact that even after so many readings of *Hagakure* I failed to discover in it the keys to my locks, although they were hanging there in plain view.

Take, for instance, the passage about the man living in China who decorated his clothes and furniture with images of dragons. So immoderate was he in this that he attracted the attention of the dragon-god. And then one day a real dragon suddenly appeared outside the Chinaman's window, following which the poor fellow died of fright. "He must," Jocho remarks melancholically, "have been one of those who utter big words but actually behave quite differently." In my life, death was such a dragon, it was the sap with which I nourished not only my books, but even my very name, writing it in the hieroglyphs for "a devil enchanted by death." I was a proud man and I promised myself that I would be able to look the dragon-god in the eye when he appeared before me, and that my deeds would live up to my words. Even more than that, I myself went out to meet him. But who was that dragon-god?

In my childhood I read and reread many times a tale in which a beautiful prince met his end in the jaws of a dragon. I repeated one passage to myself so often that I came to know it by heart:

"The dragon began to crunch up the prince in his jaws. As he was torn apart the youth suffered unspeakable torment, but he bore it until the monster had dismembered his entire body. Then the prince was suddenly made whole and he leapt out of the dragon's jaws. There was not a single scratch on him. But the dragon fell to the ground and died."

In his mouth the prince had a magical diamond, which always brought him back to life. But I cared nothing for this diamond—in my enchantment and excitement at the closeness of death, I was outraged that the prince had escaped unscathed. Eventually I hit upon a way to make this story perfect. All I had to do was cover over part of the text with my fingers:

"As he was torn apart the youth suffered unspeakable torment, but he bore it until the monster had completely dismembered his body. Then the prince fell to the ground and died."

I have attempted to deal with my life in the same way as I did with that story. I have attempted to kill the prince, in the belief that there is nothing more beautiful than beauty that is dying. That seems funny now. But the funniest thing of all is that I saw myself as the prince.

In actual fact I was that dragon. And now that the dragon has fallen to the ground and died, the prince has leapt out of his mouth and there really is not a single scratch on him. The prince cannot be killed, no matter how hard the dragon may try. He can neither be bitten nor scratched, although he has no diamond in his mouth, or even a mouth to put it in. I know this for certain, because I can see him, as it was promised that I should beside the pyre in that empty mountain village. I know that it is he, because I have seen him before.

It was a long, long time ago. A festive procession was making its way past our yard. Walking in front was a priest wearing the mask of a celestial fox and swinging a staff with copper rings jangling on it. Those walking behind him were carrying a trunk for offerings, and that was followed by a black and gold altar crowned by the golden bird Hoo, gleaming brightly in the sun. On the outside of the altar there were red and white cords, small railings and lots of bright gilt. But inside there was simply a cube of emptiness. By contrast with the brilliance of the summer day the emptiness seemed to me like a segment of the darkness of night, and I felt afraid, because I sensed that this volume of nothingness, swaying in time with the movement of the crowd, ruled over the sun, the festival, and the merry people like some primordial prince—and having sensed that, I realized that the altar was not swaying in time to the procession; it was the whole of surrounding space that was swaying in time to the movements of the cube of emptiness in the altar, because the entire world including myself, the sun, the earth, and the sky was inside it; my parents were inside it, and all the living and the dead and many, many other things. I felt afraid and I ran away from the altar and tried to hide in the house. But as though at the black prince's command, the crowd poured into our courtyard and rampaged for a long time below our very windows . . .

Since then I have been hiding from the prince. I have concealed myself from him in the same way as I covered up with my fingers the lines that made my favorite story different from what I wanted it to be. But that does not mean that he stopped seeing me—it was I who stopped seeing him.

Not only was the dragon blind, he was also rather stupid. He did not recognize the prince even when they met over a page of *Hakagure*.

Our body receives life out of emptiness, Jocho reminded us, but I had thought that was dry scholasticism; to be quite honest, I believed that he was merely paying tribute to the superstitions of his age, like Montaigne, who interrupts his deliberations from time to time in order to stand rigidly to attention before Catholic dogma. Even on the lips of Jocho, existence where there is nothing seemed to me to be a nonsense, and I took the words about a puppet show for an expression of his male nihilism. The muscular little puppet was engaged in important business—waving its sword about, preparing to rip open its own belly. What a preposterous caricature my life was. But can a human life ever be anything but a caricature?

I thought I was a guest at the Feast of Bon, but I was merely a puppet. Now that puppet will finish thinking the single solitary thought remaining to it and vanish, leaving behind the puppet-master, who once stared the puppet in the eyes from out of a palanquin with an altar one hot summer day at noon. Where should I have sought him? Where was he hiding, the one who constructed my mechanism? To hide was probably the one thing that he could never have done. But it is still not clear where he should be sought, because apart from him there is nothing. Perhaps that is why nobody can find him? Although people have not sought him now for a very long time.

But there is no tragedy in that. People are not a mirror into which he gazes, hoping to see himself; they are puppets playing out show after show under his gaze. In order to make me dance before him, he has no need to insert a whale-bone spring into me. I am simply his thought, and he can think me just as he wishes. But since I can neither see him nor touch him, he is also simply my thought. And here, in collision with itself, my mind falters to a halt.

Perhaps my attempt to reach out and touch the puppet-master with my sword was an expression of sublime revolt against the heavens? But it would seem not. More likely it resembled some monstrous joke at which one cannot stop laughing precisely because it is so monstrous. Even killing the puppet turns out to be impossible. Puppets do not die—one simply ceases playing with them. All the time the prince was pretending to be a dragon, the dragon was plotting his death. No doubt I was a wicked puppet. But he who played with me is good. And so I can see the most important thing, I can see my real self—him. Or rather, he can see himself, but that is the only way it can be. And my knowing that makes everything else unimportant.

And now, eternally beautiful, invisible to all but himself, he turns his gaze away from me, and Yukio Mishima vanishes. Only he remains. The one, the only guest at the Feast of Bon, who comes eternally to visit himself. And Mishima's head, mutilated by a clumsy sword-stroke, rolls on and on across the red carpet, never to reach its edge.

Cathy Rose

Buddha in a Box

THINKIN' ABOUT TAKING a walk down to the corner store. Thinkin' about saying hi to the Chinese lady that works there. Nice lady, pretty lady, owns the place. Saw a little gold box round her neck yesterday. Asked her what it was. Told me it was Buddha sittin' in the box. "That's Buddha!" I said. Didn't mean to embarrass her, guess I did. Tiny little fat guy in there. Chinese lady's a Buddhist.

Thinkin' about writing a letter to my mamma. Tell her San Francisco is very fine. Tell her I've adjusted, ain't got in no trouble, ain't hanging out with the wrong crowd. Thinkin' about that note she left me saying, "Walter Rountree wants to marry me, son, you gotta get outa that room." Thinkin' about getting me a telephone, doing some talking. Thinkin' about who I'd call up. Maybe call my mamma, wouldn't even have to write her, could talk to her. Tell her the Greyhound trip out here wasn't so bad 'cept for a fat ol' guy sat on top of all the sandwiches she made me. Tell her I ate 'em anyway. Tell her I found my own life like she said I ought to. Tell her it's okay she married Walter Rountree. Tell her I'm my own man now.

Thinkin' about getting me a girlfriend. Saw a few pretty ones on the stoop yesterday. Called me "big boy." I said, hi. One of 'em had red lips. Thinkin' I'd like a girlfriend with red lips. Thinkin' about buying a Bic pen. Make a list, handsome fellah, plan your future! Hey, on the bus saw *Lives of the Rich and Famous* off a army guy's TV watch. Wouldn't mind being famous, wouldn't let it go to my head, could handle it.

Thinkin' about walking down to the corner store, saying hi to the Chinese lady, saying hi to the Buddha. Thinkin' about changing religions out of First Baptist and over into Buddhism. Thinkin' about being a Booo—dist, a Boo—ooooo—dist! Get me a little guy in a gold box. Hang it round my neck and look at it in the mirror. Wave to it. "Hey, Booo-dah! Hey!"

About the Contributors

Translator **Andrew Bromfield** studied Russian at Sussex University, England. He has lived in Russia for long periods, where he was the co-founder and editor of the journal *Glas,* establishing its reputation for quality translations of contemporary Russian literature. His varied career also included teaching Russian in Ireland, and English in Soviet Armenia, and working for the Russian airline Aeroflot. He now lives and works in rural Surrey, England. He is best known for translating all of Victor Pelevin's works that are in English, several of which have been shortlisted for major prizes. His translations have been published in *Grand Street, The New York Times* and *The New Yorker.* His latest book is *The Winter Queen* by Boris Akunin (Random House, USA). Soon to appear is *Monumental Propaganda* by Vladimir Voinovich. He works with a Buddha beside his desk, and says he has no formal connection with Buddhist organizations, but is trying to build up a viable routine of Buddhist practice. "But that will take a long time."

Sharon Cameron is Professor of English at Johns Hopkins University, the author of six books and a practitioner of Vipassana meditation. The excerpt in this volume is from *Beautiful Work: A Meditation on Pain,* published in 2000 by Duke University Press and reprinted by permission.

Lama Surya Das is an authorized lama in the Nyingma school of Tibetan Buddhism, and a well-known Western Buddhist teacher, leading retreats all over the world. He has written several books, including *Awakening the Buddha Within* and *Letting Go of the Person You Used to Be*. He spent thirty years studying Zen, Vipassana, yoga, chanting, and Tibetan Buddhism, and twice completed the traditional three-year meditation retreat at his teacher Dilgo Khyentse Rinpoche's Tibetan monastery. He and his wife, Kathy Petersen, and their dog, Lily, live in Arlington, Massachusetts, and Dzogchen Ösel Ling, a new retreat center outside Austin, Texas.

Doris Dörrie was born in Hanover, Germany, in 1955. She studied drama in the United States and continued her studies at the Academy of Television and Film in Munich, where she lives and works. She's the author of several novels and short-story collections, and has directed many films including *Enlightenment Guaranteed* and the feminist comedy *Men*.

Oregon writer **Martha Gies** began publishing nonfiction in the mid-seventies and later studied fiction with Raymond Carver at two summer arts workshops. Her short fiction now appears widely in literary reviews; she teaches writing and has earned several fellowships and grants. A convert to Catholicism and an activist for human rights, Gies is connected to Zen Buddhism through the contemplative writings of Thomas Merton. She studied the Urasenke way of tea under the late Soju Moriyasu.

Francesca Hampton teaches English as a second language at Cabrillo College in Aptos, California. As a backpacking traveler in the 70's and 80's, she has made three long trips to Asia and is a long-term student of Tibetan Buddhism under Lama Thubten Yeshe, His Holiness the Dalai Lama, and others. She helped to found the Vajrapani Institute in Boulder Creek, California. Her short stories have been published in *The Sun* and *Eratica* magazines and the anthologies *Best of the Sun* and *Stories of the Spirit, Stories of the Heart*. More of her fiction appears on her website, members.cruzio.com/~cesca. "Greyhound Bodhisattva" was inspired, she says, by the life stories of Tibetan immigrants in America, including one incarnate tulku who actually did visit the bus station in San Francisco in the 1980s just to talk "casually" with those in greatest need. The story was also influenced by an account in

David Snellgrove's *Three Lamas of Dolpo* of a lama who routinely gave assistance to villagers by taking the form of a wrathful deity in a dream state.

Keith Heller was born in 1949 in Moorhead, Minnesota, and although he now lives in California, has also inhabited Japan, Spain, and Argentina. He's studied Theravada Buddhism for over thirty years and is a member of the Buddhist Publication Society of Sri Lanka. His fifth novel, *The Woman Who Knew Gandhi*, was published by Mariner Books in January 2004. "Memorizing the Buddha" will be incorporated into *A Forest of Voices*, the first in a trilogy of novellas about the early history of Buddhism.

Marie Henry is a San Francisco–born poet and short fiction writer whose work has appeared in numerous literary magazines including *Yellow Silk, Exquisite Corpse, Apalachee Quarterly,* and anthologies including *Bite to Eat Place, Only Morning in Her Shoes,* and *Full Court: A Literary Anthology of Basketball*. She's currently working on a book of prose and poetry about swimming, illness, and healing. Her journey through chronic fatigue immune dysfunction led her to Buddhism and Spirit Rock Meditation Center in Woodacre, California. Vipassana breathing meditation came as a natural outflow from life as a long-distance swimmer.

Jan Hodgman ordained and practiced Zen under Harada Sekkei Roshi in Japan from 1985 to 1993. She is now active as a writer, winning prizes and publishing widely in literary magazines. She is endlessly revising a memoir, *The Other Shore: Eight Years in a Japanese Monastery,* and is at work on a novel. She lives on Fidalgo Island, in the state of Washington.

Though **M.J. Huang** isn't a Buddhist, her personal spirituality resonates with elements from Buddhism and Hinduism. She was educated at Minnesota State University and the American Film Institute. She has traveled throughout the United States, including to the soulful stone towers of the Badlands in South Dakota. She has written six screenplays, a novel, and a nonfiction book about the creative process of screenwriting; she's currently working on a collection of short stories.

Pico Iyer is the author of several books about the romances between cultures, including *Video Night in Kathmandu, The Lady and the Monk, The Global Soul,* and *Abandon.* He wrote the text for the book *Buddha: The Living Way,* has been traveling in the Himalayas for thirty years and has lived on and off for sixteen years in Buddhist Japan.

Keith Kachtick is the senior instructor for the Lineage Project, a Dharma-based nonprofit organization, based in the South Bronx, that offers meditation and yoga classes in New York City youth prisons. He's written for *Esquire, Texas Monthly,* and *The New York Times Magazine,* among other publications. His novel *Hungry Ghost,* from which the story in this volume is adapted, was published by HarperCollins in 2003 and widely reviewed.

Anne Carolyn Klein (Rigzin Drolma), Professor of Religious Studies at Rice University in Houston, Texas, has written four scholarly books on Buddhism including *Meeting the Great Bliss Queen.* This is her first published short story. Since 1970 she has studied and practiced with leading lamas from several Tibetan traditions and was given rein to teach in 1995. Founding director of Dawn Mountain, a Tibetan temple, community center, and research institute in Houston (www.dawn-mountain.org), she teaches contemplative practices and, with Phyllis Pay, Buddhism in the Body™ workshops. She also invites and translates for eminent Tibetan lamas. She shares all this and life in general with therapist and Buddhist practitioner Dr. Harvey B. Aronson, cheered on by lovebird Longchen Luli and parakeet Pede Belden Birdie, successors to the late sainted budgerigar Ms. Mani Padi.

Jake Lorfing lives in Austin, Texas. "Old Horse" is his first short story. It was written midway through a two-week solo retreat at a Shambhala meditation center in July 2002, upon hearing gunshots in the valley below.

Margo McLoughlin is a writer and storyteller, originally from British Columbia, but currently living in Cambridge, Massachusetts. Before attending Harvard Divinity School Margo served as a cook at Insight Meditation Society in Barre, Massachusetts, where she did bake the occasional cake. A student of Pali and Sanskrit, Margo translates the *Jataka* (stories of the Buddha's former lives) from Pali and performs her own adaptations. Her first CD, with musical accompaniment by Doug MacKenzie, was released in the spring of 2004. See her website www.jataka.org for details. Her short fiction piece "Flying" was published in the award-winning anthology *Takes* (Thistledown Press, 1996). Her nonfiction writing has appeared in numerous publications in British Columbia. She has also published a little bit of fiction and nonfiction in various places.

Dinty W. Moore is the author of *The Accidental Buddhist: Mindfulness, Enlightenment,* and *Sitting Still* (Algonquin, 1997) and other books. He is an NEA Fiction Fellow and has written stories and essays for *The New York Times Sunday Magazine, Utne Reader, Crazyhorse, The Southern Review,* and *Arts & Letters*. His Buddhist practice includes study with many teachers, but he suffers from a tendency to wander.

Victor Pelevin, Hinayana practitioner for eleven kalpas, is the author of many books including *Omon Ra* and *The Life of Insects*. Born in Moscow in 1962, he has established an international reputation as one of the most interesting of the younger generation of Russian writers. *Time* magazine described him as "a psychedelic Nabokov for the cyber age." He has written for *The New York Times Magazine* and *Grand Street* and was selected by *The New Yorker* as one of the "Best European writers under 35." His novels include *Buddha's Little Finger* and the prizewinning *Homo Zapiens*. Pelevin is at work on a new novel, *The Helmet of Horror,* a retelling of the myth of Theseus and the Minotaur.

Judith R. Peterson, who recently moved to South Dakota, says: "Biography is the past story, a past moment that no longer exists. This recitation of the previous—this is who I was then—lacks relevance for me in this context, which is my exclusive context of this moment—which, of course, is the only moment that I have. So instead, I would like to share with you my present project and its purpose. I am illustrating *The Jataka or Stories of the Buddha's Former Births* edited by E. B. Cowell. The illustrations are searchlight beams that go from my heart to the material and back—they show me where I am on this Buddhist path. When I am done with that, who knows what the future holds? Like the past, it really doesn't exist."

Gerald Reilly's fiction has been published in *The Gettysburg Review, The Virginia Quarterly, Prairie Schooner,* and *Image*. "Nixon Under the Bodhi Tree" won an O. Henry Award in 1999. His fiction often portrays characters facing spiritual crises, sometimes in a Buddhist context. His Buddhist background is varied, but he started by studying with Lama Pema Wangdak at the Vikramasila Foundation in New York City, and soon attended H.H. Sakya Trizin's Lam Dre teachings in Rajpur, India. He lives and teaches writing and literature at Bloomfield College and Montclair State University in Northern New Jersey.

Cathy Rose read her first Buddhist books in high school. "I was one of those kids like in the Matt Groening "Life in Hell" cartoon," she recalls, "where the teen is sitting on the floor of his messy room meditating and the mother sticks her head in bugging him and the kid yells, 'Shut up, I'm meditatin'!'" She moved on toward a more in-depth reading of Buddhism in college and has sustained the interest ever since. Her Ph.D. in clinical psychology is from California Institute of Integral Studies in San Francisco, a school whose focus is on the intersection of Eastern and Western disciplines. During her training, she explored some of the connections between psychoanalytic thought and Buddhism. She now works as a psychologist in private practice in San Francisco. In her fiction-writing life, she's pursuing an MFA in creative writing at San Francisco State University. Other stories have appeared in the literary magazines *Rosebud, Fourteen Hills,* and *Transfer*.

John Rueppel grew up in St. Louis, and is now a Montessori teacher and budding writer living in Boulder, Colorado. He is studying Zen with Gerry Shishin Wick Roshi at the Great Mountain Zen Center in nearby Lafayette. He is working on a historical novel set in India and is also the editorial director of campaign-earth.org, an online environmental website.

Kira Salak, a daring traveler and former track star, has been studying Theravada Buddhism under Matthew Flickstein and Ginny Morgan while pursuing a Ph.D. in English/creative writing at the University of Missouri–Columbia. She is the author of *Four Corners: One Woman's Journey into the Heart of Papua New Guinea,* as well as the upcoming book, *To the World's End.* A contributing editor at *National Geographic Adventure* magazine, her work can be found in *Best American Travel Writing 2002, Best American Travel Writing 2003,* and *Best New American Voices 2001.* She has been learning Mongolian in hopes of walking across that country.

Leah E. Sammel is the proud mother of two small children. She participates in a Vipassana meditation group near her home in San Antonio, Texas; her current meditation practice is metta, or lovingkindness.

Merry Speece has published two chapbooks of poetry and been a recipient of a state arts commission fellowship in prose. A work combining prose and poetry, *Sisters Grimke Book of Days,* was published as a chapbook in 2003 by Oasis Books, in England. She has spent most of her life in rural Ohio and presently lives in the village of West Liberty. Though she has never had a desire to join religious groups or practice a particular religion, she felt some affinity with the teachings of the Buddha, which she first learned about in a comparative religion course. "That the Buddha said 'Life is suffering' made me laugh," she recalls. Through the years she has found Buddhist teachings useful not only in dealing with illness, but also as a source of poetic language and interesting stories.

Marilyn Stablein hitchhiked to Nepal when she was nineteen, and stayed for over six years living, traveling, and practicing in and around the Himalayas. Her memoir, *Sleeping in Caves: A Sixties Himalayan Memoir* (Monkfish Publishers, 2003), tells the story of that time. Her eight books include *The Census Taker: Tales of a Traveler in India & Nepal* and *The Monkey Thief* (Shivastan Publishing, 2003). She's also an artist, working mostly in assemblages and collages. She was represented in the 2003 Cologne, Germany, and Kingston, New York Bienniales. With her husband she owns and operates Alternative Books, a bookstore, and The Uptown, a jazz club, both in Kingston, New York.

Ira Sukrungruang is a first generation Thai-American born and raised in Chicago. He spent a great deal of time during his childhood at Wat Dhammaram, the first Theravada Buddhist temple in the Midwest, where he learned the teachings of Buddha. His essays, stories, and poems have appeared in *North American Review, Witness, Another Chicago Magazine,* and other literary journals. He is the co-editor of *What Are You Looking At? The First Fat Fiction Anthology* published by Harcourt Brace. Currently, he teaches creative writing at SUNY Oswego and is working on his memoir, *A Normal Thai Son.*

A native Californian and former merchant seaman, **Mark Terrill** was a participant in Paul Bowles's writing workshop in Tangier, Morocco, and has lived in Germany since 1984, where he's worked as a shipyard welder, road manager for bands, cook, and postal worker. He's published a lot of books with small presses. Some of the more recent include *The United Colors of Death,* from Pathwise Press; *Here to Learn: Remembering Paul Bowles,* from Green Bean Press; *Kid with Gray Eyes,* from Cedar Hill Publications.

Easton Waller teaches comparative religions at Saint Leo University, near Tampa, Florida. He is married and has three sons, ages six, eleven, and seventeen. He is a practitioner of Theravada Buddhism, which he studies through his spiritual mentor, Ajahn Keerati Chatkaew, a Thai monk who resides in Stockton, California. His work has appeared in the magazines *Tricycle: The Buddhist Review, Buddhadharma, Parabola,* and *New Thought,* and he's nearly finished writing his first novel, a story about a group of Theravada monks who establish a temple in gangland California with the intent of teaching at-risk Southeast Asian American kids the Buddhist virtues of nonviolence and sobriety.

Kate Wheeler has written two books of fiction, one of short stories, *Not Where I Started From,* and a novel, *When Mountains Walked;* and articles about travel as well as Buddhism for a range of publications. She has received a Guggenheim Fellowship, an NEA, a Whiting Award, two O. Henry Awards, and has been included in *The Best American Short Stories* and *The Best American Travel Writing.* She also teaches meditation, having practiced Buddhism since 1977 under a variety of Western and Asian teachers and briefly ordained as a nun in Rangoon, Burma. She currently lives in Somerville, Massachusetts.

Jeff Wilson lives with his wife in Chapel Hill, North Carolina, where he is pursuing a Ph.D. in religious studies, specializing in Buddhism in North America. He's a member of the New York Buddhist Church, and contributing editor for *Tricycle: The Buddhist Review* and *Killing the Buddha.* His first book, *The Buddhist Guide to New York,* was published by St. Martin's Press in 2000.

Diana Winston is the founder of the Buddhist Alliance for Social Engagement (BASE) Program and served as the associate director of the Buddhist Peace Fellowship in Berkeley, California. She has been practicing Vipassana meditation since 1989, including spending 1998 as a Buddhist nun in Burma. She is the author of *Wide Awake: A Buddhist Guide for Teens* and is currently teaching Dharma and engaged Buddhism while training as a Vipassana teacher under Jack Kornfield.

First Appearances

Sharon Cameron's "Beautiful Work," is excerpted from *Beautiful Work: A Meditation on Pain*, published in 2000 by Duke University Press and reprinted by permission. Copyright 2000, Duke University Press.

Doris Dörrie's piece is excerpted is from the novel *Where Do We Go From Here*, Bloomsbury Press 2000. Reprinted by permission. Copyright Doris Dörrie 2000.

Martha Gies's "Zoo Animal Keeper I, REC-SVC-ZK"was first printed in *Orion*, Summer 1995, and then in the anthology *Celestial Omnibus: Short Fiction on Faith*, Beacon 1997. Copyright Martha Gies 1995.

Francesca Hampton's "Greyhound Bodhisattva" is reprinted from *Eratica Magazine*, Winter 1998.

Jan Hodgman's "Tanuki" first appeared in *Calyx: A Journal of Art and Literature by Women*, Summer 1999 and was reprinted in *The Year's Best Fantasy and Horror, Thirteenth Collection*, St. Martin's Press, 2000. Copyright Jan Hodgman 1999.

Pico Iyer's "A Walk in Kurama" is excerpted from his memoir, *The Lady and the Monk: Four Seasons in Kyoto*, Vintage Departures 1992. Copyright Pico Iyer 1991.

Anne Carolyn Klein's "The Mantra and the Typist" was originally published in *Tricycle: the Buddhist Review*, Summer 2001, and reprinted the following year in *Hypatia* as part of a larger innovative article.

Keith Kachtick's "Hungry Ghost" is excerpted and adapted from the novel of the same name, published by HarperCollins 2003. Copyright Keith Kachtick 2003.

Victor Pelevin's "The Guest at the Feast of Bon" has not been published elsewhere in English. It is reprinted with permission of Pelevin and the translator, Andrew Bromfield. Copyright Victor Pelevin, 2004. Translation copyright Andrew Bromfield 2004. All rights reserved.

Gerald Reilly's "Nixon Under the Bodhi Tree" first appeared in *The Gettysburg Review* in 1998, and was selected for an O. Henry Award in 1999. Copyright Gerald Reilly 1998.

Kira Salak's "Beheadings" was published in *Best New American Voices 2001* after first appearing in the literary magazine *Prairie Schooner*. Copyright Kira Salak 2000.

Marilyn Stablein's dream excerpts, "The Prediction" and "Teeth," first appeared in *Night Travels To Tibet*, a chapbook published by Shivastan Publishing, Kathmandu, Nepal, 2001. Copyright Marilyn Stablein 2001.

Novice to Master

An Ongoing Lesson in the Extent of My Own Stupidity
Soko Morinaga
Translated by Belenda Attaway Yamakawa
144 pages, ISBN 0-86171-393-1, $11.95

"Part memoir, part wisdom resource, *Novice to Master* provides a lively and enlightening overview of Zen, and wonderful anecdotes on the poignance of living in the present moment."—*Spirituality and Health*

Mindfulness Yoga

The Awakened Union of Breath, Body, and Mind
Frank Jude Boccio
Foreword by Georg Feuerstein
320 pages, 100 photos,
ISBN 0-86171-335-4, $19.95

Mindfulness Yoga introduces an entirely new integration of yoga and meditation! Whether you're a beginner or have been practicing for years, *Mindfulness Yoga* is for you. Easy-to-follow sequences are laid out with over 100 accompanying photos in this groundbreaking presentation of mindfulness meditation and yoga. Special lay-flat binding makes this book even more useful as a practice aid.

"*Mindfulness Yoga* should be read by *every* aspiring Yoga practitioner."—Georg Feuerstein, author of *The Yoga Tradition*

Mindfulness in Plain English
Revised, Expanded Edition
Bhante Henepola Gunaratana
224 pages, ISBN 0-86171-321-4, $14.95

"Extremely up-to-date and approachable, this book also serves as a very thorough FAQ for new (and not-so-new) meditators. Bhante has an engaging delivery and a straightforward voice that's hard not to like."
—*Shambhala Sun*

Zen Meditation in Plain English
John Daishin Buksbazen
Foreword by Peter Matthiessen
128 pages, ISBN 0-86171-316-8, $12.95

"Down-to-earth advice about the specifics of Zen meditation: how to position the body; how and when to breathe; what to think about. Includes helpful diagrams and even provides a checklist to help beginners remember all of the steps. A fine introduction, grounded in tradition yet adapted to contemporary life."
—*Publishers Weekly*

Longing for Certainty
Reflections on the Buddhist Life
Bhikkhu Nyanasobhano
256 pages, ISBN 0-86171-338-9, $14.95

"An unusually practical, philosophical, and graceful volume, to be treasured and re-read by Buddhists of all types and stages, as well as non-Buddhists. Deep, and shining."
—Publishers Weekly

"Bhikkhu Nyanasobhano is American Buddhism's Thoreau"
—Bhikkhu Bodhi

Meditation for Life
Martine Batchelor
Photographs by Stephen Batchelor
168 pages, ISBN 0-86171-320-8, $22.95

"Among today's steady stream of new books on Buddhist meditation, most are easy to ignore. This one isn't. It offers simple, concrete instructions in meditation and the photographs are delicious eye candy. Author Martine Batchelor spent ten years in a Korean monastery and presumably knows a lotus position when she sees one—she also has a sense of humor."—*Psychology Today*

Faces of Compassion

Classic Bodhisattva Archetypes and Their Modern Expression
Taigen Dan Leighton
Foreword by Joan Halifax
352 pages, ISBN 0-86171-333-8, $14.95

This wonderful book could also be aptly titled "An Introduction to Mahayana Buddhism." Leighton guides us through the ideas and ideals of Buddhism and the bodhisattvas, showing us that their modern expressions are indeed among us.

Beside Still Waters

Jews, Christians, and the Way of the Buddha
Edited by Harold Kasimow, John P. Keenan, and Linda Klepinger Keenan
Foreword by Jack Miles, Pulitzer Prize-winning author of *God: A Biography*
288 pages, ISBN 0-86171-336-2, $14.95

"A probing, thoughtful collection of vivid stories of Jews and Christians who have gone East for spiritual study and then returned to their respective faiths much richer for the experience."—Matthew Fox, in *Yoga Journal*

The Compassionate Life

The Dalai Lama
144 pages, ISBN 0-86171-378-8, $19.95

Illuminating themes touched upon in *The Good Heart* and *The Art of Happiness,* this generous and gentle book contains some of the most beloved teachings on compassion that the Dalai Lama has ever offered. Touching and transformative, *The Compassionate Life* is a personal invitation from one of the world's most gifted teachers to live a life of happiness, joy, true prosperity.

Daughters of Emptiness

Poems by Buddhist Nuns of China
Beata Grant
256 pages, ISBN 0-86171-362-1, $16.95

"Beata Grant provides an impressively compact and readable overview of the changing fortunes of Buddhist nuns in China, beginning in the fourth century, all the way to the present. A landmark collection of exquisite poems, scrupulously gathered and translated."
—*Buddhadharma: The Practitioner's Quarterly*

Hardcore Zen

Punk Rock, Monster Movies,
and the Truth About Reality
Brad Warner
224 pages, ISBN 0-86171-380-X, $14.95

"FIVE STARS. An engrossing and entertaining Chicken Soup for the Anarchist, Over-Intellectualizing Soul."—*About.com*

"Entertaining, bold and refreshingly direct; likely to change the way one experiences other books about Zen—and maybe even the way one experiences reality."—*Publishers Weekly* [starred review]

Daily Wisdom

365 Buddhist Inspirations
Edited by Josh Bartok
384 pages, ISBN 0-86171-300-1, $16.95

Daily Wisdom draws on the richness of Buddhist writings to offer a spiritual cornucopia that will illuminate and inspire day after day, year after year. Sources span a spectrum from ancient sages to modern teachers, from monks to lay people, from East to West, from poetry to prose. Each page, and each new day, reveals another gem of *Daily Wisdom*.

About Wisdom Publications

W ISDOM PUBLICATIONS, a nonprofit publisher, is dedicated to making available authentic Buddhist works for the benefit of all. We publish our titles with the appreciation of Buddhism as a living philosophy and with the special commitment to preserve and transmit important works from all the major Buddhist traditions.

To learn more about Wisdom, or to browse books online, visit our website at wisdompubs.org. You may request a copy of our mail-order catalog online or by writing to:

Wisdom Publications
199 Elm Street • Somerville, Massachusetts 02144 USA
Telephone: (617) 776-7416 • Fax: (617) 776-7841
Email: info@wisdompubs.org • www.wisdompubs.org

The Wisdom Trust

As a nonprofit publisher, Wisdom is dedicated to the publication of fine Dharma books for the benefit of all sentient beings and dependent upon the kindness and generosity of sponsors in order to do so. If you would like to make a donation to Wisdom, please do so through our Somerville office. If you would like to sponsor the publication of a book, please write or email us at the address above.

Thank you.

Wisdom is a nonprofit, charitable 501(c)(3) organization affiliated with the Foundation for the Preservation of the Mahayana Tradition (FPMT).